XMAS ANGEL

ALSO BY JORDYN KROSS

Find all of Jordyn's books at jordynkross.com or here:

Melting Hearts Series

Prequel Novella - Jack's Frost

(free for newsletter subscribers)

Book 1 - Winter's List

Book 2 - Xmas Angel

Book 3 - Shattered Ice

The Yacht Club Series

Book 1 - The Handler

Book 2 - The Wrangler

Dirty Daisy Mystery Series

Book 1 - Dirty Daisy

Book 2 - Hell Hath No Furry

Book 3 - Bone to Pick

Book 4 - Dying the Knot (Coming in 2027)

Uhraervi Brothers

Hung with Care

Open Enrollment

Pole Position

Fool's Gold

NOAH Series

Prequel Novella - Quantum Entanglements

Book 1 - Captain's Treasure

Book 2 - Stolen Fire

Nonfiction

Demystifying the Beats

Author Survival Guide

Single Titles

A Lost Claus

XMAS ANGEL

MELTING HEARTS BOOK 2

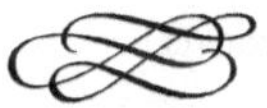

JORDYN KROSS

Published by Scarlet Parlor Press, LLC
PO Box 21786, Albuquerque, NM 87154

Library of Congress Control Number: 2022903084

Publisher's Cataloging-In-Publication Data

(Prepared by The Donohue Group, Inc.)

Names: Kross, Jordyn, author.

Title: Xmas angel / Jordyn Kross.

Description: [Albuquerque, New Mexico] : Scarlet Parlor Press, LLC, [2022] | Series: Melting hearts ; book 2 | First published as an ebook in 2020.

Identifiers: ISBN 9781733380850 (print)

Subjects: LCSH: Women artists--Fiction. | Veterans--Fiction. | Man-woman relationships--Fiction. | LCGFT: Romance fiction. | Erotic fiction.

Classification: LCC PS3611.R776 X53 2022 | DDC 813/.6--dc23

Print ISBN-13: 978-1-7333808-5-0

Ebook ISBN-13: 978-1-7333808-1-2

Editor: Colleen Wagner

Cover: Brandi Doane McCann

CHAPTER 1

Noelle Michaels masked her revulsion as the manager of the Fried Egg Tavern twirled a lock of her dark red hair in his hand. God, she hated to be touched, but she couldn't avoid him in the narrow back hallway. In the past, people she'd allowed to get that close had only hurt her.

"You know, we could talk about how to increase your percentage of the sales if you want to come into my office." Gerald rubbed his cold, moist fingertips down her bicep, getting too close to her breast.

Instead of giving in to the urge to punch him in the throat, Noelle forced a smile. "Can't. I have to get back to the studio." She retreated a step, unable to remain still any longer. "There are some things in progress I shouldn't leave too long."

There was no way in hell she'd go into a room with the creep. Where she stood, people could see her. The kitchen staff were a swinging door away, and his customers were in the dining area behind her. She could sprint out the back, but she didn't want to risk losing her show.

She squared her shoulders. Her art hung on the tavern walls—her first show ever. It wasn't a real art gallery, yet. But, no matter how many years passed, how many shows she had in the future, there'd be no forgetting her first.

A shiver of awareness rolled up her spine, and she scanned the bar. A tall, muscular man stared intently at *Blue Boy*, his hands stuffed in the pockets of jeans that gripped a perfect ass.

"Are you sure you can't stay?" The manager's voice dragged her focus away from the sexy backside. "I have time to sit with you if you're...*hungry*." His tongue peeked out from between his lips.

She tried not to gag. The bar food smelled delicious, and she hadn't eaten that day, but the thought of him staring at her across a table ruined her appetite.

"I just stopped by to check on the show." Three of her mixed-media portraits had sold already. If she could survive the month, she was tracking to sell twelve of her pieces. In addition to the cash she'd saved, sixty percent of the sale price of every purchase meant she might be able to afford a place to live when the inevitable came to pass.

One step closer to independence.

"Well, you know I can't pay you until the end of the month. We still have time to renegotiate the final split." He slithered into the gap between them.

"Sure." She shrugged one shoulder casually as if she weren't crawling out of her skin. "Just not right now. I appreciate everything you're doing, Gerald. I know you took a chance on me. It looks like it's going to work out for both of us."

"It could work out even better." He dragged his finger along her collarbone to her neck.

Note to self: Wear turtlenecks. No matter how fucking hot it is.

"We could sit by my pool this weekend with strawberry daiquiris, or we could drink some wine in my playroom one evening."

What the fuck does he mean by playroom?

"Those both sound..." *Disgusting.* "Interesting. I'll have to think about it." Before coming to the restaurant, she'd dressed as classy as she could. Stole a blouse from the back of her mom's closet and left her hair down so she didn't look like a student. It had worked a little *too* well. He saw her as a woman and probably didn't care that she couldn't legally drink for another five months.

Noelle moved quickly through the back door. If she didn't go now, she'd say something she would regret. Even though Gerald was a letch and would try to cheat her if she didn't keep track of the sales, she needed him.

One benefit to having meth dealers for parents, Noelle could calculate the commission in her head. Nothing like druggy math for figuring cuts and profits. The legal contract would protect her if Gerald tried to screw with her money. Her art teacher, Ms. Julie, had reviewed it and read it to her, at least the parts that mattered. They'd created a list with the prices for the twelve pieces she was exhibiting.

Noelle walked down the alley, sticking to the long, late afternoon shadows to avoid the Arizona heat. In a couple of weeks, school would start again. Summers were torture without access to a studio. She missed working on her art and seeing Ms. Julie every day. The story about her work in progress was an easy lie. Gerald wasn't the first man to hit on her, and he wouldn't be the last. Just another dick looking for a wet place to land. She didn't trust anyone enough for that shit. For years she'd kept herself safe from the creepy dudes who were in and out of her parents' trailer. No man would ever get close enough to hurt her.

Once she was away from the restaurant, the stench of rancid grease faded. She focused on the trash piles. A momentary reflection might be all the hint she'd get of something worth inspecting. On her tiptoes, she peered into a dumpster, and a smile spread across her face. Bare metal wire, a rare find. Discarded and unwanted bits of other peoples' lives were the medium and inspiration for her art. It was her passion, a calling she couldn't ignore, to gather those small pieces someone else considered trash and transform them into trea-sure. She tucked the wire into a pocket of the backpack slung across her body before moving on.

July in Tucson was a beast. Nick Christoph felt like a rotisserie chicken at the grocery store, slow baked. The Fried Egg Tavern was blessedly cool, and he paused at the entrance to let the air-conditioning wash over him. His buddy Gabe had suggested the place when they'd agreed to meet. A black granite bar flanked by dark metal stools ran the long length of the room. The golden wood floors were similar to his own home. But the espresso-stained tables and chairs that filled the rest of the place were darker than anything he owned. It was nicer than he'd expected.

A couple of men were at the bar enjoying a beer and the game on TV, but the tables were empty. Three o'clock on a Thursday was apparently a slow time. If the food was decent, he could drop by on his way home after school for an early dinner on occasion.

A server stopped. Dark hair pulled into a ponytail, she raked her predatory gaze over his body and grinned.

"Just one?" She stood too close and leaned into him.

"Two. I'm meeting someone."

Her smile dimmed, but she nodded. "Follow me." She paused at a table against the far wall and dropped the menus. "Grab me when you're ready to order."

Nick pointedly ignored her swaying retreat and pulled out a chair. As he sat, he stilled.

The artwork hung above the table was like nothing he'd seen before—a child playing with a plastic truck, the face painted in flawless detail as if it were a commissioned portrait. Bits of layered fabric provided the clothing. The toy truck was real, rising out three-dimensionally from the canvas. It looked like it had been salvaged from the bottom of an old toy box, its shattered pieces glued together with lines that weren't perfect. It had the feel of a classic portrait pushing its way into real life. It was stark and emotional and priced much too low based on the small white square stuck to the wall beneath it.

There were more portraits and some still-lifes throughout the restaurant, but his inspection would have to wait. His buddy was in the doorway.

"Hey, *Saint*. How's it going?" Gabriel stuck out his hand.

Nick flinched at the nickname. Ignoring the hand, he grabbed Gabriel in a man-hug, finishing with two strong pats to his back. "*Thor*. Good to see you."

"It's been a while. Figured I should take advantage of my road trip. Catch up in person for a change."

Nick waited while Gabe perused the menu. When he finally looked up, Nick asked the question that sat in his chest like a molten rock. "How's the leg?"

"The aftermarket part is great. They finally got the fit perfect—no more rubbing and such."

"Glad to hear it." Nick grimaced.

"Stop it. We've been over this. You did the right thing in a fucked-up situation. It was never going to have a better outcome."

Nick didn't agree. Two of their team members had died. Gabe lost half his leg. And the girl Nick had tried to save was a stain on the buildings in that desert village.

Gabe was quiet until Nick met his gaze.

"Going to the shrink again?" Gabe asked.

"Group. Twice a month." Nick ran his hand over his head as if he could wipe away the pain of the memories.

"Nightmares still?"

Nick shrugged. He deserved to remember. He deserved the shame. And he deserved the sleepless nights. They'd been rare until his last security assignment earlier that summer, before he'd quit to teach. Thank goodness it hadn't ended badly. The woman was fine, living her life in New York. His failure to act hadn't led to death. Again.

The waitress interrupted his spiraling thoughts. After they ordered, Nick struggled to find a different topic of conversation.

"So, teaching? How's that going?" Gabe asked.

"So far, great. Of course, I don't have any students yet. Just prepping and getting used to the environment."

"Any hot single teachers?" Gabe waggled his eyebrows. The man was a walking hormone and never had trouble getting the ladies. His olive complexion and dark hair couldn't have been more of a contrast to Nick's silvering crew cut and light blue eyes. Out of habit, Nick wore the military cut his buddy had left behind.

"More like milk and warm cookies. I'm surrounded by women who look like models for Mrs. Claus."

"Well, how perfect is that for 'Saint Nick.'"

"Funny." Nick took a long swallow of his cold beer. "Doesn't matter. I'm not looking for love. I had that with Helena. That part of my life is over."

"Sorry, man, I forgot. I…" Gabe turned red and clamped his mouth shut.

"Don't worry. It's been years." Nick stuffed down the memories that clawed their way up. "So, what are you doing with your life? In your email, you said you're on your way to Colorado?"

"Yeah. Apparently, my uncle decided to leave me his property. A lodge up in the mountains near Aspen. I used to go there when I was a kid, but I haven't seen it in over a decade." He shrugged. "Might as well take a look before I decide to sell it. I'm not doing anything else."

The waitress slid two plates onto the table and hung around, flirting and pouting and asking as many questions as she could. Did they have everything they needed, did it look good, and was there anything she could get them? Finally, Nick gave her the *look*. The icy stare that made her stutter and move along. What did she expect? A threesome on the table?

He and Gabriel bullshitted and ate their way through the enormous sandwiches and drank another beer. Too soon, his buddy decided he had to get going. It was a good visit, and Nick was more at peace than he'd expected to be when Gabriel had asked to see him. Gabe was doing well, moving on with his life. Nick hoped his friend found something worth saving in Colorado.

Nick remained behind to check out the art show after Gabe left. He rose from the booth and inspected the tag on the piece over the table. *Blue Boy*. The child's face dug into his memory, familiar and foreign all at once. It made his soul hungry in a way he couldn't understand or explain. He wasn't a huge art fan—that was his parents' thing—but there was something about it that called to him.

Should he start from the front of the restaurant and work his way to the back or the reverse? Electing to go from the back so he could leave when he was done, he turned and froze. A crimson mane of fire cascaded down the back of a slight woman with sensuous curves. She faced a man standing too close to her, stroking her arm. Nick swallowed a growl. *Where was this coming from?*

It'd been forever since he'd felt the stirrings of desire, and, besides, he'd always preferred tall brunettes like Helena. He hadn't even seen the redhead's face. None of that mattered as he moved toward the couple. But before he'd taken three steps, the woman darted down the darkened hallway. A square of light filled the corridor as she thrust open the exit. He blinked at the blaze of sunlight on her hair before she disappeared and the door closed behind her.

He took another step, hesitated. He couldn't chase some random woman. That was a good way to end up explaining his behavior to the police. So, with a deep breath, he resumed his original mission. He put the woman out of his mind and focused on the art. Perhaps he could find something for his home. The walls were a little bare. Since he was going to be staying, he might as well decorate.

CHAPTER 2

$\mathcal{N}$ick glanced up at the clock on the classroom wall. The end of the day came too quickly, never giving him enough time with his students. He stood up from his desk. "Make sure you have your things together."

Two students rushed to the door, as they did every afternoon.

"William. Lucas. The final bell hasn't rung. Clear your desks."

Lucas turned back and sneered. He was fifteen, sixteen at most, and had a prison-yard stare. "We gotta go. We're supposed to leave early for the bus."

"After you've cleared your desk." Nick's tone allowed for no dissent. Two weeks of repeating himself, after years of working with soldiers who'd obeyed on the first command, was making him crazy.

The young tough guy returned to his desk and tucked the stray pencil behind his ear, folded the sheets of paper, and stuffed them in the back pocket of jeans that hung off his ass.

Nick nodded. "See you tomorrow, Lucas."

The kid, fists clenched, looked at the ground as he left. William hurried to catch up. Two down, six to go. The bell rang, and the all but one of the remaining students moved like zombies out of the classroom. Jeez, what meds were they on?

His one female student sat at the back of the room, seemingly oblivious to all the activity around her. She sketched with her pencil on some lined notebook paper.

"Noelle?" Slowly, he made his way down the aisle. It didn't matter what she was working on—it was time for her to go. He put his hand on her desk. "You'll miss the bus."

Her body jerked and she hunched. Despite the near triple-digit weather, her hair was wrapped in a knit cap.

"The bell rang. Don't you need to catch the bus?" Usually she left with the rest of his class.

"No." With a precise sweep of her arm, she tucked her drawing into the cardboard folder she carried. A makeshift artist portfolio, he supposed. Art was the one class she was mainstreamed into.

Rising from the desk, she avoided him, still not making eye contact. She inched toward the open classroom door. The sounds of students thundering out of the building had died down. As though crossing a highway, she looked both ways, then darted out without saying a word.

Nick shuffled the papers on his desk. Time to get reorganized and make some notes on his students. He'd also need to pull their files soon to work on the individual education plans required for each of his exceptional-needs kids.

"Nick?" The teacher from next door stuck her head in his classroom. "Congratulations, you survived another week."

Nick abandoned his efforts to edit his calendar. "Mrs. Stafford."

"It's Ms., not Mrs. I ditched Mr. Stafford years ago. Call me Laura." She smiled flirtatiously, a pointless effort. Not because she was older than him by several years—he had no interest in a romantic relationship with anyone.

"Laura." Nick took a deep breath. "Yes, I survived. Are there always so many interruptions? PA announcements, assemblies, kids getting pulled out of class?"

"You won't get into a rhythm for at least a month." She waved a hand. "A bunch of us are celebrating two weeks down and only forty to go at O'Grady's if you want to join us."

"I might do that." He didn't particularly want to socialize with the other instructors, but he should go. He was new, and it was kind of her to reach out to him.

"If I hadn't seen your car still in the empty parking lot every day since we started back, I'd believe you." She shook her finger at him as if he were a naughty child. "But you, sir, are a workaholic."

"I just want to do my best for the students."

"You'll be fine. You only have what, six? Or is it eight this year?"

"Eight. I should have a teaching assistant."

She chuckled as if he'd told a joke. "I have a hundred and twenty-five, in five different classes. But I don't get any help. Give you some kids with 'special needs,'" she said as she made air quotes with her fingers, "and you need a TA."

Nick looked at her blankly.

"Well, not *you* specifically, but special education teachers." She tittered nervously and smoothed her top over her hips.

"It's for their safety, as well as meeting the requirement to provide individualized education."

"Oh, of course. I don't mean anything." She spoke slowly, drawing out the words. "I'm just dead from the first days. It doesn't get any easier, even after all these years."

"You have one of my students in your third-period class." He flipped to the front of his calendar, searching for the note he'd made, frustrated that he couldn't remember the detail or find it quickly. He usually retained little things like that.

"That's my prep period. You must be thinking of Mrs. Harris, Glenna. Have you met her?"

"I don't think so."

"She'll be at the pub tonight. Come for a beer." She smiled at him. "It's just a few of us, but it's the best way to get to know the others."

"You've convinced me." Nick pasted a perfunctory smile on his face. "I'll see you there."

He made a few more notes, reviewed the state of his classroom one last time, locked his desk drawers, and forced himself to have one drink. If he had to play nice to make a difference in even one of those kid's lives that year, then so be it.

NICK DROPPED his keys on his dresser and emptied the change from his pocket into the dish on the side table. Still buzzing from the day and an evening with his co-workers, his intention to take a hot shower was interrupted by the ring of his cell phone. One glance at the screen and he answered with a smile. "Thor. What's up, man?"

"Wanted to see if you're still alive after your first couple weeks." Gabriel's voice settled his restless energy.

"No actual skirmishes. So, I'm good."

Gabriel laughed. "Is it everything you expected?"

"Not exactly." Nick huffed out a breath. "I have the training and the mission, but the team is lacking. My aide won't be assigned for another week."

"You're just mad 'cause you aren't in charge."

"I'm not agreeing with you." But Gabriel had a point. Nick did like to control the situation, plan for all possible outcomes. When he'd envisioned teaching, it hadn't been in such a chaotic environment. "How's the lodge?"

"Let's just say it isn't what I remembered."

"You gonna sell it?" Nick couldn't imagine Gabe making muffins for travelers.

"I'm not ready to declare defeat. Yet."

Gabriel and Nick chatted for a few more minutes before Nick's loud yawn interrupted the conversation. He apologized to his friend.

"I'll let you go. Call me." Gabriel sounded as tired as Nick felt.

Under the spray of the hot water, quotes from *The Art of War* flickered through his mind. The weekend would provide the opportunity to prepare for his success.

Noelle checked her cap reflexively, making sure none of her hair showed. The other students loved to give her grief, using nicknames like Flaming Retard. It was like they'd never left middle school. But her hair was really gross. Only three weeks into school and her parents had let the water get turned off *again*. One more day before the weekend when she could haul enough water to take a real bath and wash her hair. With any luck, her parents would be gone, and she could have the trailer to herself.

She'd spent a couple of hours in the art room like she did almost every afternoon, and Ms. Julie had offered to give her a ride home as usual. But no way would she let her favorite teacher see where she lived. It was none of her business anyway.

Noelle picked up her homemade portfolio and slung her backpack over her shoulder—everything that mattered under her control. The weight was comforting. She adjusted the straps and headed outside.

After almost five years at the high school, she could walk the grounds without thinking. The faces of the other students changed, but the hallways and the campus never did. Head down, she concentrated on her current project and kept an eye out for useful discarded items. When two football players erupted from between the buildings, there was no opportunity to avoid them.

"Ask her out. Ask out Red Sped," Kyle Murphy hollered as he pushed Mike Kenner into her. Mike's sports drink dowsed her shirt in orange stickiness as she fell. Her knee scraped the sidewalk, and her pants ripped.

"What the *fuck*?" Noelle screamed.

"Smooth move, asshole." Mike regained his balance and kept walking. "Now I gotta wait till I get home to rehydrate."

Her portfolio was dangerously close to the orange puddle that had spilled out of the abandoned bottle. Heart pounding, she pulled it to safety and checked for any damage.

"Are you okay?" The deep voice resonated down her spine. Mr. Christoph.

Noelle groaned internally. Did it have to be him? Couldn't she experience her humiliation with the tie-dye-wearing history teacher or the ancient janitor? "I'm fine."

"You're bleeding." He leaned over, and his hand hung in midair. "Let me help you."

She ignored Mr. Christoph's perfectly sculpted hand. There was already a tightness in her chest, making her breath shallow. Without touching him, she stood and tried to right her clothing. Every bit of her ugly white bra was on display through her wet shirt. She rounded her shoulders and dropped her head to hide the heat that rushed into her face.

"Well, you can't clean up here. The building's locked. Come on, I'll give you a ride home." Mr. Christoph turned and walked toward the parking lot.

Home. Right. She rolled her eyes. *Never.*

"Noelle. Let's go. It's hot out here."

She shifted on her feet and peered past him, considering all avenues for escape. It wasn't just the matter of where she lived but what state her parents would be in. Why couldn't she tell him no? Anyone else, she would have already walked away.

"Noelle. Move. Now."

She jerked at his tone. He sounded like he was commanding an army in a life-or-death situation. For fuck's sake, nobody was dying. She was sticky and needed to wash her knee. But words escaped her, and, unable to argue, she followed him. There had to be a way to get out of Mr. Christoph seeing where she lived. Somehow.

He covered the tan upholstery with a towel he'd pulled from the trunk.

Noelle perched on the edge of the seat to avoid touching anything. The car smelled like him. Leather with a hint of something lemony. It wasn't one of those plug-in scent makers—she'd smelled him the first day of class and promptly taken the desk farthest from his. His scent, his voice, his commanding attitude—there was no way a teacher should be so...much.

The car's air conditioner gasped as it tried to overcome the Arizona heat. Sweat poured down her back, but her front was bonding with the orange-stained fabric that was baking dry. Blood seeped into the edges of the hole in her jeans. She gritted her teeth. How had her day gone from so good to so fucked in the blink of an eye?

"What's the address?" He paused at the exit to the parking lot.

Noelle glanced at him, not quite making eye contact. "The water's off," she blurted.

"What?"

"At my house. There's no water to get cleaned up." She grasped the strap on her backpack tighter to resist the need to slap her forehead. She usually didn't have any trouble remaining silent around teachers, but something about being alone in the car with him was cracking her walls.

Mr. Christoph's eyes practically bugged out of his skull.

"What am I going to do with you?" He gripped the steering wheel so tightly that she thought it might rip off in his hands. Large, powerful hands.

An itch to pull out her pencil and sketch threaded down her arm. Noelle forced herself to sit quietly and think about something else besides her teacher. At least the air had cooled off, but now her shirt pulled where it was stuck to her skin, and her knee throbbed.

"How long has it been off?"

Noelle shrugged. Weeks, but he didn't need to know that. It was a half mile from the trailer to the dog park. The public restroom toilets and sinks allowed her to maintain some cleanliness. It wouldn't be easy to get the mess out of her clothes and clean her wound, but she'd figure it out. "It's fine."

"No. We'll get you cleaned up at my place, then I'll take you home." He rolled up to a stop sign, snapped on his blinker, and turned down a street she'd never seen before.

Noelle scowled. She never should have gotten in his car.

Too soon, they pulled into the driveway in front of Mr. Christoph's home. The place looked like something from a magazine. It wasn't huge, but the front was landscaped with different native plants, cacti, palm trees, and sandy gravel. A couple of trendy stained-concrete steps led to a large front porch. Her crappy, paint-peeling double-wide was the total opposite of his home's pale olive stucco with perfect dark trim.

He opened his car door. "Come on."

"I can use a hose," Noelle offered. If she could just rinse off, she could walk home and be dry by the time she got there. It wasn't that far.

"No, you're cleaning up *inside*. Let's go." Mr. Christoph walked around the car and opened the passenger side. She gripped the edges of the seat. Instead of yanking her out like she'd expected, he grabbed her backpack and trotted up the steps. He unlocked the wide front door and left it standing open.

Noelle clenched her jaw. She left her portfolio behind on the seat and shuffled up the path. Toes on the threshold, she poked her head in. Wood floors and leather furniture. So nice. A slatted table sat on a multi-colored rug in front of a stone fireplace. On both sides of the hearth, books filled built-in shelves beneath the windows. No way was she walking in there.

"Mr. Christoph?" she yelled.

"Back here. Just come straight down the hall." His deep voice echoed through the house and settled low in her stomach, tempting her to obey.

Was he out of his mind? If she went in there, she'd track blood and dirt through his pristine home. And she'd be alone with him. There was too much that could go wrong. Nerves had her pulse racing and her feet itching to run.

But she had to get her backpack.

CHAPTER 3

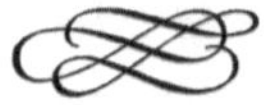

$\mathcal{N}$ick placed fresh towels on the rack and a clean, dry bath mat for Noelle in front of the tub. What was taking so long? It's not like she could get lost in his little two-bedroom bungalow. It was less than fifteen hundred square feet, for god's sake.

Noelle stood on the porch. "Where's my backpack?"

"The shower's ready."

She didn't move.

Letting out a frustrated sigh, he moved behind her and herded her into the house and down the hall, using her aversion to touch against her. "Are you going to wash yourself? Or am I going to have to do that, too?"

"I'll wash." She crossed her arms, a scowl on her face.

"There's soap, shampoo, and conditioner. Toss your clothes in the hall. Don't forget the hat. I'm going to get the towel from the car so I can do them all together. When I get back, they'd better be in the hall or I'm coming in here to get them. Do you understand?"

"Yes."

It was amazing how much disdain she was able to convey with just one word. Nick shook his head. He wasn't any happier with the situation than she was. "I put out clean towels. My bathrobe's on the back of the door. When you're finished showering, you can watch TV until your clothes are done." He shut the door behind him. "Two minutes, Noelle."

After a quick jog to the car, Nick returned to scoop up the pile of rags outside the bathroom door and started the front-load washer in the laundry alcove off the kitchen. Her clothes were completely inadequate. Yeah, it was Arizona, and it was warm, but the autumn mornings were cool. She should have a sweater or hoodie at least.

There came the telltale sound of the water shutting off. Nick waited. Several minutes went by, but she didn't emerge. He knocked on the bathroom door. "Noelle? Everything okay?"

"Ye-yes." Noelle opened the door and tugged the tie on his robe tighter.

Their eyes met, and he faltered. Long dark lashes, still slightly damp, framed beautiful brown eyes filled with intelligence. His chest tightened, but he was too young for a heart attack. He fought to take a breath, to break the spell, but he couldn't. His bathrobe was long on her, bagging at her wrists. With the belt tightly tied, her delicate curves were no longer hidden. Her wet hair was dark red, almost black. It curled into soft waves that were lighter where it had begun to dry.

She was fire, and he was a moth. Unable to stop, he angled into her and smelled. For a moment, he forgot she was his student, could only see a wet, naked woman draped in his robe. His cock stirred.

Stop.

He spun and walked back to the kitchen.

"I have some snacks on the coffee table. What do you want to drink? Water or milk?" His voice was tight.

"Soda?"

She was right behind him, too close. He opened the refrigerator and leaned in to let the cold air cool his ardor. "Don't drink the stuff," he said over the door, keeping it between them. "How about juice?"

Noelle frowned. "Sure."

"Have a seat. Your clothes are in the washer; it's going to be a little while. These front-loaders are energy efficient, but the cycles take forever." He didn't normally babble, but having a woman *undressed* in *his* house made him nervous. The plan had made sense, help an injured student who had no access to running water. He'd failed to integrate critical details when he'd come up with the solution—she was a woman who ignited his long-dead desire. With one hand, he pulled out the carton of OJ and rubbed his forehead with the other as if he could wipe the situation away.

Until he could take her home, he would at least try to get some information. The facts he had weren't adding up.

Noelle stood at the edge of the living room, one toe digging into the rug. He set the drinks on the coasters on the table. "Sit down, Noelle."

She drew her hands inside the sleeves of the robe and crossed her arms. Her gaze flitted between the chairs, the sofa, and the front door.

"Here." He pointed at the couch. "I'll get a comb for you." Keeping her there for any amount of time was the worst of plans, but he couldn't suppress the compulsion to care for her.

When he reached the bathroom, Nick gripped the edge of the sink and glared at himself in the mirror. *She's your student. Off-limits. Not a career-limiting move, a career-ending move. Get her dry, dressed, and out of here. Not one minute longer.* Nick sighed. He was arguing with himself, a clear sign the insanity was well and truly entrenched. *Okay, so I'll feed her, too. Then straight home.*

Nick grabbed his comb and returned, handing it to her.

She took it and drew it down from her scalp but halted abruptly when she encountered a knot. Nick expected her to gently tease it out, but she yanked the comb, and his own scalp screamed in sympathy.

"Let me help you." He held out his hand for the comb.

"I can do it myself." She lifted her chin.

"I used to do this for my cousins." If he knew how to stop arguing with her, he would.

For several seconds she stared at him. He'd been ready to give up when she shrugged and then held the comb out to him. Instead of sitting with her, which his entire body demanded, he walked behind the couch, trying to keep some distance.

Starting with the ends, he gently drew the comb through her clean but tangled tresses. He methodically worked a section at a time from the bottom, then farther up, caressing each silken strand. Noelle released her stiff spine, a soft moan escaping her lips.

"You like having your hair brushed." Nick was entranced by the flames.

"Can't remember anyone doing this for me." Her voice was low and soft. The warmth of it grazed him like a lover's hand.

Nick combed and stroked until Noelle's hair was nearly dry. The dark red locks took on a golden cast now that they were clean. He should stop. It had gone beyond taking care of her. If he continued to indulge his attraction, his inevitable erection would be obvious, and her hair was turning him on big-time.

Her hair...

Nick straightened. Adrenaline coursed through his body. The tavern. That's where he'd seen her before. She was the woman who'd been talking to the manager.

"You're done." He stepped back from the couch and retreated to the bathroom. Several deep breaths and another stern lecture to his libido later, he forced himself to leave the safety of the white-tiled room. Everything would be okay as soon as he got her out of there.

She stood in the middle of the living room again, out of place in his tidy world. Her arms crossed around her middle, avoiding his gaze.

"Let's get you fed." Nick closed the distance, intending to wrap his arms around her and offer comfort. The last thing she wanted and the last thing he should do. He halted at a safe distance instead. "Is there anything you don't like?"

"Um, that's okay. I need to go." Noelle peered around him as if plotting her escape.

"Well, your clothes aren't done, and I'm hungry." He turned toward the kitchen. "I'm used to an early schedule, and if I start cooking now, we should still be able to get you home at a reasonable hour. Do you need to call your folks?"

"We don't have a phone." Noelle had followed so silently that he hadn't heard her take a step.

He retrieved a pan from the cabinet next to the stove and shoved it under the kitchen faucet.

～

NICK REFOLDED HIS NAPKIN, adjusted the silverware on his empty plate and glanced at Noelle's nearly empty plate. He'd served baked chicken with rice and peas because who didn't like that, and she might have food allergies. Were his culinary efforts good enough? Was he over-thinking?

"It was really good. Thank you." Noelle kept glancing from the front door to the dryer. It was obvious she wanted to escape.

Some perverse part of him wanted to delay, to keep her there with him. Bad plan. He cleared their dishes from the table, loading them into the dishwasher. "Your clothes are done, but I need to get you a different shirt. Yours is ruined."

"You sure?"

"Am I sure about what? That the shirt is ruined or that I'm giving you one to wear?"

She shrugged.

"You can check yourself. It was on its last legs before your accident. One of your favorites?"

"One of my only."

"You don't have other clothes, Noelle?" He ground out the question between gritted teeth. Anger built the more he learned about her situation.

She glared up at him, defiance rolling off of her. "The charities stopped coming around once I turned eighteen. After all this time, they've worn out, and I've outgrown everything else."

"From what I can see, you outgrew this one, too." Nick couldn't get a handle on how she lived. No water, no phone, no clothes. What else did she lack? How did she survive? "Stay here. I'll be right back."

Nick snagged a long-sleeved, olive-green henley he hadn't worn in years from the back of his closet and tossed it on the bed. It had always been a little small. In the third drawer of his dresser, he found the concert t-shirts he'd hung on to. His nostalgia wasn't stronger than his need to care for her. It would be easy to part with a few.

He selected a few of his favorites: U2, Nirvana, and one from a Styx concert he'd gone to when the band was already over-the-hill. Giving them to her wouldn't put a dent in *his* wardrobe.

Shaking his head, he opened the dryer. Her shirt went into the garbage. He retrieved the rest of her clothes and realized there was no way they fit her correctly. The bra in his hand didn't match the curves currently encased in his robe.

"Here're your things and a shirt to wear. I'll take you home and talk to your parents about the accident and your need for school clothes."

Red crept up her cheeks. "No."

"You can't run or hide from the problem, Noelle."

"This isn't my *teacher's* concern."

"The charities aren't donating to you anymore. The clothes you have won't last through the school year. I can't ignore it. Now, get dressed."

Nick ushered her back to the bathroom and shut the door. He held on to the handle a moment, his conscience wrestling with his desire to keep her and care for her. As soon as she came out, he must take her back to her parents. In some ways she was right—it wasn't his place to save her. But somebody had to.

Nick opened the car door for Noelle and placed the rest of the shirts in her hands. He hadn't anticipated the pleasure in seeing her wrapped in his clothing. The U2 concert had been memorable, but it would never compare to seeing her come out of his bathroom wearing the t-shirt.

The shirt revealed how her bra struggled to contain her breasts.

How had he found himself in the situation of talking to a student's parents about bras for their daughter—a woman who inspired unwelcome dirty thoughts? One quick conversation and he'd walk away, to see her only at school and never think of that night again.

CHAPTER 4

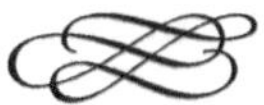

Nick drove slowly while Noelle indicated the direction to her home with her finger. They passed tired trailers and junker cars parked along the edges of the narrow road. There wasn't a tree or plant to break up the hard-packed dirt. Not even weeds wanted to live in the place. Whoever had named the trailer park Happy Valley had a sick sense of humor. There was nothing happy about the place. And if "Valley" was a euphemism for "hell," then, that at least made sense.

"Shit," Noelle said as soon as they came around the final corner. She put her head in her hands. "It's too soon."

Red and blue lights atop police cruisers strobed over the chaotic scene.

"Is this your…" What should he call it? Her nightmare?

She lifted her head. "Yeah. Home."

Police officers were everywhere. Nick turned off the car and watched as cops dragged a handcuffed man out of a dilapidated trailer.

A woman bolted out the door, stark-ass naked and screaming like a banshee. "You fuckers! You can't take me from my home. You don't know who you're fucking with. I own you. Get the fuck off my property."

She sprinted toward Nick's car. Flashing lights illuminated Noelle's emotionless face as the crazed woman stared through the windshield like a wild animal locked onto prey. Hatred filled her bloodshot eyes.

Two uniformed police dropped her naked body down to the ground hard. She kicked and punched while rolling in the dirt. It took both muscle-bound cops to overpower the drug-fueled strength the little woman wielded. They handcuffed her and threw her in the back of one of the squad cars, then tossed a blanket in behind her.

Nick expected Noelle to start crying, but she remained stoic despite the fact her life had gone from terrible to catastrophic. He waited until only two officers remained.

"Stay here," he told her before he stepped out of the car.

Noelle's trailer appeared to be one of the sorriest in the lot. At some distant point in the past, the outside might have been painted with blue trim, but the shade was no longer identifiable. More cardboard than glass filled the metal window frames, and a ragged screen door hung on by one hinge. The front stairs were attached by a lone half-tightened screw. A tetanus shot should be required to use them. One cop pasted a large red notice on the front door and then added a huge *X* of yellow crime-scene tape. As if someone would miss the warning.

Nick approached the other officer. "Excuse me?"

The woman tucked her clipboard under her arm and rested her hand on her holstered gun. "Sir, you can't be here."

"I tea…I work with the daughter of the people who live here."

"There's a daughter? I thought that woman made it up. She kept ranting that we couldn't arrest her because her daughter was coming home from school."

"Is she allowed to go in there?"

"No way. The place is a pigsty, and they were cooking meth in the bathroom. Normally, it would be weeks or months before they clear a scene like that, but in this case, I don't think the trailer will be salvageable. Most likely, it's going to be removed and destroyed."

"What about her things? Where is she supposed to stay?"

"You said you work with her?"

The officer sounded interested in Noelle. Nick wasn't sure if it was as a witness or suspect. He'd better fix that fast. "She's classified as special needs. She still attends high school."

"How old is she?"

"Nineteen or twenty, I think."

"Any chance she's involved in this?" The officer nodded toward the trailer.

"No, she's a good student, just has some learning issues." Nick raked his hand over his head. Although possible Noelle was involved in drugs, he wouldn't cause her more pain by not defending her.

"I can call a social worker. It might take a while for someone to get here. But if she's a functioning adult, meaning she can feed and dress herself, they aren't going to be able to do anything but try to get her a spot in a shelter." The officer jerked her head toward Nick's car. "Is that her?"

Nick nodded.

She frowned. "The spaces in the female-only shelters are gone before they even open up. If there's anywhere else she can stay, she should."

"We'll figure something out. Thanks."

What was he going to do? Nick dropped into the driver's seat and started the car but remained parked. Noelle's face was still stony, maybe in shock.

"Was that your mom?" he asked.

"You mean the screaming naked woman? Yeah, that's her." She rubbed the bridge of her nose with her finger.

"And your dad?"

She stopped rubbing. "Stepdad. He was the one in handcuffs when we first pulled up."

"They aren't going to let you back inside. It's too dangerous."

"Doesn't matter. I don't leave anything there I care about, ever."

"Do you have any family you can call? Grandparents, aunts, uncles?" He reached for her, unable to resist the attempt to comfort.

Noelle leaned away. "No."

"Do you have a friend you can stay with?" He prayed she had a friend, anyone, because if not, he was about to make a very bad decision.

She shook her head. "I have enough for a cheap hotel."

"That's not safe. You'll stay with me for tonight. One night, and I'll find another, more permanent solution." The hotel was a terrible idea, but staying with him was worse.

The drive back to his place was quiet. Noelle fell asleep sometime before they arrived. How had he ended up with a student in his car, soon to be asleep in his bed? It wasn't that she was beautiful, even though she could be an angel with her creamy skin and fiery locks. He'd gone years without sex or even the desire. It was something else that called to him. She needed to be rescued.

Nick parked in his driveway and dropped his head to his hands on the steering wheel. There was only one problem.

Every other time he'd tried to save a woman he'd failed.

CHAPTER 5

"Noelle? Hey, Angel, we're here."

Noelle jerked awake at the sound of Mr. Christoph's voice. The scene from earlier rushed back like a movie on fast-forward. She'd be lucky if she held down the dinner he'd fed her. Her home was gone. The meth lab in her trailer hadn't exploded, but it might as well have. At least her mother and the creep she'd married were in jail where they belonged, hopefully for a very long time. But she wasn't ready, didn't have a contract with a gallery or even another restaurant show. The cash she'd saved would run out too quickly without a way to replace it. She had no clue where to go or what to do.

"You don't have to keep me." She risked a glance at him.

He stared out the windshield as if he were still driving and not parked in his driveway. Stubble roughened his profile. His chin dropped, and he closed his eyes.

"I can find a place to stay." She'd figure out something. She always did.

"We'll worry about that tomorrow." He jingled the keys, clasping them in his strong hand, his forearm flexing. "You've had a rough day. Just for tonight."

The gentle invitation in his deep voice soothed her rattled nerves. Noelle opened the car door and followed him to the front porch. If it were *her* home, she'd never have to go back to the trailer park or deal with her parents again. She could put out red flowers in a navy-blue pot to break up the sterile expanse and complement the olive structure. *No.* She crushed the image and threw it away. If a wish was going to make that happen, it would have happened years ago when she'd first become aware of what her parents were and how little she had compared to others. Wishes didn't do shit.

As soon as they were inside, Noelle collapsed on the tufted leather sofa, unable to keep her eyes open. Her body ached like it had been dragged behind a truck. Instead of trying to move, she curled into a tight ball.

"Hey, sleepyhead." Mr. Christoph nudged her with his knee. "I'm bunking out here. You've got the bedroom."

"I'm fine." She'd struggled to form the words. Given a blanket, she would sleep for a week.

"No, I love sleeping on this couch. Got it big enough so I could. Don't deny me my God-given right as a man to sleep on my sofa." He bumped her again.

Twice he'd saved her, and he meant to give up his bed. It made no sense.

"Come with me." He held out his hand.

Could she trust him? She'd learned a long time ago people liked to grab vulnerability and deliver pain, but somehow he was different. He waited for her to allow the connection, as he had that afternoon. Noelle finally set her fingers in his palm, and he led her to his bedroom. Heat from his skin spread up her arm, wrapping around her shielded heart.

The room, like his hand, was warm and masculine. He had a big bed with a wooden headboard made of thin vertical slats capped by a larger shelf. The chocolate-brown bedspread was soft and inviting under her fingertips. A vision of him in the bed, with her, formed so quickly that it left her stunned and breathless. Uncomfortable, she turned away.

And froze, locking her jaw to hold in a gasp.

One of her pieces from the bar show was hanging on his bedroom wall. Her angel. She'd spent hours just on the wings. The soda cans cut and flattened and cut again. With a small engraver, she'd etched in the feathers. She'd painted the face, but the rest of the angel and the background was a collage of copper wires, cobalt tiles, and wire mesh netting layered with tissue paper and other bits and pieces.

Her best work was in Mr. Christoph's bedroom.

"You like my angel? I just bought it. My first piece of art for this house."

Noelle couldn't respond. She nodded, not taking her eyes from the work she loved.

"I fell in love with it." He inhaled a slow, shaky breath and she turned to him. His voice was lower, shot with pain. "She could almost be my late wife. The likeness is...uncanny. And the artist's name is Angel. It felt like fate."

Ms. Julie had suggested the name when they were finalizing the selection for the show. It was the first time an image had come to Noelle in a dream. Not the body but the face. She'd worked nonstop for weeks until it was perfect, exactly what she'd seen.

A lump formed in her throat, and she choked out her words. "I'm sorry. About your wife."

"It was a long time ago." Mr. Christoph gazed past her at the painting. "She was sick when we got married. I'd hoped to have more time with her. After she passed, I joined the military."

He clenched his jaw, and she crossed her arms to keep from reaching out to comfort him. He probably hadn't meant to tell her that. Sometimes she did the same thing with Ms. Julie—said too much. But it wasn't like she would tell anyone. Hell, he'd witnessed her messy life unravel into shreds. For some reason, she trusted that he wouldn't use it against her. He might not know it, but he could trust her, too.

"We should go to bed. I mean *you*. You need to get some rest. Before school." Mr. Christoph's face turned as red as her hair. "I like to go in early." He drew an oversized t-shirt from a drawer in his tall wooden dresser and thrust it in her direction. "Here." His hand shook as he held it while keeping his gaze directed away. "You can sleep in this."

Noelle brushed his fingers purposely as she took the offering. A touch she meant to reassure and thank him. He snatched his hand away like she'd burned him.

"I…I have to go. Find you a toothbrush."

Noelle held the shirt up, but her eyes never left his body. She followed him as he went to the hall bath, forcing herself to pause in the bedroom doorway.

His muscles moved and bunched while he hunted through the drawers and cabinets in the bathroom until he found a sealed tooth-brush. He barely slowed as he handed it to her before continuing on to the living room. A breath of his scent teased her as he passed. The lines of his thighs and ass held her rapt until he moved out of sight.

He was beautiful, and he liked her artwork.

If she imagined a life with a house and a husband, like normal people, he would be a part of that dream. She snorted out a breath. *Right.* Normal people didn't spend their time exploring dumpsters or carry all their belongings in one sack on their back. Besides, she had other goals, and they didn't include ties to any place or anyone, especially Mr. Perfect Christoph.

After she brushed her teeth and took off her clothes, she slid the cool, faded cotton t-shirt down her bare torso. It caressed her skin with its over-washed softness.

She should say thank you and good night. It was only polite. So, slowly she tiptoed down the hall to the living room. She paused at the edge of the wall as Mr. Christoph's bare feet came into view below the edges of his jeans. Maybe he was already asleep. But a single lamp cast a shadowy light over the room.

Inching forward, she peeked over the back of the couch. He lay shirtless, one arm thrown over his face. The darkness settled on him, deep into the edges of each muscle while the light licked at the peaks. A thin covering of golden hair gilded his chest, making his dark nipples stand out. She rolled her lower lip between her teeth.

She must have made a sound, because he moved his arm. Ducking back behind the cover of the wall, she returned silently to his bedroom. She locked the door and crawled into his bed, still panting for air.

She hugged the extra pillow to her body. His unique citrusy smell surrounded her, filling her lungs. Her breasts tingled with desire. She tried to mentally work on one of her unfinished pieces in the studio, but a new image formed in her mind, a naked man sprawled on a couch. She shook her head and attempted to focus on anything else. What would she find in the dumpsters during her next search-and-rescue mission, as she called them? How was her old friend who lived on the streets doing? Even where she might stay the next night, but that led to thoughts of sharing the bed with *him*. Mr. Christoph, with his defined muscles and Prussian-blue eyes, owned her thoughts.

Her spine tightened, and her legs twitched. Maybe when she was no longer in school, they could date. He would touch her, kiss her. Press himself inside her. Her fingers slipped into her underwear. Wetness eased her way. She circled her clit slowly, imagining his tongue. What would it be like to have his face buried between her thighs? His short hair brushing against her tender skin? His tongue delving inside, tasting her?

Back arched, she penetrated herself, grinding on the palm of her hand. With her other hand, she tugged on an aching nipple. Her legs fell open, and she dove in deeper, searching for the release that would allow her to sleep. Faster. She tweaked the other nipple. Sizzling energy squeezed through her as she clenched around her own fingers, pretending they were his. She turned her head into his pillow and muffled the sounds, working her body until boneless relaxation washed over her.

His scent clung to her. Would he smell her when he returned to his bed, or would he wash the sheets before he realized what she'd done? Her pussy spasmed as she imagined him drawing the fabric to his face, smelling her the way she breathed him in. Wanting her.

Right.

Not going to happen. He was beyond her, and being an artist was the only thing that mattered. Slowly, she exhaled and promised herself: *One night, never again.*

CHAPTER 6

*N*ick pushed through the students crowding the school's administrative office on their lunch hour.

"Alice? I need a file." He projected his voice to get the attention of the overworked secretary.

"Mr. Christoph! Just come back here. You can get whatever you need." Alice rolled her eyes before she turned back to the students clamoring for her attention.

Nick darted through the gate, relieved to be out of the crush. In the back room, he tried to make sense of the organizational system. *Why isn't all of this available on the school database?* It would be easier and logical, but for some reason, the special education students had paper files, too.

After several minutes of searching, he found Noelle's. It was thick, one of the largest in the drawer. It would take hours to comb through. He stacked it on top of his planner and returned to the quiet of his classroom, anxious to uncover the explanations it might hold for all the questions he had.

Nick kept his class busy with self-directed tasks through the afternoon while he devoured the information on his mystery student. Noelle had a dual diagnosis. In second grade, she'd tested as dyslexic and struggled with all things related to reading or spelling. She'd been held back in third grade. Toward the end of seventh grade, she had been recommended for reevaluation and found to have an emotional disability, specifically "an inability to build and maintain satisfactory interpersonal relationships with peers and teachers, inappropriate types of behavior or feelings under normal circumstances, and a general and pervasive mood of unhappiness or depression." Had the girl ever *lived* "under normal circumstances"? Armed with a second label, they'd kept her for a couple of years before sending her on to high school.

Because of the combination of disabilities, she was eligible for services until she graduated or she aged out of the system at twenty-one. A milestone she would hit in a matter of months—on Christmas, in fact. Did she know the school would no longer have to provide for her? Why was she still attending? She could have left, gotten a job. The setup made his scalp itch. The same thing he got when the intelligence didn't add up before a mission.

He was clueless about social services and the support money, but the file stunk. Nick ran the facts again, searching for a logical explanation. Noelle wasn't dysfunctional. She was working around not having water and clothing and taking care of herself with drug-addicted parents. The police had said they were manufacturing methamphetamine in the trailer, and Noelle hadn't seemed surprised. Yet she was surviving and came to school every day. The person in the file was weak. Why had she concealed the fact she was strong, resilient, adaptive?

The school bell signaled the end of the day and broke his train of thought.

"Noelle! Please come see me," Nick called before she moved for the door. He said goodbye to each of his other students, calling them by name and wishing them a good weekend. Although his current focus was on Noelle, it didn't prevent him from connecting with each individual in his class.

Noelle stood in front of his desk, her backpack slung over her shoulder with one strap and the cardboard portfolio under her arm.

She'd worn a different knit cap—her gorgeous mane hidden from him.

"Why do you cover your hair?" he asked before he could stop himself. At least he'd managed to keep from reaching for it.

She turned red. "It keeps it out of my face when I'm working on a canvas."

"But you could tie it back." An alarm rang in Nick's head. No matter how much he liked her fiery mane, he needed to stop arguing with a student about her appearance.

"It's just easier." Noelle stared at her feet and pressed the toe of her tennis shoe into the floor. "If they don't see my hair, they don't notice me. At least, not as much."

She glanced up, and her fierce brown eyes made his heart pound and his cock harden.

"Your hair is beautiful." *And I want to wrap my hands in it while I kiss you, make love to you. No! Absolutely not. Not now. Not ever. Student, Christoph, student.*

Too bad his body wasn't listening.

"I should go." She looked toward the door.

"Did you find a place to stay?" Nick stood. The telltale bulge in his pants be damned, he couldn't let her leave. But if she had shelter for the weekend, there would be no reason to hold the meeting he'd scheduled.

"I'll get a motel room." Noelle stepped away from his desk.

"Wait. I called a meeting this afternoon to address this. You need to stay."

Noelle scowled and turned away.

Nick put his hands in his pockets to restrain himself from reaching for her. He was dealing with an adult, not a child. Ordering her around was going to backfire. "I mean, would you please stay?"

Noelle stopped, but she didn't answer right away. When she did turn, her eyes flashed with anger, lips mashed together in a thin line. "It was nice of you to keep me last night, but there isn't anyone who can fix this. If you need to have a meeting to figure that out, fine. I have to catch a bus."

"I thought you didn't ride the bus."

"A city bus. There aren't any motels around here I can afford."

"If you stay, I'll make sure you have a ride." Seconds passed while she considered his offer. He kept an impassive expression while the mental calculations played out across her face.

"Fine." She returned to her desk and dropped her things. She slumped into the seat and crossed her arms over the Nirvana t-shirt he'd given her.

Before Nick could chastise himself for noticing how good the band logo looked draped over her breasts, the classroom door opened and two women entered.

"Ms. Julie?" Noelle came to attention. The woman was never invited to those meetings. She looked out of place with her paint-splattered overskirt and swinging ponytail. More like a student than a teacher.

Her art teacher smiled. "Hey, Noelle. Mr. Christoph asked me to stop by. What's going on with you?"

Noelle refused to explain the latest mess in her life. Instead, she'd wait for Mr. Christoph to do it. Silence was never a bad plan.

The door opened again, and her stylish middle-aged school counselor, Mrs. Harwood, walked in. The counselor she'd expected.

"Ms. Balinchek, Mrs. Harwood. Thank you for coming." Mr. Christoph indicated that they should take a seat. "There's been a change in Noelle's living situation. I need some ideas for a temporary residence."

"What happened?" Mrs. Harwood asked Mr. Christoph.

Ms. Julie tried to make eye contact. Noelle dropped her gaze to the ground.

"Noelle's parents were arrested last night, and her home is…uninhabitable."

"You're kidding." Ms. Julie put her hand to her chest.

Noelle clenched her jaw.

Mr. Christoph straightened the open calendar on his desk. "Do you have any ideas about a safe place to stay?"

"What about…" Mrs. Harwood's voice trickled off.

After so many meetings over the years, the counselor knew almost as much about Noelle as she did about herself. No family and over eighteen. Even though she attended high school, she wasn't a minor. Noelle felt a dark chuckle well in her throat. All those smart people and they couldn't solve the problem any better than she could.

"I'm not sure what options are available." Mr. Christoph leaned back and gripped the edge of his desk, arms flexing. The sexy pose threatened to distract Noelle from the conversation.

"Where did you stay last night?" Ms. Julie, forehead wrinkled in confusion, sat in the desk next to Noelle.

"At a friend's house," she answered, accustomed to concealing the details of her life. "But it was only for one night. I can't go back."

Tears stung her eyes, threatening to fall. She'd give anything to be curled up in Mr. Christoph's bed. Never had she slept so well or felt so safe. Maybe if she wasn't his student… *Stop. Get it together.* One night and she was ready to fall over herself for a warm bed and a nice man.

Mrs. Harwood tapped her sparkly fingernails on her leather planner. Her braids, shot with bright red, draped down her back as she peered at the ceiling. Noelle assumed the counselor was trying to come up with an answer. Every time Noelle had been forced to sit through a standardized test, she repeated the same actions. They didn't help.

"We don't have a lot of options," she finally said.

No kidding. Mrs. Harwood summed up Noelle's life perfectly.

"You can stay with me for the weekend. I wish it could be longer, but Dave—that's my husband," Ms. Julie said, looking over at Mr. Christoph, "he went to get his mother. She hasn't been doing well lately. We're moving her in with us."

"Do you want to stay with Ms. Balinchek, Noelle?" Mr. Christoph came out from around his desk and stood in front of her. He was *asking* her?

"You can call me Julie." She aimed a glossy smile at Mr. Christoph, and a pang of jealousy shot through Noelle. Maybe she should reconsider her refusal to use makeup.

"Do you want to stay with Ms. Julie, Noelle? Even if it's just for the weekend?" He focused completely on her, and the unwelcome green-eyed monster retreated. His irises had faint lines of violet radiating out from the center in a sea of clear blue. It made them appear darker.

She dropped her gaze, not wanting to maintain eye contact in front of others. She nodded her agreement to stay with Ms. Julie. A sucking void built in her stomach. Ridiculous. He wasn't abandoning her.

She wasn't his.

Didn't want to be.

"I really appreciate it," Mr. Christoph told Ms. Julie. "Perhaps you can do some thinking over the weekend. Any ideas would be helpful."

"I'm sorry I can't make the same offer. If I had the space I would." Mrs. Harwood tucked away her pen and closed her notebook. "I'll make some calls. See if we can find something for Monday."

"Thanks," Mr. Christoph stood when Mrs. Harwood rose from her chair.

"We should get going." Ms. Julie stood and waited for Noelle to do the same. "We can stop at the grocery store on the way. Maybe rent a movie?" She moved toward the classroom door. "You know, this works out well for me. I needed a hand with the house to get ready for living with my mother-in-law." Ms. Julie grinned.

Noelle was unable to reflect the cheerfulness.

Mr. Christoph followed them. Ms. Julie walked out into the hall. Noelle lingered in the doorway. He put one hand on her shoulder. A small part of her prepared to fall into his embrace and beg him to keep her. She steeled her spine. He couldn't do it and probably didn't want to.

He was still holding her shoulder when he leaned in and told her quietly, "I'm sorry, Noelle. I wish… You'll be okay for the weekend. Monday, we'll have another meeting. See what can be done." He handed her a piece of paper. "My number. If you need anything, call. I'm not abandoning you. It just…has to be this way."

She stared at the writing.

He released her shoulder and rubbed his hand down her back as he nudged her through the classroom door.

She wouldn't have been able to force herself to go if he hadn't. Her fingers tightened around the scrap, and she shoved it into the front pocket of her jeans. With a deep breath, she blanked her face and followed Ms. Julie.

CHAPTER 7

$\mathcal{N}$ext Monday at 9:45 a.m., Nick escorted Noelle to a small conference room. A scarred oval table surrounded by utilitarian seating filled the space. Slatted metal blinds on a narrow window cut the harsh light in stripes across graying white walls.

All weekend he'd poured over Noelle's file and the laws regarding special education until he was bleary-eyed. Noelle's second diagnosis had to be wrong. Not only that, she'd received insufficient support in a regular classroom for her dyslexia. But the paperwork offered very little in the way of explanation. A transition plan done a couple of years ago languished in the file. Her parents hadn't attended that meeting, but they had signed off on the individualized education plan. It might be enough to propel Nick's solution forward. Despite the risk to his credibility if he was wrong, he had to take the chance.

Noelle sat in the black plastic chair he'd pulled out for her. She crossed her arms on the edge of the table, her eyes averted.

"Any problems this weekend with Ms. Bal...I mean, Ms. Julie?" Nick asked.

She shook her head.

"Why are you still here?"

Noelle's eyes snapped to his.

"I mean, why haven't you left to get a job or done a work-study program?" The question had burned in his mind for days. She didn't belong there.

"There aren't any programs for me. I don't fit. I'm not a super geek. I could drop out, but I'd lose access to two meals a day, air-conditioning, running water, a studio, and all the art materials. I can sell what I make."

"You think you'll earn enough to support yourself?" The words stung his own ears, but it wasn't a practical plan.

"I think a minimum wage job—if I could even get one—would give me rent for a room in a crappy house and no future. Art *is* my job—my *only* chance of success. This school is all I have, and even it's going away soon." Her eyes filled with sadness and longing, and his heart seized.

"Noelle," he said softly and took a step toward her. But he froze when the door opened and Principal Lopez, Mrs. Harwood, and Ms. Julie filed in.

Principal Lopez flipped on the fluorescent lights. Her skirt suit was drab beige, the perfect color for doing battle in the desert. Somehow the older woman made it look classy.

Nick cleared his throat. "Thank you all for coming. I know this was short notice."

"Thanks for scheduling during my planning period." Ms. Julie chuckled and dropped into a seat.

"Did you find everything you were looking for in that file, Mr. Christoph?" Principal Lopez closed the door.

"I have a plan. But it'll need support, and I'm not sure how feasible it is."

"I'm always willing to back my educators' well-thought-out academic designs for our very special students." Principal Lopez took her seat and smiled warmly at Noelle. "Where are your parents? They should be here for this."

Noelle looked up at Nick, wide-eyed, with her hands clenched tightly in her lap.

"The goal of this meeting is to update and accelerate a previous

IEP plan for Noelle's independence before she loses eligibility in December. It's been made more urgent with the arrest of her parents last Thursday night and her home being condemned."

Principal Lopez froze in the middle of crossing her arms. She placed her hands on the table instead.

No one said anything. He'd expected more surprise, especially on Lopez's part. Instead the woman nodded as if what he'd said explained everything. Apparently, the administrator was aware of the situation, if not the current events.

"We could go through the motions of having her retested and mainstreamed, but we don't have the time for that to be effective. Instead, I propose an intense course of work in the four fundamental areas—reading, math, science, and social studies—using techniques based on current research in learning and, specifically, learning disabilities." Nick passed around the document that listed the details. "The plan ensures Noelle is prepared to take the GED after she ages out."

Nick left out the part that she should have been mainstreamed years ago. Based on the documents buried in her file, her parents had fought it. Noelle, for her part, had only insisted on having access to the art class. She was a minor then, and he couldn't blame her. The adults in her past had let her down.

"What else?" Lopez asked.

"She needs to get a bank account and learn how to manage that. She needs to learn to pay bills. I'm not sure what she can qualify for, but she'll need a job and probably some government assistance so she has a place to live."

"Where is she living now?"

Julie updated Principal Lopez on where Noelle had stayed for the weekend.

"Noelle, do you have anything to say?" Nick was worried about how quiet she was. It couldn't be comfortable to have people talking about you and your future.

"I need access to the studio. And I want to get my diploma." Noelle clenched her hands into fists as she looked around the table. "I'll do whatever else I have to, to stay in art class and graduate."

"Of course," Ms. Julie said.

"I don't want you to give up anything before you have to. I'll help you, and so will everyone else in this room," Nick said. Noelle did nothing to acknowledge him. "But you're not eligible for a diploma. I thought you knew that."

"What?" Her eyes locked on him. "Why not?"

Nick cleared his throat. He hated having to break it to her in front of everyone. "The individualized graduation plan that was put into place years ago was never completed or modified. With the time we have left, the only viable option is the GED test."

Principal Lopez held out her hand. "Let me see that file."

Nick held his breath as she flipped through the pages of systematic failure. Noelle slumped in her chair, no longer looking at anyone at the table. Lopez had started at the school right before he'd been hired. He'd heard rumors about the previous administration's lack of concern for the students.

"What about her living arrangements?" Principal Lopez asked as she slid the file back to Nick. "I'm sure we can work through the educational and transitional plan, but we have a homeless student whose guardians are in jail. Technically, we can't even authorize this plan without them."

"We can assume that the documentation is sufficient for Noelle to be treated as her own guardian for our purposes. There is some final paperwork to do to complete it, but any other student at her level would have already been acting as their own guardian for the last two years." He paused and made eye contact with his boss.

"Go on." The principal wasn't giving her approval, but she hadn't shot him down either.

Mrs. Harwood cleared her throat. "I sent an email to our homeless-student liaison for the district." The counselor checked her phone. "She responded right away, but Noelle's age blocks her usual solutions. She's doing some more research. But I did find a charity facility with an open bed in their women's section."

Nick's stomach dropped. That wasn't what he wanted for her. There had to be something else. "I could—"

"Don't say it." Lopez shot a pointed look at Nick. "Noelle, you'll stay at the shelter until you have a job and assisted housing. It's only temporary. But for now, make it happen, people."

Noelle didn't look up, just nodded. Her arms were wrapped around her stomach, and her shoulders were rounded. She couldn't fold into herself any deeper. Her pain sliced through Nick's gut. He ached to hug her against his body and tell her everything was going to be okay and then hide her away. If he could keep her from ever being hurt again, he would, but she was off-limits no matter how hard she gripped his heart.

"Are the details documented?" Principal Lopez pulled the file back across the table.

Nick met his boss's gaze unflinchingly, glad she couldn't read his thoughts. "Yes, ma'am."

"Are we done? Because I have three hundred and ninety-six other students who need my attention today." She held out her hand for a pen, scrawled her signature, then stood. "I believe in you, Noelle. I know that underneath all these challenges, you're a smart young woman." The principal left the room.

Mrs. Harwood added her name to the document. "I'll meet you after school and give you a ride to the shelter."

"You can store your portfolio in my supply closet. Come in early. I'll be here." Ms. Julie signed her name and left.

Nick waited for Noelle to acknowledge he was still in the room. She stared intently at the document on the table, her lips pressed so tightly together that they were white. What was going on in that mind of hers? The silence was a mystery he burned to unravel. He blew out a harsh breath and rose.

"Noelle, you need to sign the form." Nick handed her the pen, sick with impotence. Was that all he could offer her?

CHAPTER 8

The ball of dread in Noelle's stomach grew the farther Mrs. Harwood drove down the empty street toward the shelter. Chain-link fences flanked both sides, an occasional battered dumpster the only thing breaking up the nothingness. She turned into a driveway, past a spindly tree doing its best to grow from concrete and decomposed granite. Set back from the street, a two-story building loomed. Evenly spaced windows along both the ground and top floors broke the expanse of beige. There were no details, nothing of interest. Just a plain building with a metal door. Not even a sign.

"This is it," Mrs. Harwood said as she stopped at a random location in the dirt lot. Other cars were parked in ragged rows farther away.

Noelle got out and calculated how early she'd have to get up to catch a bus. She planned to take advantage of every minute of studio time she could get. Yanking her backpack higher on her shoulder with one hand, she checked to make sure her cap covered her hair with the other. With a deep breath, she followed her counselor inside.

A staff member recited the facility rules as she showed Noelle to a cavernous room, barren except for rows of metal beds with thin mattresses. In a sad attempt to make the place more appealing, someone had painted the walls a drab peach color. Her tennis shoes squeaked with every step across the light blue flooring that reminded her of elementary school. A sickly hint of pine-scented cleanser, buried by the overwhelming scent of poverty and bodies, stung her nose. She would do whatever it took to get out of the shelter as quickly as possible.

Over the next few hours, women straggled in, clones of her mother. Too skinny, hair too scraggly, faces with yellow, pockmarked skin. Only one way to deal with those ghosts: don't talk, don't turn your back, don't show fear.

At least the place was free and she wasn't on the streets, and none of the women actually *were* her mother. Noelle would be indoors while she lay awake all night and figured out what to do next.

Thankfully, she'd opened a bank account with Mr. Christoph on his lunch hour or those women would've smelled the money on her. If she'd known how easy it was, she would have opened one sooner. She'd had to hold in a laugh as her teacher's eyebrows met his hairline when she'd taken out the three thousand dollars she'd saved. Some of that was from Mr. Christoph's purchase from the art show, but he didn't know it. Despite Gerald attempting to cheat her, she'd made over six hundred dollars on eight paintings. The shelter was temporary. She'd find a way to make enough to live on her own.

Three long days later, Noelle dragged onto the city bus. She hadn't slept. At least at home she'd had a door she could lock in her tiny bedroom. The shelter offered no privacy, and the lockers they provided were a joke. After the first day, she'd refused to repeat the experience of eating breakfast in their cafeteria with the other residents. Everyone ate together, men and women. She'd learned how to be invisible at school, but there didn't seem to be any way to avoid the focus of all those strangers, people mostly older than her, harder than her, and with less to lose. The food wasn't worth being on display. Instead, she ran through early and grabbed whatever was out—an apple, a small box of cereal—and tucked it away. She'd wait to eat at school and then spend forty-five minutes in the studio before going to class.

The bus on that side of town wasn't much better than the shelter.

But the driver had kind eyes and was older—she could tell by the amount of gray in his close-cut afro. "Sit by me, young miss." His deep warm voice had guided her when she'd boarded for the first time. She'd sat next to him each day since. Men streamed on at each stop, wearing dirty jeans and dirtier work boots. She held her backpack in her arms like a shield. It didn't stop them from staring, but it limited the view. Most of them got off before her stop.

When she stepped off the bus, she made sure no one followed her. Too early to be on campus, she checked the dumpsters on the way. There was a good one behind a tile store. Sometimes the ones behind the restaurants had old kitchen equipment. That was rare, but it was worth checking daily. That day, she didn't find anything for her art, but she found her best friend.

"Hey, Joe."

The old man lifted his craggy sandstone face from his knees and pulled a dirty blanket tighter. Watery brown eyes met hers, and his lips parted to reveal aging yellow teeth. "Little No-No."

Nostalgia rushed over her at his greeting. He'd called her that since she was a little girl, because the only word she'd used for the longest time was *no*.

"I got some stuff for you." She reached into her backpack. Joe had taught her so much about salvaging materials and using tools when he stilled lived in the trailer park.

"I got some stuff for you, too. Was waiting to see if you'd be here."

"Hulk's the best dumpster in Tucson." Noelle had nicknamed the giant green bin when she'd first seen it years ago.

"You betcha.'" He rolled to his knees and thrust his upper body into a tiny tent. In moments, his arms were full with a dented, slightly rusted sheet tray, pieces of pottery, and a few loops of silvery wire.

She dug into her pack and retrieved two boxes of cereal, an apple, and an orange. Joe might have less resources than the people at the shelter, but he didn't stink of despair. Or if he did, she didn't smell it.

"That's a fine trade, *mija*, but I don't expect nothing from you."

"Didn't expect anything either, but thank you." She sat with her friend while the sun rose in the empty blue sky.

"Time for you to go to school, no?"

"Yeah."

"*Bueno*. You go get smart. Get that diploma."

She tapped her forehead briefly to his shoulder. He'd repeated the same words to her since she'd started school. Joe had gone into the military before he'd finished and always regretted it. How was she going to explain to him that it couldn't happen? Not the way they'd planned. She'd find a way to tell him—soon. His gifts secure in her pack, she rose and walked down the alley.

"Morning, Ms. Julie." Noelle sat on the floor outside the classroom, where she'd been waiting for her teacher. She stood, ate the last bite of toast from the school breakfast, and brushed the crumbs off on her jeans.

"Hey, Noelle. How's it going?" Her teacher noticed every detail. Noelle was a mess, but there was nothing she could do, so it wasn't worth answering.

Noelle followed Ms. Julie into the classroom and dumped out her treasure. It wouldn't take long to clean, sort, and store it in her art locker. She retrieved her current piece as soon as she was done and got to work.

"This is different," Ms. Julie said from right behind her. Noelle continued to add more blue. "You usually stick with people, portraits."

"It's a portrait."

"It looks like two planets in a starry sky."

"It is. It's a portrait of two people who can't escape their orbit. They're attracted, but they can't come together."

"Wow. I can't wait to see it when it's finished." Her teacher didn't move. "Is this the piece you're going to put in the senior show? The competition is the first week in November."

She'd do everything she could to win. Five hundred dollars was motivation enough. But besides the prize money, it was an award she could use to convince an art gallery to hang her work.

"Not sure." Whichever piece was in progress was always her favorite. In a month, she might not like it as much. In the limited time she had left, she'd make as much art as possible so she'd have plenty to sell when she did find a gallery.

Time passed in a blur. After a glance at the clock over Ms. Julie's desk, she rushed to clean up and put her things away.

"Noelle, you're late." Mr. Christoph waited at the door for her. None of the other students even looked up from their work.

She set her backpack down at her desk, missing her portfolio that she used to store her random sketches or to work on designs during free time.

"We have a lot to accomplish. I need every minute with you I can get." He checked his watch. "What should we start with?"

Mr. Christoph's idea of preparing her for the GED was painful and exhausting. Reading out loud, vocabulary, and lots of written work, piled on top of math, science, social studies, and more reading. He shouldn't have been able to focus on her so hard—he had other students. But somehow, he managed to give them almost the same amount of attention he gave her. She'd never seen a special education classroom run with such precision. Even his new teaching assistant rushed around, efficiently following orders.

And Noelle was working her ass off, too. Every bit of knowledge she acquired for the test required her to repeat and review over and over again. Not like art, which flowed out like water from a faucet. At least, if the bill had been paid, the water flowed, not like at her trailer. Noelle stifled a hysterical giggle. Maybe all the GED work would pay the bill. Maybe life would get easier. She'd give anything to take a nap. Instead, she dragged her body over to her teacher's desk. She was so grateful when the end of the day finally arrived.

"I want you to stay after class today." Mr. Christoph's voice pounded into her achy head.

She froze in the midst of lifting her backpack to her shoulder. "I can't miss my bus."

"I'll give you a ride. We didn't get as much reading time in as I planned."

Lucas had lost his shit that morning about having to work on math with the TA. Again. And he'd threatened to cut the man's balls off and produced a knife. Mr. Christoph disarmed him easily and got the resource officer to remove the crazy asshole. At the time, Noelle had been happy to get out of reading.

"Fine." She dropped her bag. "But do we have to read *Huckleberry Finn?*"

"We need to get through the reading list for the GED."

She hated the book. It was about the child of an addict, a boy, who had missed out on getting an education. He kept getting offers from people who wanted to help him, and he refused all of them. The kid *enjoyed* having no future, no plan. Then there were words she couldn't figure out, some misspelled on purpose. Mr. Christoph wouldn't let her skip any she didn't know, and he wouldn't tell her what they meant. It took hours to read a couple of pages. The whole thing was bullshit.

The temptation to argue with Mr. Christoph welled up, but she wasn't stupid. Turning down a chance to change her life would be the dumbest thing she'd ever done. Besides, she craved more time with him. His kindness and his stern bark, the perfect mix. He was patient, never hurried her. It was like he believed she could accomplish whatever task he assigned. When he touched her shoulder, her body never failed to react. And the way he smelled. Did he notice when she leaned in to sniff him? God, she hoped not. Talk about embarrassing.

Noelle slumped in the desk after she pulled out the book. Mr. Christoph, still busy with his calendar, hadn't prompted her to start, so she put her head down on the desk. She'd rest for a few minutes. Reading aloud took all of her energy, and she didn't have any to give.

Someone touched her, shook her. She threw the desk back from her body and automatically assumed a defensive stance.

"Whoa." Mr. Christoph stepped back, hands up. "I tried to wake you, but you were sleeping so hard you didn't hear me call your name."

"Sorry." She righted the desk but couldn't face him. Heat crept up her neck to burn her cheeks. Another thing that sucked about being a redhead.

"You don't have to apologize." He wiped a hand over his mouth, gripping the stubble on his chin. "I shouldn't have touched you when you were sleeping. I know better."

"What time is it?" Noelle wanted to change the subject before her blush darkened to deep tomato red.

"About four-thirty. I had some paperwork to do and thought you'd wake up on your own. Are you sleeping at the shelter?"

"I'm fine." She shouldn't lie to him, but what could he do about the fact she was afraid to fall asleep with all those women around her?

"How about you read to me for an hour before I take you to get dinner." He sat down in the chair at his desk. "I can drive you to the shelter afterward."

Noelle nodded. Maybe he'd change his mind and let her go home with him again. For one more night, she'd do almost anything despite her promise to herself that she wouldn't return to his place. She'd made it before she'd slept at the shelter. Before she'd found out what true, deep sleep was in his bed. She yearned to go back there.

Next time, with him.

CHAPTER 9

$\mathcal{N}$ick escorted Noelle to his car. The butterflies in his stomach were unexplainable. It wasn't a first date. She wasn't his girlfriend. She was a student. A student whose voice was so soft and silky that he couldn't get enough. While she'd spent the last hour reading a Mark Twain novel, struggling with the words, he'd forced himself to focus on something other than the lushness of her lips and how nice it would be to kiss them. He was out of his mind. *Student, Christoph, student.* And he was taking his student to dinner.

"Have you eaten at Mario's?" He glanced at her as he pulled out of the parking space.

"No."

"Do you like Italian food?"

"I guess. I mean, I eat whatever they serve in the cafeteria, spaghetti or pizza or whatever." She picked at a loose thread on the inseam of her jeans, drawing his eyes to the V of her legs. He snapped his attention back to the road.

Nick cleared his throat. "I don't think what they serve in the school cafeteria should be called Italian."

The rest of the drive passed in silence. He studied her each time they paused at a light or when he needed to change lanes. Mesmerized by the tendril of hair that had escaped her knit cap, her light spatter of freckles, the delicate bones in her hands. He ached to touch her, caress her skin, run his fingers through her hair. Instead, he gripped the wheel tighter and focused on driving.

The hostess seated them at the little melamine table with two red vinyl chairs. The place was one step up from a greasy spoon, but Nick liked their food. He told himself that because it wasn't a fancy restaurant, if they were seen together, no one would accuse them of dating. They were just grabbing some dinner on a Thursday night before he dropped her off. No big deal.

Noelle held the laminated menu and squinched her face up while she read it. He hadn't thought about how hard it might be for her to make a selection. Jumping in wouldn't help her. He relaxed and let her take her time. If she needed help, she'd have to ask.

"Can I get you folks something to drink?" an older woman, who was probably one of the owners, asked.

"Coffee," Noelle said without looking up from the menu.

"Noelle. You should have milk."

Her gaze snapped to his. The argument ran across her face like newsprint. She glanced at the waitress.

"Fine."

"Water with lemon for me." Nick turned his attention back to his… dinner companion. "Do you want water, too?"

"I want coffee," she said under her breath. Louder she added, "But I'll take a water also. Thank you."

The woman left without comment.

"What is your deal with coffee?" Noelle asked him.

Besides the fact that she obviously had sleep issues like he did? "You're studying hard and that burns a lot of calories. You can't live on coffee and cafeteria food."

"I have until now."

"A lot of things are going to have to change. Even the finest tools will rust if not cared for."

She returned to studying the menu. He studied her.

She wore one of his shirts, the long-sleeved henley with the sleeves pushed up. The olive fabric complemented her pale skin. Her hair would have made the picture perfect. Now that he'd seen her hair down, he had to keep himself in check or he would snatch that cap off her head. It was better that her mane was covered. They weren't on a date.

The woman returned with the waters and milk. "Have you decided?"

"Noelle, do you need more time?"

"Um, can I have the pasta prim…prima…primavera?"

The woman corrected her pronunciation automatically and wrote it down. Nick ordered the same thing.

"Damn. I got it wrong." She scowled and stared out the wall-sized window.

"People mispronounce foreign words all the time. She knew what you wanted. So mission accomplished."

She didn't say anything, as usual. He wished he could read her thoughts. Instead he decided to pry more information out of his enigma. "This summer. Were you at a bar called Fried Egg Tavern?"

"Yeah." She turned back, but her gaze was lowered.

"What were you doing there? Do you know the manager?"

"I know Gerald. He's the owner's son." She dragged her finger across the table in small patterns.

"Was he the man touching you?" Nick tried to keep the growl out of his voice.

"You saw us?" Her chocolate eyes widened when she met his gaze.

"I did. You left right after that."

"I don't like people touching me. Usually." Noelle's voice faded so low that he almost missed the caveat.

"But why were you there?"

"For the art." Her answer made sense. Obvious once she'd said it. Her entire life centered around art.

"It was a spectacular show. I bought that piece for my house." An image of his angel popped into his mind.

"I know."

"Do you know the artist?" He should probably contact his parents if she did. They'd love to get introduced to an emerging artist with that much talent.

"Yeah."

"Is it someone Ms. Julie introduced you to?" Was it a man? Why did he care? He sipped at his water, trying to cool the burn building in his chest.

"It's mine." She lifted her chin and glared at him. "The art."

Nick put down his glass of water. "The portrait of the angel in my bedroom. You did that?"

A quick nod was all the confirmation she gave him.

"Noelle, your work is amazing. You're incredibly talented." And the knowledge made her more beautiful. Beautiful, talented, wild, and fierce. Every box checked. If he had a list. If being with her were acceptable.

Their dinner's arrival interrupted the conversation. Nick let her eat in peace. He needed time to absorb the fact that not only was she the gorgeous woman he'd seen in the bar, she was the artist who'd inspired his purchase.

"Noelle?"

"Hmm?" She was focused on her dinner.

"I need to ask you a question, and I want you to be honest. I won't be angry." It might not be the right time, but ever since her parents had been arrested, he'd had a seed of doubt.

Noelle put down her fork. "What?"

Nick sipped water so he could speak. "How did you get all that money? For the bank account?"

"I've been saving since I was ten." Noelle laughed. "I thought you were going to ask me a hard question."

"Since you were ten years old?" He shook his head.

"Yeah, I started doing odd jobs around the trailer park earlier than that. But I didn't learn to hide my money until later."

"So, it isn't drug money," Nick said, almost to himself.

"*No.*" Noelle's voice was loud, and the diner went quiet. She turned beet red and clamped her lips closed.

Nick leaned over the table and in a low voice said, "I'm sorry. I didn't mean that. It was the cop. She asked if you could be involved. Of course, I denied it, but I didn't know. And then you had all that cash."

"Never." Noelle bent toward him, their foreheads nearly touching, her eyes cold and steely. "I would *never* do that stuff. The reason I started hiding my money was because, before that, my mother, or maybe my stepfather, stole every penny unless I spent it first."

He leaned back in his chair. "How did you hide it?"

Noelle sat back, too. "My backpack has a false bottom." She shrugged. "One of the neighbors, Anna, taught me to sew. Her eyesight was bad and her hand shook, and she'd pay me to mend things."

"And you saved everything." Nick was in awe—she did anything to survive and even thrive.

"Every dime I could. It was only a matter of time before my parents died or were arrested."

"Still a lot of money."

"Another neighbor, Joe, used to have me help him recycle. He's the one who taught me about the value of things people throw away. At first I traded what we found for cash, then I started using it in my art. Which I sold, so some of it came from my showing."

"It's rare to make money selling art. Most never get a taste of the success you've had." Nick had seen artists, even with talent, not be able to translate their art to sales. But Noelle's had a realness which made it easy to relate to.

"The senior show is coming up. It has a cash prize."

Nick nodded, but the money couldn't be much. "I hope you win."

Noelle went back to eating. The rest of dinner passed without a word.

In the car afterwards, Noelle curled up in the passenger seat, eyes closed. She'd eaten almost her entire plate. It pleased him how much she'd enjoyed the dish. If he could, he'd take her to more restaurants, and movies, and museums. But they'd arrived at the shelter. She'd been through so much that it was no surprise that she needed to rest. He stifled the urge to turn around and drive her back to his home. He had to leave her. His job and his other students depended on him to do the right thing.

Unable to stop acting like he was on a date, he came around the car and opened her door. She took his hand and let him help her from the car. They were too close. He should back away, but he didn't. Noelle hesitated, then stepped forward and kissed him lightly on the lips.

"Thank you for dinner, Mr. Christoph." Her voice whispered across his tingling mouth. She adjusted the strap of her bag and strode into the shelter. His mouth hung open, and his dick tried to point him in her direction.

He forced himself to get back in the car and leave her at that godforsaken shithole. A military-issued tent in the middle of a war zone had been nicer.

Nick drove home in a daze. He ached to wrap her in his arms, take her home, and never let her go. He'd kiss her, and not a chaste peck on the lips. A passionate kiss, which owned her and claimed her as his. They'd make love for days, and he'd watch her work on her art after a lazy Saturday morning spent between her legs.

His house was cold and empty without her fire. He undressed as a sexy future formed in his mind. Noelle. His to touch, protect, provide for. A feisty warrior, wrestling with him. Heating him. Loving him. He stepped under the shower spray and soaped up his hand. His cock hardened, throbbing for her touch, but that would have to wait until after she'd left school. Would she do more than kiss him then? He stroked himself, pretending it was her paint-splotched fingers.

In his fantasy, she worked in an art studio attached to their house, her flaming red hair like a messy halo around her head. Dressed in one of his old white button-down shirts, she would lift her arms to apply more paint and her cute naked ass would peek out below the hem. He'd go to her and take her on the studio's daybed, unable to resist her beauty and talent. He'd dive between her legs and feast until she came all over his tongue. Then slowly, he'd slide up her body, dragging the shirt to expose her breasts to his mouth. As his fantasy built, he worked himself faster. His cock pressed into her tight, wet pussy. They would make love until he couldn't hold back any longer.

His balls rose up against his heated skin, and he erupted onto his hand, hips thrusting uncontrollably, searching for Noelle. For the real woman. But she wasn't there except in his mind. He sighed and washed himself.

Tomorrow. He would see her then. It wouldn't be enough, but he'd make it work until she finished school, and then maybe there would be room for him. But her life and her needs came first, no matter how much he desired her.

NOELLE SNAPPED up into a seated position, and the scratchy blanket slid down her torso. There wasn't supposed to be daylight streaming into the cavernous room empty of its usual occupants. She'd been so tired that she'd slept and slept hard. She'd dreamed of Mr. Christoph —Nick—that part she remembered. Could almost feel his hard cock pressed against her, his arm wrapped around her middle, holding her close.

But the rest of the night was a black hole of sleep. It must have been deep, because one of the ghost women had stolen the shoes off her feet. *Why the fuck would someone steal my shoes?*

They weren't great shoes. Just the cheapest, on-sale tennis shoes she'd allowed herself to afford. Now she had socks. Kind of. Her big toe poked through the left one.

She'd heard it could happen. Supposedly, if she left them on, it would prevent the theft. *Not.*

All of her money was in the bank, so she couldn't even buy a new pair. She grabbed her backpack from under her pillow and went downstairs to see if the staff could help.

It was after noon before Noelle had acquired a sexy pair of white plastic shower shoes and found something to eat. Going to school wasn't happening. She sat on the bus and stared at her big toe, avoiding the crazy man who wanted to talk. Crazy Man seemed to be looking at two different things at the same time, and she was one of them. Drool spilled out of the corners of his creepy grin, and his hand opened and closed repeatedly as if he were squeezing an orange. Crazy Man was in bad shape, needed help from somebody. But that couldn't be her. She had her own pile of shit to deal with. Her usual bus driver was off duty. She sat close to the new driver, but he didn't seem to care what happened in the passenger area. Noelle threaded the keys she carried, keys that opened nothing, through her fingers. A primitive but effective weapon. Hopefully, Crazy Man would stay on the bus.

First, she'd buy new shoes and socks. Why not splurge? The problem with getting new shoes was that she wouldn't be able to sleep at the shelter again. Not that she planned to.

After some banking and shopping, she'd spend the rest of the day on the hunt for inspirational discards among the dumpsters. Not exactly a fancy lunch and spa day like she'd seen on TV, but it wasn't bad.

And she needed a break from Mr. Christoph.

Nick.

She'd kissed him.

Done it and hadn't checked to see if he was shocked or mad or grossed out. It didn't matter since she couldn't take it back. The Labor Day holiday would give her four days away and might give him time to forget. He probably already had. It hadn't been much of a kiss, barely a peck.

Yeah, it was all working out for the best. New shoes and time away from school. Start again on Tuesday after a few nights in a cheap hotel room. The shelter sucked. There was nothing the principal and the counselor could say that would make her go back there.

And it wasn't like she was *never* going back to school. After all, the art room and Nick were there. She rang the bell to stop the bus and wove her way past Crazy Man. He followed her with one eye but remained seated. Noelle kept her keys at the ready and walked to the bank.

CHAPTER 10

$\mathcal{N}$ick stuck his head in the art classroom. "Ms. Julie?"

"People, please continue with your sketches." She stepped out and shut the door behind her. "Have you seen Noelle?"

"That's what I came to ask you."

"She never misses school." Julie's forehead wrinkled. "I've seen her come so sick, I've sent her to the nurse's office."

Nick ran his hand down his face. "I'll call the shelter and see if they know anything. If she isn't there, we should look for her." Why hadn't he thought to buy her a phone? "Can we meet after school?"

"I wish I could, but I have to get home. We hired a home health aide. If I'm late, I get charged time and a half."

"Your mother-in-law is sick?"

"Dementia. We didn't know how bad until my husband went to get her." Julie checked on her class through the small window cut in the door.

"I'm sorry."

"Me too. Will you let me know what happens?" Her fingertips brushed his arm. He held still, suppressing his instinctive recoil. She was a co-worker. And not Noelle.

"Give me your number." Nick programmed it into his cell phone.

A call to the shelter aggravated his concerns. Noelle's shoes had been stolen, and she'd told them she wouldn't be back. That was a problem. Where could she have gone? She'd need money—the bank.

The end of the day couldn't come fast enough.

~

"Mr. Christoph. Nice to see you again. How can I help you?" The bank manager clung to his hand. She was probably his age and, by the contact she was maintaining, single. He could use this to his advantage.

"Call me Nick, Lucy." He gave her his best panty-melting smile.

"It's my pleasure," she purred.

Nick followed the manager into her office, all glass walls and catalog furniture with a single plant. "Do you remember the young woman I brought in last week to open an account?"

"Of course, your…foster daughter?" She tapped his shoulder.

"Sure." He forced himself to step toward her and lowered his voice. "Is that account still open?"

"Let me check." Lucy walked around her desk, her ass swinging to an unheard bass line, and punched the keys on her computer. "Is she in some kind of trouble?"

"I'll know more based on what you can tell me." Nick avoided eyeing the cleavage on display as she bent over her keyboard.

"Well, I can't tell you much, and I really shouldn't tell you anything, but it will be just between us, right?" She winked at him and smiled.

Nick leaned forward over her desk and met her eyes. "Absolutely."

Lucy took a quick breath and blinked a couple of times before facing the monitor. "The account is still open, but she did make a withdrawal earlier this afternoon—two hundred. And it looks like she had a debit card issued."

"You're a lifesaver." Nick picked up her hand from the keyboard and gave it a quick squeeze. Just as quickly, he dropped the manicured flesh and double-timed it back to his car.

Noelle had money. He considered his conversation with the shelter staff. She'd have bought shoes first. Food and shelter next. She'd been ready to rent a motel room the night her parents had been arrested. A cheap motel, in a shitty part of town. Where criminals trafficked in victims and drugs. Nick scowled. When he got his hands on her, she was going to be very sorry for not bringing her problem to him.

There was no point trying to track down the shoe store, and it was probably too early for her to check into a hotel. It would still be light for hours. Where would she go? He called Julie's cell phone. As soon as she answered, Nick pelted questions at her. "Julie, what does Noelle do in her free time when she's not in the studio? Where does she hang out?"

"Nick?"

"Yeah, sorry. I think I know what she's up to. Renting a hotel somewhere. But not right away. What would she do to kill time?" Nick fired up the engine on his car.

"I know she hunts for materials for her work. Dumpster diving, so to speak."

Nick glared at the face of his phone as if he could see Julie in the screen. "Seriously, she's crawling in and out of dumpsters?"

"Yeah. I think she tends to focus on tile stores, home-improvement stores, and restaurants based on the stuff she brings in."

"Right." Nick hung up. Did no one care about Noelle? Her favorite teacher knew she crawled into trash bins and didn't see a problem? He hadn't put two and two together either when he'd admired the artwork at the bar. It was so far removed from being trash. And at the time, he hadn't known it was Noelle making the art. Nick slammed his hand on the steering wheel. *Where is she?*

He drove up and down alleys and behind all the big box stores, especially the DIY stores. Behind a Mexican restaurant, a stray dog loped down the packed-dirt path, tongue lolling. Nick continued to drive, eyes peeled for any sign of Noelle. Two men leaned together, exchanging something, likely drugs. His stomach soured as he searched behind a hamburger joint, a plumbing store. He closed the vents in his car to block out the hot stench of decay. A woman rolled a shopping cart laden with detritus, talking to people only she could see.

After a couple of hours searching, panic welled and the urgency to find her rode him hard. He couldn't stop. He crept down a long, narrow track behind a dated strip mall. Flashes of rolling through another desert city, oceans away, flickered in his vision. He stopped the car until his breathing evened out.

A hunched old man extracted a tent from his horde and began assembling it. The sun had dropped low, turning the light blue sky gold and the clouds fiery orange. Time to canvas the hotels. He'd start at the cheapest he could find and leave his number so they could call him if she checked in. A quick stop at the ATM and he was armed with incentive for the clerks to talk.

Nick parked at the third hotel in his quest. It was better than the last two, but not by much—one half star, according to the website aiding his search. His rage was white-hot, and he hadn't found her yet. At that rate, he'd burst a blood vessel and die in his car.

"Hey, man, how's it going?" Nick asked the clerk through the door of the private area where the young man watched a pornographic cartoon on a crappy television.

"Be right there." The guy stood up and hit a button somewhere, freezing the animated woman with her tits full screen.

Charming.

He palmed a folded twenty out of his pocket and settled his hand on the counter with the edge of the money showing. "I'm looking for someone who may have checked in today."

"Had a few people check in." The kid scratched his chin as if he had a beard.

"You'd remember her."

"Oh yeah. Her." The kid rolled his eyes.

Nick's chest pounded, and his throat got tight. He slid the money farther out. "What'd she look like?"

"I don't know, my age? Wearing a hat. It's too fucking hot to be wearing a hat, man."

"Yeah, I hear ya, bro." He put the money in the kid's outstretched hand but didn't let go. "What room?"

"Sixteen." The clerk tugged on the bill. "But she can't have her money back."

"I'll handle it." Nick released the twenty and marched out of the grimy glass box that acted as the lobby. He jogged down the unlit sidewalk under the sagging overhang. Some of the rooms had numbers tacked on the faded green doors, others had been inked in with a marker. Number sixteen was close to the end.

A gunshot sounded, and he dropped to a crouch—scanned the open parking lot. Not a gun. A truck had backfired. He closed his eyes, took slowing breaths, and visualized his safe place. Rising, he moved the last few steps toward where he'd find her. He halted and pounded on the flimsy barrier.

"Noelle! Open up. It's Nick Christoph. Noelle." Desperation colored his voice. He continued his assault on the flimsy wood-paneled door until it opened. Finally. Her face appeared before him, loose hair grazing her shoulders and eyes wide. She was alive.

"What are you doing here?" She had one hand on her hip and one on the door.

"What am I doing here? What are *you* doing here?" The part of the room he could see wasn't from that century. Old, faded pastels that had probably once been a Southwest palette. He could swear the mud-brown carpet she stood on was moving. Disgust rolled up his spine. "Have you lost your mind?"

"I needed a place I could sleep."

"Get your stuff." He clenched his fists and crossed his arms, widening his stance to take up more space like he'd learned to do when he'd commanded troops.

"I paid for the night." Noelle mirrored his pose. "I'm staying."

"No. You aren't. Get your stuff." It was all he could do not to take her over his knee right there. If he didn't think they'd catch a disease by sitting on that bed, he would. "Now."

Noelle blanched. She dropped her fists and picked up her back-pack. "Let me get my things out of the bathroom."

"You have three minutes." He had to get her out of there so he could fix her thinking.

Two minutes and a brief text to Ms. Julie later, letting her know Noelle was safe, Nick marched Noelle to the car. His hand still shook as he opened the passenger door for her and took her backpack. The bag had to weigh thirty-five pounds at least. He tossed it in the back seat. Sliding in the driver's side, he tried not to slam the door.

"Mr. Christoph…"

Nick stared out the windshield and slowed his breathing to clear the red from his vision. "We'll talk when we get home. Until then, not a word."

CHAPTER 11

*N*oelle expected Nick to rage and scream. Instead, he drove the speed limit. Used his blinker. Didn't slam to a stop. His control sucked away every bit of hers. She sat, lips pressed together to keep from babbling, hands tightly clenched in her lap to resist flinging open the car door and running for it. To nowhere.

There was no way to predict what he would do next. She tried to take comfort in the fact that all he'd done since she'd met him was help her.

They pulled into his driveway. Nick turned off the car. He removed the key. Noelle remained frozen, waiting for instruction. The fact that he'd taken her to his home and not somewhere else confused her. Almost as much as him tracking her down.

"We're going to go into the house. I'll put your things in my study. Then we'll discuss how poor your choices were today."

Noelle opened her mouth to argue. She'd made excellent choices. Mostly.

He held a hand up. "First, you're going to listen. Then you can have your turn."

Noelle nodded because if she stopped biting her tongue, the excuses would flow. He was still eerily calm, but his jaw was tight, and the veins in his neck bulged. Her hand shook as she opened the car door. When she stepped out into the arid night, her legs wobbled and threatened to collapse.

In the living room, the shaking worsened while she waited. Maybe she should have called the school or even gone in late. But she was an adult and could make her own decisions, even bad ones. Was Nick going to keep her or take her back to that shelter? No matter what he said, he couldn't make her go. He could storm and threaten, but she wasn't going to spend another sleepless night in a room with twenty strangers looking to steal her stuff. That was bullshit.

"Here."

Nick's voice made her jump, almost knocking a glass out of his hand.

"Steady. You don't have to be afraid, Noelle."

"I'm not." She accepted the glass and quickly drank it down, surprised at how thirsty she was. "I didn't hear you come in."

"Doing some deep thinking?" Nick sat down in the armchair next to the couch.

Noelle didn't say anything while she took her time setting the cup on the coffee table. Faced with the disappointment and anger of a man who'd only treated her with kindness, her bravado slipped away. A man who attracted her far too much to ignore her feelings. Even though he was an overbearing ass most of the time, it was obvious he felt something for her. One of the few people in the world who did. But his expectations—

"Noelle, I know you're an adult."

"I'm not go—"

He held up his hand to stop her. "Let me finish. You'll have your opportunity." He paused, and his gaze bored into her brain. "You're an adult, but with very little experience. You've taken care of yourself, but you always had a mom and dad and a home, even if none of them were very desirable. This whole thing with your parents' arrest thrust you into the world unprepared. I know I'm only supposed to be your teacher, but I care about you. Probably more than I should." Nick wiped his palms along denim-clad thighs. "I know you had some trouble at the shelter—"

"I'm not going back there." She crossed her arms. "I can't sleep. They take my shit."

"I'm not sending you back. But that's not the point."

The knots in Noelle's shoulders released. If he wasn't going to try to force her back there, she could deal with anything else.

"You could have called me from the shelter. Or at least called the school to get a message to me. I could've helped you. I *want* to help."

Nick's intense gaze demanded a response, but what should she say?

"You didn't call. You disappeared." The hurt in his voice was unexpected.

"I was late, and all I had were plastic shower shoes." She glanced down at her new navy canvas sneakers.

"Being late and having crappy sandals is no reason to avoid the one place where there are people to help you." Nick ran his hand over his head. "Ms. Julie was worried. I imagined the worst but couldn't leave the classroom." His deep blue eyes pierced her. "Waiting until the end of the day to find you was…torture."

The graveness of his voice scraped her nerves, and she hung her head. "I'm sorry."

No one ever gave a shit where she was. She went to school because it provided food and art. She didn't have friends there. Ms. Julie had her own life, and they didn't talk about anything but art. Nick—he was her teacher. She shouldn't be attracted to him. He made her feel things she'd avoided. Guilt was the latest emotion, and she didn't like it at all.

"When I saw you in that ratty motel room, I nearly lost my mind. What if something had happened and I wasn't able to…" He closed his eyes for a moment before locking them back on her. "I wanted to throttle you for putting yourself in such a risky situation." His voice dropped to a rough whisper. "I wanted to hold you."

The nearly inaudible words hit Noelle low in her belly, and her knees went weak. Nick raised his head slightly and pursed his lips.

"I don't want you to ever put yourself in that kind of danger." His grip tightened so hard around the arms of the chair that the leather was going to bruise.

"Well, what am I supposed to do?" She threw her hands in the air. "They condemned my trailer. I don't have any other family. I don't have a lot of money. That crappy hotel room was a fuck-ton better than the druggie-packed shelter. What the fuck was I supposed to do?" Her eyes burned with unshed tears. The past week had been brutal. She wrapped her arms around herself and rolled her lips between her teeth.

Nick rose to stand right in front of her. "I'll tell you what you're supposed to do. What you're going to do." He held up one finger. "Number one, you're going to stop swearing at me. I won't tolerate it." He held up a second finger. "Number two, you're going to stay here. We'll keep it a secret for now, but I'm not letting you out of my sight again." He put up a third finger and raised his eyebrows at her. "Number three, you need to decide what you want to do with your life."

Noelle's head swam with his words.

He held his open hands out to the side, as if he had nothing to hide and every truth to give. "Part of being an adult is deciding what your goals are. Going after them. I know you've done some of that with your artwork, but you have some big decisions to make."

Nick dropped his hands and stared at her.

No swearing. That made sense—it was rude. And he wanted her to stay with him, but what did that really mean? And number three? She had a plan. But how could she make it happen after her world had unraveled too soon? She wasn't ready.

"What, Noelle?"

"I'm sorry I swore at you?" Noelle wasn't sure how to answer; her thoughts were as jumbled as her emotions. She reached for his hand and savored its warmth.

"What else?" Nick's fingers enclosed hers.

"If I stay here, where am I going to sleep?"

"For tonight, in my bed."

"Where are *you* going to sleep?" Hope speared through her, leaving a singed path of need. She peered up at him through her eyelashes, hoping she wouldn't blush.

"On the couch."

No.

"What if I don't want you to sleep on the couch?" The words escaped in a whisper. She put her fingertips over her lips. Since she'd stayed the night what felt like weeks ago but was only days, Nick and his bed had been a constant desire no matter how she tried to push it from her mind.

"I'd say…I appreciate the invitation. For now, I'll take the couch. I can rearrange the study and put a bed in there. We have options. You don't have to sleep with me. That isn't what this is about."

Noelle cringed and couldn't meet his eye. He didn't want her that way.

"Noelle." Her name was a growl on his lips. Nick tilted her chin up with the fingers of his free hand. The heat of his touch ignited her desire.

"Don't be embarrassed. Please. I'm trying to do the right thing. I've been attracted to you from the moment I saw you." His fingers traced down her neck before he let them drop.

A shiver trilled up Noelle's spine.

"But there's a lot happening right now. There's a lot at risk."

Noelle nodded. She raised her gaze to his, trying to figure out what could make him care for her when he could lose everything.

"Angel…" He squeezed her hand. "You're so special. And, if you still want me in your bed *after* we figure all this out, there's no place I'd rather be." He lifted her hand and kissed it before letting it go. "You honor me."

Noelle stopped fighting the urge to lean into him and put her arms around him. He pulled her closer. She tucked her head into his neck, breathing him in. He smelled so good, like Nick. Several minutes passed, the heat from his body warming places inside her that had always been frozen. The magic broke when her stomach growled so loudly that it probably roused the neighborhood dogs.

Nick stepped back laughing. "Guess I should feed you."

Noelle nodded. The loss of him was already letting the chill return.

He guided her to the kitchen. "We'll eat, and then you're going to get some sleep. In the morning, we'll figure out your life plan."

For the first time, Noelle considered adjusting her dreams to include someone else.

NICK SAT in the darkened living room, his cell phone screen the only light. He had to make the call. It was only fair, but the explanation would be weak at best. Sucking in a fortifying breath, he dialed.

"Saint." Gabe's voice crackled with sleep.

"Sorry, man, forgot it's later there."

"No worries. Still coming out tomorrow? I got brats and beers and a shit-ton of work to do around here." Gabe chuckled.

Nick ran a hand over his head. "Yeah, no. That's the thing. I had to cancel my flight."

"Everything okay?" Gabe's voice filled with the alertness of a soldier coming on line.

"Fine." How could he explain it? "A student had an emergency. I took her in."

"Her?"

"Um. Yeah. It's complicated. She's almost twenty-one. But she doesn't have a place to live at the moment. Kind of a sudden thing."

"What are you doing, man?"

"The right thing. I think. But I won't be there to help with the renovations this weekend."

"Two of my brothers are here. I'll be fine. Wanted to see you. But—"

"I know." Nick cleared his throat of the chagrin threatening to choke him.

"So, this girl, *woman*—are you...I mean..."

"Attracted to her?"

"I shouldn't even ask."

"It's not about that."

"If anyone could live with a woman and keep his hands to himself, it's you, Saint."

The name stung. He was anything but. He promised to reschedule and offered more apologies to his friend before he hung up.

Nick dropped the phone on the table and flopped back on the couch in total darkness. Once again, he'd put himself in a no-win situation. For a woman. But for Noelle, he was willing to burn everything to the ground.

CHAPTER 12

$\mathcal{N}$ick rolled and caught himself with one hand on the carpet before he fell off the couch. The previous day came back to him in a series of images, no sound, no emotion, until he got to the part where Noelle slept in his bed. His morning wood strained, sending shots of need down his thighs. He pressed the heel of his hand down on it, over his sweatpants. No relief.

Bathroom. Eyes barely open, he shuffled down the hallway.

Noelle rushed out of his bedroom and knocked into him.

Arms full of soft, forbidden woman, his erection pressed into her belly. *Yes.* He could return her to his bed and heal the pain of wanting her. *No.* She wrapped herself around him, restricting his escape from his insane urges. He had to stop it. "I'm going to use the bathroom, then you can have it."

Noelle pressed her nose into his chest. "You smell so good," she whispered.

He tightened his hold on her.

It would be the wrong move to escalate the situation by pressing his face into her neck and kissing his way to her lips. He arched away, holding her at arm's length. Her skin darkened to a deep, hot red.

"Sorry," she mumbled. "I thought—" Her gaze dropped to where his erection bridged the space between them.

Scalded with embarrassment, he snapped his arms free. Her grip loosened. He practically ran, calling over his shoulder, "I'll be right out."

Slamming the bathroom door between him and temptation, Nick panted as if he'd just completed an obstacle course. Damn. She couldn't get her GED fast enough. Gabe was right. Living with a student was bad. But living with Noelle? There was no possible way he was that much of a saint. He stood away from the toilet and pressed his aching dick down so he could relieve himself.

Why? Why had his libido decided to wake? A lack of sex drive, gone cold since his wife's death, had earned him the "Saint" nickname. That, and a few honest moments when Nick had questioned the moral compasses of those around him. "Saintly" didn't describe him anymore.

Thankfully, his hard-on disappeared in a wave of self-loathing. He washed his hands and brushed his teeth quickly.

Noelle waited outside the door.

"It's all yours. Clean towels in the cabinet. I'll make some eggs." Nick walked away from her as he rattled off the list. "We'll talk over breakfast."

The only response was the clack of the wooden door closing against its frame.

First order of business, find out what her plans were after she left school. In his experience, most people had no idea—at least, the ones he'd met in the service hadn't. A few of them had always intended to serve, but the majority had joined when the parties were over and they'd been left at loose ends. Noelle could join the military if she wanted. It provided a healthy, disciplined life with job training. But the barracks didn't include art studios. He doubted his defiant artist would enjoy the life as much as he had—until everything had gone sideways.

He shut down the memories and retrieved a carton of eggs and butter from the refrigerator. Going through the domestic motions of making scrambled eggs packed with veggies and a bit of cheese, along with whole-grain toast, brought him back to center. Mostly. Group met on Wednesday—but that was a long five days away. He could always call the counselor in an emergency. But the recollection of his combat failure didn't make the situation urgent, just uncomfortable.

Noelle appeared at the opening of the kitchen, dressed, hair wet. No matter how she appeared, the magnetic draw to her was nearly impossible to resist.

"Coffee?" Noelle spun in the kitchen searching his empty counters. "I can't function without coffee."

"Looks like you're breathing to me." Nick hid his smile at her frustrated groan.

"I'll make it, just show me where you have the pot."

"Don't own one."

She narrowed her eyes at him, and while he might have won that skirmish, the war clearly wasn't over.

Noelle whipped open the door to the refrigerator and pulled out a carton of orange juice. She held it up to him with a questioning glance. He nodded and pointed at the cabinet with the glasses. She pulled out two glasses and filled them, a drop of juice hitting the counter. Nick quickly wiped up the spill while Noelle put away the remainder.

"Butter the toast and we're ready to eat."

She followed his instruction and then sat with him at the table.

When he'd bought the Craftsman house, it had seemed like more than enough space. With Noelle there, filling the room with her spirit, it was too small. He couldn't avoid her. And every time he brushed up against her energy, he wanted to coat himself in it, like it would make him invincible to reality. He choked down a bite of cooling eggs. It would be difficult to let her go, but he had to encourage her to make plans. He'd deal with the loss when it came like he had in the past.

"HAVE YOU THOUGHT ABOUT YOUR FUTURE?"

"Every day since I was ten." Noelle tried not to sound sarcastic. Nick didn't know her. He'd based his question on concern, not judgment.

"What do you want, Noelle?"

"A place to live." The flicker of hurt that flashed across Nick's face had her quickly clarifying. "I mean a place of my own. Nothing fancy. Safe. With good light, so I could paint there until I get a studio."

Nick nodded. "How are you going to pay for that?"

"I did pretty good with the art show at Fried Egg this summer."

"That's only one show. That's not going to pay the rent very long."

Ouch. His statement was accurate, but it still stung. "It's a start. Obviously, I need more shows. Maybe something permanent where I can keep work up year-round. And I could teach some art classes."

"Have you taught before?"

"Couple times. Girl Scout troop. Visiting middle schoolers." Noelle had loved showing younger students basic techniques and how to blend their colors. Getting them to put their imagination on the canvas.

"Wow." Nick's eyebrows shot up. "That's great."

She looked down at her breakfast, unsure how to respond to his praise.

"Those aren't bad plans. But you might not make enough to sustain an apartment, food, and transportation."

"I know how to live cheap." She chomped her toast, daring him to contradict her. Cheap living was like a religion for her family. And she had at least part of what she'd need for rent saved up.

"Aside from your savings, what are you doing specifically, right now, to make this happen?"

Nick's words sliced deep. She dropped her toast to her plate and wiped the crumbs from her hands. Nothing. She wasn't doing anything. Except the living-cheap part since she hadn't paid for the breakfast she was eating. Things came to mind that she should do but hadn't—look for a job, look for an apartment, look for a gallery. A spark of competency flashed. "I'm making art. Every day. Art I can sell."

"What else?"

God, he wouldn't let it drop. The spark faded. Fucking life plan. No pressure at all. What else *should* she be doing? "I guess I need to look for a gallery. Maybe one of the shops in the old-town area would take my work?"

"Possibly. But they might want art that screams, 'Tucson desert.' Are you willing to paint something that sells versus expresses?"

"I don't want to." The thought of painted saguaros, like rows of middle fingers flipping fuck-yous across the landscape, made her stomach turn.

"What about an out-of-state gallery?"

"Not sure how to go about that."

Nick crossed his arms. "So, you have some research to do."

Noelle nodded, lips pursed. She'd talk to Ms. Julie on Tuesday.

"We should work on GED prep," he said.

Noelle sighed. The man never quit. "Fine."

"Also, I like to run. You can come with me."

"I don't run." Not unless she had to.

"Exercise is good for the mind. Helps with creativity."

He must be right, because her imagination created an image of sweaty, shirtless Nick. And it was very inspiring.

"I can show you the studies."

Seriously? She released a sigh as the sexy image disappeared. He was going to show her research on why she should work out. And probably make her read it out loud, too. And analyze any math or science in the article. "I'll go."

"Great. You clean up the kitchen since I cooked, then we'll read for an hour to let our food settle before we head out."

Oh boy! Noelle didn't let the sarcastic words slide out of her mouth. Nick had the best intentions, and she had a free place to stay. At least while it lasted, she would try to get along. But why couldn't he offer sex as a workout? It had almost happened earlier in the hallway. Two steps and they'd have been in the bedroom. She'd be so on board with that. Instead, she followed him into the kitchen with her dirty dishes.

She expected him to leave as she loaded the dishwasher. But he wiped down the dining room table, then came back and cleaned the stovetop. He scrubbed the already-sparkling counters. Didn't he trust her to clean up after a damn meal?

"I'm going to take a shower," Nick announced.

Before a run? Didn't matter. Not her water bill. She retrieved her sketchbook and a pencil from her pack and tried to come up with ideas she could paint for an old-town gallery. What ended up on the page was the back of a naked man under a spray of water. It might not work for tourists, but she'd buy it.

CHAPTER 13

Nick dropped into his office chair. He'd given up pretending to sleep. When he'd leaned his head against the closed bedroom door, Noelle's soft snuffles reassured him she wasn't suffering like him. No surprise. She'd worked hard, doing everything he'd asked the entire holiday weekend, including three runs that proved how much she needed regular exercise and better gear. And maybe some defense training. He'd add that to their schedule. Peaceful times were the time for preparation.

He typed another search into the browser on his computer. Previous searches for art gallery jobs, art teachers, and postings looking for artists didn't bode well for Noelle's plan. Nobody was begging for artists. Especially ones without college degrees or teaching certificates. And Noelle hadn't yet graduated high school. He pulled up the requirements for the GED and perused them again. What Nick found didn't help him fall asleep. The plan he formulated required sacrifice, and if he wasn't careful, Noelle would abandon the GED, and him, completely. It was risky to ask her, because she'd lose access to the school studio—unless… He needed to talk to Ms. Julie.

Tuesday morning, Nick stuck his head in the empty art classroom. "Ms. Julie? Got a second?"

"Hey, Nick. Come on in. Good holiday?" Julie sat at the back of a room packed with stuff he would've thrown away. Easels and paintbrushes were stacked haphazardly. Paint spattered the walls and tables. The room screamed for gloves and garbage bags. To start.

But he needed Julie's help. He squashed the criticisms and moved to requests. "I've got a delicate situation. Hoping you can work with me."

"Noelle? She seemed okay earlier. Apologized for missing school and making us worry."

"Yeah." He brushed a hand over his head. There was no way to ease into the conversation. "The thing is, she can't be a current student and register for the equivalency exam."

"What?" She tilted her head.

"To take the GED, Noelle has to—"

"You want her to drop out?" Julie's voice quivered with horror.

"No." He reverted to the words he'd planned. "It has to *appear* that she hasn't been in class so when the time is right, she'll already have been disenrolled and can take the test. But she'd still be coming to class. Mine *and* yours. But we wouldn't report it."

"You want me to lie?"

Julie was right. It had sounded reasonable when he'd come up with the idea. But he was asking her to lie. "If she loses access to the studio, she could quit *everything*. The school failed her—for years. I'm trying to find a way to make this right. It's for Noelle. And if anything…if there's any backlash, I'd say I didn't let her come to art class. Take full responsibility. It won't come back to you."

"I mark her absent, even though she's here."

"Yeah." Nick rubbed the back of his neck. "She'll be dropped automatically."

"No. A truancy officer is assigned. And a dropout prevention plan is developed."

"The officer will get her home address. They won't find her there."

"They'll know she's at the shelter. Mrs. Harwood notified the homeless-student liaison."

"Pretty sure it only matters for students under eighteen." And she wasn't living at the shelter. "But all of this regulation stuff aside, in the end, it will help Noelle."

"How does this help her? And why would you be willing to risk your career over one student?"

Both good questions. He only had a sane answer for one. And he might be mistaken about the sanity of that one. "She can still do her art, which she needs if she's going to have something to sell later. She can still practice for the tests. Turns out, there's a special civics one for Arizona, so we have more work."

"Have you talked to Noelle about this?"

It was a fair question, one he'd expected. "No, I don't want to interrupt her progress or add any more stress. With everything she's been through—her parents, the shelter—it's just a paperwork challenge. Not a big deal."

Julie stared at him. Nick stood firm despite the niggling trail of guilt that wound its way up his spine. No fidgeting, no speaking. At least she hadn't questioned his urgency. The classroom clock ticked loudly while he waited for her answer. He had nothing else to convince her. If she wouldn't go along with it—well, he'd build that bridge when he came to it.

"Fine."

"Thank you."

Julie pointed a finger in his face. "But if this blows up, it's on you."

He raised his hands in surrender. "Absolutely."

NOELLE WAITED OUTSIDE ART CLASS. She still came early, like she was staying at the shelter. Nick had offered to drive her, but she'd insisted on taking the city bus. He'd looked relieved and guilty when he'd handed her the prepaid pass. Neither of them addressed the fact that he followed the vehicle each morning. He'd even waited the day she got off the bus early to check her favorite dumpster. When they arrived, she would go to the cafeteria, and he would go from the parking lot to the classroom. All the man did was work. With her, with the other students, and even when he was home. Studying files or working with her. Except for a couple of Wednesday nights when he'd had an "appointment," he worked.

"Noelle." Ms. Julie's voice dragged Noelle back to the present. "I'm so glad you're here."

Where else would she be? Ms. Julie had been acting weird the past couple of weeks. Maybe she knew Noelle was living with Nick. Nerves prickled the back of her neck.

"I have something for you." Ms. Julie unlocked the classroom door.

Noelle followed her into the sanctuary. The smell of drying paint and dust soothed any worries. She felt more comfortable at Nick's every day, but the studio was home.

Ms. Julie set a paper shopping bag on the metal stool in front of Noelle. She peered inside. Clothes. She lifted her eyes to Ms. Julie.

"I'm sure they'll fit. We're practically the same size," her teacher said, excitement lacing her voice as Noelle pulled out a silky, cobalt, short-sleeved top and then reached back in the bag. A black skirt followed, along with a pair of low heels. The shoes were brand-new. No scuffs on the bottom. "You'll need them for your job interview."

"Job interview?" Noelle swallowed down the flutters in her stomach. What kind of job could she qualify for that needed her to dress up that much?

"A woman I know from my old book club has a friend who owns a gallery downtown. She needs an assistant. Two evenings and Saturdays."

"Really?" A bubble of excitement built. It filled her with the unfamiliar sensation of...hope.

"Good news, right?" Ms. Julie fluttered around. "The interview is today. After school."

"Today?" Bubbles burst in a wash of dread. "That's great." *Liar.* She'd never interviewed for anything.

"You can change here, and then I'll drive you over. My husband's meeting our caregiver, so I can wait until you're done. We can grab a bite and celebrate. I'm sure you'll get it, then I can drive you to the shelter."

Crap. Up until Ms. Julie had said the part about the shelter, Noelle had been excited, nervous but thrilled. She needed the job interview, but how could she get out of the ride?

"Noelle?"

"Um, yeah." She forced a smile to her lips. "Thank you."

Ms. Julie tucked the bag of clothes away. A million questions and doubts swirled in Noelle's brain. What did gallery assistants have to do? How was she supposed to act during an interview? She silenced the stream of questions. A solution would come. Nick would help her.

Noelle got her planet project out. The painting part was almost done. The thin layers of paint built up just as she'd envisioned, giving the piece a "celestial" quality according to Ms. Julie. The tiny metallic tiles and wires would add the sparkle the piece needed. Noelle let herself get lost in her work until she had to go to class.

The day passed in a blur. Noelle focused on slow, deep breaths as Ms. Julie drove into the heart of the city.

"Noelle, be yourself. Be honest. Let the owner know how much you love art and how dependable you are. I already gave you a reference." Ms. Julie glanced from the road to her. "You look very professional. Perfect for the job."

Noelle tugged on the end of the ponytail they'd tied her hair into. Her teacher sounded as nervous as she was. Too soon, they were there.

Ms. Julie leaned across the front seats. "I'll be right over there, at the coffee shop. Just gotta find parking."

Noelle nodded and closed the door. She could do it. Had to. It was part of her life plan. First get the job, then she'd negotiate for a small space. A place to hang her work for sale year-round.

She pulled open the glass door by the hot metal handle. The front of the gallery featured two stone sculptures displayed in large windows. The rest of the space was long and narrow, broken up by random pieces of wall unconnected to anything but the floor. Noelle stepped off the entrance mat, and her shoe slid on the polished concrete, nearly taking her down. Recovering, she smoothed her skirt with a shaking hand and tugged her hair. The room had that captive air smell she associated with museums. With slow, mincing steps, she made her way toward the back, where she assumed the office would be.

Two different artists' work hung on the walls. An abstract painter who used bold black brushstrokes on white canvas, and another who seemed to favor the encaustic process in desert pastels. Didn't expect to see that technique in Tucson. Maybe they were using a resin that would set and be resistant to heat, not the beeswax she'd had to use in school.

"You must be Noelle." A harsh voice snapped Noelle back to her reason for being there.

"Yes." She held out her hand to the trim, dark-haired woman as she'd practiced with Nick. Hopefully, the woman wouldn't notice the tremor.

"I'm Greer Davis." She was dressed from head to toe in black except for a large silver necklace. "You may call me Greer."

The name on the door—*Greer Davis, Fine Art.*

Crap. She was the owner. Noelle smiled. "Nice to meet you."

Nick's training seemed to work. Greer nodded, and Noelle followed her into an office. It was minimally furnished with a glass-and-chrome table for a desk and two black-and-chrome chairs in front. The only color in the room came from an individually framed abstract diptych. Noelle sat in the closest seat, and they talked about art and what her expected duties would be. The pay wasn't great, but it was a job, in a gallery. Hours she could work around school. Noelle sighed with relief when the meeting was over and she stepped outside. The harsh heat warmed her like a hug. She clacked across the crosswalk to the café. Would Nick be there? He was supposed to offer to drive her back to the shelter.

The heavy scent of coffee made Noelle's mouth water. God, she missed it. Her eyes adjusted to the dim interior, and she glanced around. Ms. Julie sat at a round, wooden table to the left of the door, but she wasn't alone. Nick. He was there. Relief settled over Noelle and the nerves holding her hostage for the last hour released.

When his eyes landed on her, he froze mid-sentence. His gaze licked down from her tied-up hair to her pointy black heels.

"How did it go?" Ms. Julie's perky voice broke their connection.

"I got the job." Noelle's body lengthened as pride stretched along every muscle.

Ms. Julie jumped up and squealed. But Nick's quiet "The first victory of many," resonated deep, infusing her with confidence.

"Mr. Christoph?" Ms. Julie calmed enough to speak. "Do you want to join us? We're going to do an early celebration dinner."

"I'd be delighted." Nick stood and tucked his chair into the table.

Noelle couldn't wait for dinner to be over so she could be with Nick.

Alone.

CHAPTER 14

Noelle dropped into the passenger seat of Nick's car. She'd been amazed how easily he'd talked Ms. Julie into taking Noelle to the shelter himself. But her art teacher had it rough. So much responsibility caring for her family and yet she was still looking out for Noelle's best interests. Getting her a job and taking her to dinner. It surprised Noelle, but in an awesome way.

Noelle wiggled her toes in the uncomfortable pointy heels. The new boss, Ms. Davis—Greer—scared the crap out of her. Her rough voice and direct ways made Noelle nervous that she would screw everything up. She couldn't lose not only a job, but potential gallery space. Not to mention disappoint Ms. Julie. *No pressure.*

"What's going on inside your head, Angel?" Nick's deep voice broke into her spiraling thoughts.

"Thinking about the new job." Noelle tugged at the hem of her skirt.

"Anything in particular?"

"Greer liked my outfit. Said it was perfect for the gallery except when they have openings. Then I'll need a black cocktail dress. I'm not sure I know what makes a dress 'cocktail'."

"Not surprised you'll need a dress. It's an upscale gallery."

"I guess."

"We'll have to go shopping."

Noelle cringed at the word. But Nick was right. She couldn't get by with concert t-shirts and holey jeans. But the hit to her budget… She sighed and slouched deeper into the seat.

"It won't be that bad." Nick stilled her tapping leg with a touch. "I'll take you tomorrow."

"Okay." The heat from his fingers faded too quickly.

Quitting the job over clothes before she'd even started was stupid. If she stuck to the bare minimum—a dress, two more tops—it wouldn't kill her savings. And she'd be getting a paycheck. She'd make it up. Especially if she got to hang her work and sell the occasional piece. But there was one other problem.

"The owner also said I have to have ID for the employment eligibility verification. Not the one from the school."

"You haven't learned to drive?"

"I don't exactly have a car." That couldn't be the only way to get official identification.

"Not a problem. I can take you to get a state ID card. You have your birth certificate?"

Lead settled on her shoulders. Of course she'd leave the one thing in the trailer she needed. Not that she would've known where to find it. But her mother must've had a copy. "No."

"Were you born in Tucson?"

"Yeah." At least she'd never been told she wasn't.

"Then no problem. We'll get online and figure out what we need to do." Nick glanced over at her. "What about learning to drive?"

"I'm fine with the bus." The routes and timing were as natural to her as mixing colors on her palette. "Let me get through the GED first."

NOELLE FROZE in the cool filtered-air entry as she tried to take in the enormity of the mall. Light and color and sound surrounded her. The white tile floors reflected the glare of the store signs and skylights and overhead fixtures. There were escalators moving people in colorful clothes between the multiple levels of the cavernous building, hands filled with bulging bags. Voices echoed off every hard surface. A full-size carousel spun to a tinny melody, making children laugh while doting parents hovered.

"We should start with a haircut." Nick's voice drew her back from the vibrant tableau.

Hair? That wasn't what she was there for. "I do it myself."

"You have a job now. You'll get tired of the ponytail."

Nick had a point. She had to look professional. No knotting her hair into a knit cap. "Fine."

He led her toward a salon. The place smelled like fake flowers and chemicals and was all angles and mirrors. Parts of her own reflection were multiplied around the shop. Like a cubist painting, but live.

"Hi, I'm Mark. How can I help you?" An older hairstylist greeted them with a warm, welcoming smile. He was dressed in burnt-orange pants with a western-styled snap-up shirt that had a huge flower graphic all over it.

Nick turned to Noelle, and she stared back at him. The salon was his idea.

"My friend Noelle here needs a new haircut for her new job."

"Congratulations." Mark dragged the word out as he pointed at her cap. "Let's see what you got."

Noelle slid it off and shook out her hair.

"Look at all that gorgeousness. You've come to the right place. I'm going to take extra-special care of you." Mark waved at her to follow him. "What'd you have in mind? You don't need highlights, what about layers?" Mark spun the chair so she could sit. Without pausing, he took a cape and snapped it out, letting it fall over her and securing it around her neck.

Noelle wanted to ask what it would cost.

Nick paused and met her eyes. "Something professional. But leave as much length as possible."

She nodded, her movement reflected in the mirror. The lighting made her skin paler and the freckles stand out across her nose. Maybe she wasn't beautiful, but she was unusual, and she didn't hate how she looked. Her appearance was simply a luxury in which she rarely indulged.

"All right. Let's make you even more gorgeous." Mark spun the chair again and led her to sit in front of a tilting sink.

The stylist finished sooner than she'd expected. Noelle turned her head, holding the small hand mirror in one hand and fingering the ends of her washed, cut, dried, and sprayed hair. Instead of the coarse dryness she was used to, it slipped like satin through her grasp. Almost black underneath with the deep darkness of the red, it naturally lightened to fiery-orange flames on the upper layers. Her reflection was unfamiliar and startling. Was that who she was? Who she was meant to be? A professional adult with a job?

Nick pulled a tendril through his fingers and sighed before tucking his hand in his pocket.

"Is it okay?" Did he hate the cut?

"Too perfect," Nick answered before turning to the stylist. "Can you get us the shampoo and other stuff you used on her hair so she can do this at home?"

"No," Noelle blurted. She couldn't afford the expensive salon products. Her money had to go for clothes to match her new look.

"Listen to your man, honey. Long hair requires good product."

Her man? Butterflies flew away with her common sense and worries for her bank account. She nodded stupidly, and Nick whipped out his wallet before she could form words again. Seeing the total, she cringed. Nick was a teacher, and everyone knew they didn't make any money. "I'll pay you back."

"What are you talking about?"

"You don't have to buy me things. I have money. And a job." They hadn't even started to buy clothes. But like hell was she going to let him pay.

"You can add it all up as a math lesson if it makes you feel better." Nick laughed. "Come on. My mother says a good foundation is the key to a woman's wardrobe. We'll start with underwear." He grabbed her hand, squeezed it, then quickly dropped it.

He hadn't agreed to take her cash. But any fight she had vanished when he touched her.

~

NOELLE FOLLOWED Nick deep into the back of a huge department store. Past racks of men's clothes and fancy shoes until they came to an area with fuzzy printed pajamas hung on the walls and tables filled with lace and silk. That wasn't the six-pack of cotton briefs she'd been expecting when Nick had said underwear.

"What are we doing here?" Noelle hissed at Nick.

"You need bras that fit. They do measurements." His voice was matter-of-fact, full volume. Like they were discussing a math problem.

How does Nick know they measure boobs? And can I disappear into a rack of flannel right now?

"May I help you?" An older woman, wrinkly, with poufy gray hair, and a thick waist, appeared in front of them. She looked like she could be someone's grandmother.

"Yes, with sizing," Nick answered.

Noelle hoped the woman he addressed would be the one to figure out her size.

"What?" The clerk peered past Nick's shoulder. She made eye contact with Noelle and quickly adjusted. "Oh, of course." The woman held out a hand, and Noelle moved in the direction indicated.

"Let's go in here." She nudged open one of the doors in the dressing room area. "Take off your shirt. I'm going to take two measurements." She shook out a plastic tape measure.

Noelle hesitated, but it was what Nick wanted. For him she took off the concert t-shirt and stared at her feet, heat darkening her pale skin.

"Raise your arms."

Noelle put her arms in the air, and the woman quickly wrapped her in the tape measure twice. So fast that Noelle barely had time to register the contact.

"I'll be right back." The woman darted out of the oversized closet before Noelle could respond.

Alone in the room, she avoided her reflection. Instead, she focused on the geometric pattern in the beige carpet.

The clerk returned with two basic, white bras, not that different from the ones the charities had given her. The woman turned her back and didn't take any interest in her toplessness. Noelle tried them both on as quickly as she could.

"So, what kind of bras do you want?" The clerk adjusted the straps and took more measurements. Noelle let the woman tug her this way and that, like a dog on a leash. It was so impersonal that it didn't even feel like touching. "Do you like lace, padding, any colors?"

"I don't know." She'd had two bras in her entire life, both white and cotton. Well, the bra she had was more gray than white, but it had been white when she'd gotten it.

"Do you want me to ask your father?"

"He's not my dad." Noelle looked at the woman through the mirror, her hands balled into fists. Nick had some gray ,but they couldn't be *that* far apart in age.

"Sorry, shall I ask your friend?" The woman wrapped her tape measure into a tight circle.

"Yes." Noelle was relieved there'd been no more questions. She dropped onto a little bench made to look like wood. What word should she use for her relationship with Nick? Was it even a relationship? Hell if she knew.

She peered at her image in the mirror. Russet hair caressed her shoulders, a perfect contrast to her creamy skin. The new bra lifted her breasts, bringing them closer together and creating cleavage she'd never had. *Sexy*.

She didn't know what her relationship with Nick was, but she was going to take the first opportunity to find out.

CHAPTER 15

$\mathcal{N}$ick sat with his head in his hands and his elbows on his knees. He was buying his student *bras*. Maybe it was time to make another appointment with the VA shrink because that wasn't the kind of thing he could discuss at group. At least his insanity plea might be believable if he ever needed it. But it wasn't as if talking—to *anyone*, not even Gabe—would change his attraction to Noelle. Nick was committed to his course of action. To her.

The saleslady approached him.

"She thought you might pick some things for her to try." She gestured toward the racks of bras centered amongst tables of panties.

The situation had deteriorated. From buying to selecting Noelle's underwear. She needed them, but he shouldn't be the one picking them. He groaned internally but followed the kindly woman, who should be selling cookies, not G-strings and push-ups.

"She's been wearing a 32A, but she measures at 34. And if she wasn't so underweight, I'm sure she'd be a full C cup. I tried her in both a B and C. It's going to depend on the style," the woman babbled as she led Nick around the displays. The silky fabrics brushed his bare arms as he walked through the racks. It was like he was in a naughty kaleidoscope. If Noelle were his lover, he would savor every minute.

With her. Instead, she was hiding, and his insides churned with the stress of potential exposure.

They selected a basic white bra with a light underwire, a lacy pink bra, and a navy-blue demi-cup that would make any woman's tits look amazing. But especially Noelle's. After he picked the last one for himself, he stopped. He was out of control, following a grandma through a panty maze with a hardening cock, ready to have Noelle try on a corset.

"She'll need underwear to go with whatever she selects," he choked out.

"Of course, dear. One step at a time." She patted his shoulder and went back to the dressing room with two sizes of each bra.

Nick retreated to the bench. How soon could they get out of there?

"Hello? Is there anybody working here?"

The woman who called out wasn't visible, but he knew the voice well. Too well. It was the unmistakable piercing roar of Principal Lopez—designed to be heard over four hundred talking teenagers. His dick went limp and tried to take shelter in his stomach along with his balls.

He was so dead.

Crouching as low as possible, he darted into the dressing room hallway. At least he wasn't out in the open, waiting to be caught, but he was trapped. He rose and pressed his spine into the drywall as if he could embed himself into it. Too bad he didn't have an invisibility cloak like that wizarding kid.

The clerk stepped out of the dressing room. "Oh. I was coming to get you. She's having a little trouble deciding." The woman shook her head and fidgeted with her tape measure, not meeting his eye. "We got the right fit, but she's unsure what to select. She asked me to get you, and normally I wouldn't, but there's no one else here and—"

"Actually, there's a customer calling for you. We'll be out shortly. Thanks." Nick darted into the stall, looked into the mirror—

The air in his lungs froze. She wore the navy demi-cup bra, her lush, perky breasts framed and presented for his approval. A hint of peach teased above the edge of the fabric, and her nipples hardened under his gaze. He forced his focus to her eyes. She stared back at him through the reflection, head cocked to the side and her lower lip between her teeth.

Nick stepped closer to her and spoke softly into her ear. "Noelle, you're stunning. What do *you* think?"

She wrapped her arms around her middle, and he fought not to do the same. Danger lurked on the other side of the full-height door.

"I like it, I like all of them. But…"

"But what, Angel?"

"Can I show you?" Noelle's voice was soft like silk.

"Show me?" He closed his eyes briefly while he prayed for strength.

"The others." She took a deep breath, dropped her arms to her sides and arched her back.

Nick had no breath to answer, so he merely nodded. His gaze glued to her body in the mirror.

She released the clasp between her breasts. The fabric opened but did not fall away.

Later, he would blame his extreme lack of good judgment on the fact that all the blood in his brain had retreated to his straining cock.

Noelle's brown eyes lit with fire, burning his through the glass.

Sweat formed on his upper lip. It would take every bit of control he had not to lose his job, busted by the school principal in a department store dressing room, plowing his cock into Noelle as if it were his last day on earth.

She freed her breasts from the cups. He groaned and pressed into her back, his hands plastered to her hips to keep from moving them to her bare breasts. Her sweet nipples begged to be sucked, to make her come. And his boss was right outside the door…

"Which one?"

"Both, Angel, both." Nick's eyes tracked from her right breast to her left in the mirror.

"No, which bra do you want me to try on next?" She smiled coyly at his predicament. The little vixen rubbed her sweet ass up and down his throbbing groin once.

"You have to stop that right now, no teasing. Put on the white one." Nick released her and tried to regain his composure. His back to her, he braced one arm on the wall and rested his forehead against it. With the other hand, he adjusted his erection, trying to find some relief without coming in his jeans. The situation constrained him in a cage of passion-laced paradise and sulfurous sin. There was no leaving the stall until he was sure Lopez had gone. But if he stayed, he couldn't guarantee his control.

"Okay."

Nick turned.

Noelle bent over and lifted each delicate mound into the cup of the bra before standing slowly.

No longer did he have the mental separation of an image through a mirror. She was right in front of him. Not even the plain, full-coverage contraption could cut his desire. He'd seen her nude from the waist up—and he ached to have her.

"It's very nice." Nick grunted as pre-cum dampened his boxers.

Noelle nodded. She put her back to him. "Can you help me?"

"Huh?"

"The clasp. It's tight."

Nick choked as he lifted his hands to her warm back, slowly sweeping her silky red hair over her shoulder before he undid the clasp. As soon as it opened, he yanked his hands away as though she'd burned him, and closed his eyes. Was she teasing him on purpose? If they were somewhere private, he'd spank her for tormenting him so cruelly.

His erection pulsed. The image of him spanking her was more fuel on the fire. He was the torturer. He should spank himself. Yeah, a good spanking session. But masturbation wasn't going to solve his problem long-term, especially since she was in the room. He had to get out of there before he came in his pants without even touching himself.

Nick opened his eyes just as Noelle knelt in front of him, nipples peeping through pink lace, and reached for his belt. Nick grabbed her hands. "What are you—?"

"I must not be doing it right if you have to ask." She twisted her hands free and opened the buckle on his belt.

"Noelle, we can't," he whisper-grunted. He stepped back and leaned against the wall. His belt was undone, his zipper was halfway down, and his erection poked out of the top of his boxers, begging for him to let her do what she wanted.

Noelle crawled forward, her warm brown eyes locked on his. She licked her lips. "Please." She took his zipper down the rest of the way, grasped his cock tightly in her hand, and lowered his boxers with the other. He locked his hips to not thrust into her heated grip. Her gaze held temptation and promise.

Nick dropped his eyelids and tilted his head back. He was going to hell, and there was no place he'd rather be. He wrapped his hand around her fingers and moved over his erection, using his pre-cum to lubricate their combined grip.

She closed her hot, wet mouth around his swollen crown and swirled her tongue. From deep inside a groan rose in his throat.

"No," he choked out and yanked his hips back, keeping her hand in his grip around his cock.

"I want to."

"Not here. Not now." *Not anywhere, not ever, and not even a hand job* was what he should be saying, but he couldn't force himself to release her or stop the stroking motion that had his whole body going languid with pleasure. He braced himself against the wall and stroked harder.

Noelle's other hand grazed up his abs and then down his still-covered thigh. Electricity followed her fingers and gathered at the base of his spine. His balls drew up hard and tight. He was going to blow. He froze their movement. He couldn't.

She pushed his hand away and took him deep. Her throat squeezed his head, and he bit his lip to keep from roaring out his pleasure. Nothing he'd ever done before was so erotic.

Her dark red locks curtained the view. Unable to resist, he dragged his fingers through her flames from the base of her skull and pulled them back harder than he should have. Her sweet pink lips were glossy and stretched around his shaft.

A low noise like an animal in pain escaped his lips. He wanted to scream her name and howl with the pure ecstasy. His hips pressed forward and back without conscious effort, a tiny movement compared to what he wanted to do. It was enough to make him erupt.

Noelle gripped his hips and pulled him close, swallowing down everything he gave her.

Nick fell back against the wall. Noelle released him, and he missed being inside her.

Decimated, he weakly helped her up. He dropped his mouth to her reddened, swollen lips. She opened for him, tangling, touching. Dancing to the pounding beat in his chest. His taste was still on her tongue. He had to stop before he got hard again. Liberating her from his desperate grasp, he righted his clothing.

Noelle didn't move to get dressed. "Was that okay?"

"Beyond perfect. I don't deserve you."

Her eyes were locked on his crotch. She licked her lips again.

"Stop." Nick groaned.

"What?" Noelle raised her eyebrows.

"You know exactly what." The words came out sterner than he'd intended. He ran his hand down his face, over the scruff of his stubble. "We're in a ladies' dressing room. This isn't right."

"Sorry." The tears forming in her eyes tore at Nick's heart. He would do anything for that woman. She was smart and brave and beautiful. She was also dangerous to his future, but he couldn't walk away.

"I want you so much more than I should." Nick wrapped his arms around her. He held her close and stroked her hair.

"How we doing in here?" a voice called from the opposite side of the dressing room door, and they jerked apart.

"Fine," Nick replied putting his hand over the door in case the woman tried to enter. "I'll be right out." Nick kissed Noelle quickly. "Get dressed. I'll meet you out there."

Nick paused at the exit to the dressing rooms and scoped the area.

Principal Lopez was nowhere to be seen. He made his way to the checkout counter and tried to pretend nothing had happened while he paid for all three bras plus two more of the white ones and matching panties. A crystal-clear image of Noelle in nothing but the navy-blue lace bra and underwear wrapped around his brain and his body responded like he hadn't just had the most amazing orgasm of his life.

Noelle came out of the dressing room, doing a much better job of looking normal than he was. Not a hair was out of place despite what he'd done to it while she was on her knees. "Where are we going now?"

"I need a dinner break before we continue this insanity." Nick wasn't sure what could go wrong with buying her work clothes and some better running gear, but taking a breather seemed like a really good plan.

Fortunately, dinner and the rest of shopping went smoothly. No more dressing room blow jobs. No more bare nipples. No more near misses with the principal. Nick drove slowly home. He had to say something. Reestablish the boundaries. But the thing between them… There were no words that would stop the way he reacted to her.

"Why are you attracted to me?" Noelle's voice dropped like a bomb in the car. "I mean, I don't look anything like your wife, if she really looked like my painting."

Nick cleared his throat. A meaningless sound that filled the space, acknowledged her words, but gave him time to formulate the response to a question he hadn't asked himself. "How I feel about you has nothing to do with my late wife. I told you, the moment I saw you, I was attracted, but it's more than your looks. Your art, it's a reflection of your soul, and it captivates me." He swallowed down the words of desire that rose in his throat. "You're resilient, a fighter. I'm astonished with how you've been able to thrive in spite of your situation. But I shouldn't—"

"How did she die?"

"Cancer." The interruption and change in topic had him responding more honestly than he normally would have. "She was supposedly doing better. But she was having a bad morning. Said it was nothing, a cold. I didn't want to go to work. She insisted. I came home and…found her." And the impotence and anger rushed back. She'd lied. She hadn't been in remission, just denial.

"You think that was your fault?"

"I should have done something more. Made her go back to the doctor."

Noelle laid her hand on his thigh. "It wasn't your fight to win. You weren't even in the battle. You can't make people choose the right action. I should know. The only reason I'm not going to get a real diploma is because I refused to stay in the classes that made me uncomfortable."

He glanced over at her, and his heart clenched. Her warm brown eyes weren't pitying or judging. They held understanding, of him, of the situation. No one had ever put it that way. Maybe because he'd never been so honest. He didn't own the failure. An overwhelming need to wrap himself in her acceptance and bury himself inside her so they could never be separated rolled through him. *Wrong. So wrong.*

They arrived home before he could make her promises he shouldn't. He walked through the front door, handed her the bags, and ground out the only words he had: "I'm going to shower. I've got the couch."

He ignored the look of hurt that crossed Noelle's face before she disappeared into his bedroom, and he stripped to punish himself, or at least his once-again-hard cock, in private.

CHAPTER 16

oelle embraced the roommate role Nick had thrust her into for the last several weeks. She still went running with him and studied. But she held her tongue on anything related to their relationship. The tongue that had been happily wrapped around his cock. But he'd made it quite clear that wasn't happening again. At least, most of his body did. She still spied his sleep pants tented far too often, no matter how he tried to hide. And it wasn't her imagination that he lingered in the shower. She'd taken to timing him. It was a small drop of satisfaction that she nursed deep inside. No matter how far away he stayed, he wanted her.

Almost as much as she wanted him.

In addition to the haircut and clothes, he'd bought her a cell phone. For emergencies. Her entire life was an emergency, but whatever. At least it served a useful purpose. The mental tally of money she owed Nick was growing, but it was stuff she'd have to buy anyway. And she had a plan to pay him back.

She set another of her older, completed works on the easel in the art room and snapped a picture.

"Did you get the planets?" Ms. Julie called from the small storage closet at the back of the room with the student lockers, where she kept Noelle's finished pieces.

Noelle pulled the portrait off the easel. "I'm not selling that one."

"Oh. So keeping it for the—"

Noelle slid the photographed canvas back in its slot and pulled out the next one. A little girl in a garden made of reclaimed trash. "It's gonna be a gift. I think."

She took the last photo and hurried to make it to class. Avoiding Nick's sour you're-late attitude added to her urgency. She slid into her desk as the bell rang, breath coming too fast, not from running, but from the sexy-ass man at the front, glaring from her to the clock. He unbuttoned his shirtsleeves and rolled them as he spoke. Like she could process anything he had to say when he was teasing her with the part of him she found most attractive.

"Noelle, you're working on social studies at station three."

Wait? What? Station three. There were six stations around the room. Some for individual studying. Some for pair or group work. But three was for the TA. She opened her mouth to protest, but Lucas, who'd been allowed back in class, was taking a seat at Nick's desk.

She smiled sweetly at Nick, stood, and slowly swished her way over to her assigned spot, not doubting for a second that Nick's eyes were locked on her ass. He may have the power in that room. But she had all the power in their relationship. The more he avoided her, the more it confirmed he wanted her. She dropped into the chair and leaned close to the TA, asking about the assignment.

"Get to work, people."

Did anyone else hear the possessive growl in Nick's voice? It was going to be a long day.

She'd make sure of it.

NICK'S CLASSROOM had turned into an instrument to test his will. He couldn't take any more of Noelle's thinly disguised teases. A few minutes ago, she'd lined herself up in the aisle, centered on his desk, and carefully bent over. His cock woke up as her perfect ass swayed while she checked every single page in her new portfolio. The oversized art sleeve he'd bought her to protect her amazing work used against him. He rushed from the room, making an excuse about needing another file.

Every minute of his life was saturated with the forbidden object of his desire—Noelle.

A commotion coming from the office erased his lascivious confliction as he double-timed it to the source.

Noelle's mom.

Clothed, but barely, in a stained tank top and dirty jeans. And still crazy.

"Where the fuck is she?" she screamed so loudly that Nick was sure Noelle would hear her and come running. The worst possible scenario. There was no way he'd let her get anywhere near Noelle.

"You get my goddamned daughter in here right the fuck now." She swiped her arm across the counter and sent all of Alice's carefully organized piles flying. "You people don't know who the fuck you're dealing with."

How Noelle could have come from that demon boggled Nick's mind. The woman ripped a poster from the wall and then started toward the gate that separated the lobby from the work area. She froze mid-push when Principal Lopez stepped out of her office and picked up the handset on the nearest desk. A few button punches later and her voice boomed through the phones and speakers throughout the school. "Shelter in place. This is not a drill. Shelter in place."

Surprised that she hadn't called for an evacuation, Nick blocked the east entrance to the office as the responding resource officer filled the west entrance. He supposed the management of the unarmed lunatic wouldn't be aided by the movement of four hundred people toward the school exits. But the lunch schedule would be totally jacked.

"Our trailer is gone. Where the fuck am I supposed to live?" Spit flew from her mouth as she screamed.

"Ms. Michaels, the police are on their way." Principal Lopez could have been reading a recipe from a cookbook for all the emotion she showed.

"No, you don't get to call the cops. She's my daughter. *Mine.*" Noelle's mom beat her fist on her chest.

"She's an adult." Nick couldn't hold back the words.

"The hell she is." She glared at Nick like she was stabbing him. "If we don't have a trailer, we don't get mail at the park. They stopped my money 'cause I didn't get the notice. She had one job. Get her in here!" The woman spun in circles like a hissing feral cat recognizing it was caged.

"Noelle will not be coming." Lopez crossed her arms and arched a brow. "Only the police."

A flash of awareness crossed Ms. Michaels' face. She darted for the resource officer, catching him completely unaware. For a small woman, she was strong. In the next moment, the officer was on the floor and she was sprinting for the exit.

The police came. Classes were escorted to the cafeteria as the entire building and grounds were cleared. The woman had disappeared, hopefully for good. Noelle didn't believe her mom would come back to the school, but he wasn't convinced they'd seen the last of the crazy hag.

Nick dropped into his desk chair. The end of a long day and the only good that had come from the earlier scene was he hadn't thought about Noelle in anything other than a protective mode all afternoon.

NOELLE CROSSED the floor of the gallery to the back office as quietly as she could. She'd finally worked up her courage to talk to her boss about thirty minutes before it was time to leave.

"Greer?"

The woman made a grunt of acknowledgment without looking up.

"I know we have new artists coming in. And you'd said if there was leftover space, I might be able to hang something. I..." Noelle took a deep, steadying breath. "I'd like to show you my portfolio, if you have a minute."

Greer looked up slowly and slid her black-framed reading glasses off. "Of course."

Noelle gulped. "Do you want to see the pictures of the finished work or the sketches?"

"Start with the sketches."

Noelle opened her portfolio on the bare desk and retrieved the papers. Greer slowly walked around to join Noelle. She slid the first sketch over—a woman seated in a café, framed by a window and crying. She flipped through several others. Pausing on the drawing of Nick in the shower before she moved on.

"This. This is good."

The tension coiling in Noelle's gut with each page turn exploded, and she nearly levitated off the ground. "Really?"

It was a sketch of a woman on her knees with a man's hand in her hair. A shattered mirror in the background reflected their broken image. Noelle had a huge collection of mirror shards. She planned to start painting that piece next.

"Let's see the pictures."

Noelle whipped out her phone and selected the album with her shots. She placed the cell in Greer's outstretched hand.

Greer flipped through several of the images before handing it back. "Tell me about your method."

Noelle stuttered through an explanation of her acrylic-paint images enhanced with three-dimensional salvaged pieces as Greer walked back around her desk and sat, replacing her glasses. She nodded when Noelle finished.

Noelle waited. The woman looked down at her paperwork.

"So, can I have a space if there's room?"

"If there's room."

"Thanks, Greer." Noelle fought not to dance out of the office and out of the gallery. A space. She had a space to hang her work. Maybe not right away, but soon. Her plan was becoming a reality.

CHAPTER 17

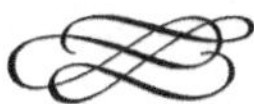

$\mathcal{N}$oelle poured a glass of juice while Nick cooked chicken at the stove. "I showed Greer my artwork yesterday."

"What'd she say?" Nick flipped the browning meat.

Noelle put the juice back in the wrong location in the fridge on purpose. A theory about Nick brewed in the back of her mind, and she'd been testing it in small ways. A left-out toothbrush. Shoes in the living room. Once again, when Nick went to retrieve some dressing for the salad, he automatically rearranged the carton. He never said anything, just quietly put things away or tidied already-clean spaces. She'd wondered if it was just things that could be seen out in the open, but no, he adjusted the contents of the refrigerator on autopilot. As she updated Nick on her job, she decided to work with him on keeping things the way he liked them. If it was important to him, she'd stop because *he* was important to her.

Finally, Noelle found the guts to ask the question that had been burning in her mind for two days. "Why'd you put me with the TA?"

"It wasn't about you. I need to work with Lucas." Nick pulled out plates and started arranging their food. "I had to do some fast-talking to get Principal Lopez to allow him to return."

"Why bother?"

"Everyone deserves a second chance. Lucas was acting from fear. Some people respond to fear by controlling themselves. Some by trying to take control of others. He'll learn better ways to handle his fear of failure."

Noelle usually avoided things she feared, but maybe that was a form of controlling herself.

After dinner, they cleaned up. Noelle took special care to wipe down every surface and put things away in their proper place.

"I have a meeting tonight," Nick said.

"Therapy?" It was a risk to ask, but she didn't want secrets between them.

"How'd you know?"

"Lucky guess. I assume for your obsessive cleaning."

Nick laughed. "Not directly."

"Usually you go on Wednesday." Noelle waited, but he didn't explain. That was okay. He would eventually. Even though he'd retreated from her after the shopping trip, she wasn't giving up. They had the rest of the year, at least. Unless her paintings started selling fast.

Nick glanced at his watch. "I gotta go."

"I won't wait up."

NICK RESISTED CHECKING ALL the windows and rechecking the doors before he left. Noelle was safe. He blew out a slow breath and left her with her books. As he turned out of the neighborhood, his cell rang. He pulled over and put it on speaker.

"Nick, it's Patricia."

"Hi, Mom." Nick smiled. She always used her professional voice on the phone. Even with him.

"I got your message. Something about an artist? Since when do you do scouting?"

"Don't get used to it. I saw a show a couple months back—"

"You went to an art exhibit? Voluntarily?"

"Funny. And no. It was at a bar."

"That I believe." His mom's light laugh was like champagne bubbles, lightening the heavy mood he'd been in since the shopping disaster. "But you don't drink."

"Met a buddy there, had a couple of beers." His mom knew that limiting caffeine and alcohol had been one of the ways he dealt with his anxiety. "Anyway, I bought a piece. And then I met the artist. She's amazing."

"She?"

"Technically, she's my student, but her work—you should see it." Nick ran his hand over his head. He *so* didn't want to tell his mother he was living with Noelle. It sounded bad, even to his ears.

"Does she have a website?" Of course his mom would want to scout out an unfamiliar artist.

"Not yet, but I can send pictures."

"Send them in an email to the work address so your father can look at them, too." The pause in the conversation grew heavy.

"What?" His mom didn't usually stop to breathe when she called him.

"When you say…student?"

"She's nearly twenty-one. It's a complicated story."

"So she means more to you?"

He'd never been able to keep a secret from his mom. "One thing at a time."

"Do you want me to talk to Alan about putting up a website?"

His mom was amazing. She didn't have one drop of artistic talent in her entire body, but she knew great art and loved promoting artists. But she hadn't even seen Noelle's work—she was offering for him. For who Noelle might be to him. "That'd be great."

"When are we seeing you?"

"Soon. I'll let you know. But I gotta run. I have group."

"Oh. Are things bad?"

"Nope, just trying to keep them from getting that way." A white lie. "Plus, I like to support the new guys."

"All right, love. Send me the email. Talk soon."

"Love you, Mom." He ended the call, relieved he'd avoided some of the facts about Noelle. His mom would understand, but he didn't have the right words to explain yet.

NOELLE ARCHED INTO THE STRONG, warm hands that glided across her skin. His citrusy, masculine scent enveloped her. Fingers ran through her hair, caressed her face. He whispered how beautiful she was, how much he wanted her. Afraid to touch him, she left her hands under her pillow and let him explore her body. If she begged, would he touch her where she ached?

His hot breath warmed her through her shirt before his hands slid the fabric up and exposed her breasts. He flicked his tongue across her ruched nipple, then sucked it deep into the wet heat of his mouth. He toyed with her flesh. She turned to get closer to him. One hand kneaded her other breast. When he pinched her bud between his fingers, she moaned. There was an empty, hollow space she wanted him to fill. He needed to touch her there, where her entire being focused. Instead, he released one breast only to fall on the other, treating it with the same detailed attention. His mouth on her tit only made her ache more intense.

She moaned again, but it was laced with a whine. He could end her suffering. His caresses lit her up, but she needed more. Her inner thighs were slick with desire. If only she could feel his body pressed against hers—inside. With him, she wouldn't be afraid of the unknown. "Please," she cried out.

She heard him moan, too, but it wasn't a happy sound and it wasn't with her in the bedroom. Noelle jerked up, alone in the bed. Her shirt remained in place, and her rock-hard nipples were dry. *What the hell?*

Nick cried out again. He was in trouble. She leapt from the bed and ran to the living room. On the couch, he thrashed in his sleep.

Noelle knelt quietly by him. He babbled unintelligibly, but he wanted someone—someone who'd left or was leaving. She touched his shoulder with her fingertips.

"Nick," she whispered. Before she could blink, she was flat out on the ground with his entire body weight on top of her. He wrapped his hands around her throat.

"Nick!" She grabbed his wrists. When he didn't let go, she lifted her hips and trapped his arms, then flipped him over.

His eyes were open but unfocused. She still straddled him when he finally recognized her. His eyes bulged, and he rolled away as if he were on fire, dumping her on the floor. Freed, he sprang to his feet and left her lying there.

Wow, defense training works.

NICK SHUT the door to the bedroom, breathing hard and barely able to see until he focused on the bed. The unmade, rumpled bed where Noelle slept. Drawn to it with a force he couldn't resist, he slid a hand under the bedding. Her warmth lingered on the sheets, seeping into his frozen fingers. He lifted the pillow, where a strand of her fiery hair lay abandoned. Bringing the cushion to his face, he inhaled her scent, carnations and coffee. Spicy and strong. Alive.

He dropped to his knees, his body cradled around the down-filled form that smelled like her but wasn't. A knock roused him. God, how long had he been curled on the floor? Was Noelle hurt? Why hadn't he stopped? Or stayed? Or helped her? But he couldn't save anyone. Not even himself.

The knock was louder. "Nick?" she called.

He forced himself to stand, abandoning the pillow on the bed. He went to the door, resting his forehead on it. He shouldn't open it. She shouldn't be there.

"Nick?" Her voice was almost a whisper, like she knew he was there on the other side.

Sucking in a deep breath, he turned the handle, breaking the barrier but not allowing her in.

Her hand rose, and she placed it on his chest right over his heart. How could she stand to touch him after what he'd done?

"I'm sorry." Her voice was quiet, gentle, full of the same warmth passing into his chest. "I know better."

He should step back.

Close the door.

He couldn't.

"You should be afraid of me." His voice raspy, as if he'd been the one who'd been strangled.

"No."

"I had my hands around your throat." Saying the words out loud reinforced what a sin he'd committed.

"Yes." She nodded but didn't back away.

"You can't be here."

She stepped forward, narrowing the space between them. "I'm not leaving."

He gripped her wrist, loosely, unwilling to remove her from his body. "I'm dangerous."

It wasn't a threat. It was a confession.

"It's not aggression in your eyes when you look at me." Her sweet brown eyes met his.

"It's just as deadly—"

"No." She touched his cheek with her free hand, her softness undeserved. "I've seen the eyes of people who want to hurt me."

"What do you think you see?" He couldn't imagine, because all he saw when he looked in the mirror was failure.

"Desire."

"Not possible." *Not allowed.* Not something he should ever feel for her.

"Desperate, flaming, desire. And fear."

"*You* should be afraid." Because she was right. He was being consumed by his feelings for her.

She pushed on his chest, the change in pressure barely perceptible.

He dropped his gaze, unable to look her in the eye. "There's no guarantee I can do this right."

She took a step closer, her body pressed to his.

"Why?" he pleaded, hoping she would have the words that would make sense of it all.

"Because. I need you, too."

CHAPTER 18

Noelle moved into the empty space Nick left as he let go of the door. He continued retreating, his gaze on the ground. Noelle shut the door behind her with a click. Nick froze and met her eyes. His were filled with anguish. She closed the distance between them and wrapped her arms around his neck, pressing her body into his. Slowly, she locked her lips to his mouth.

Oh god. Firm and warm. The slight stubble on his chin rasped her skin. She peeked the tip of her tongue out to taste him. He parted his lips, and she slipped inside. When they'd kissed in the dressing room, Nick had been in charge. But there in his bedroom, she had control and was noting every sexy detail. Sexy, but foreign. Then he moved, and she forgot everything about the kiss that didn't make sense, because his arms wrapped around her and pulled her tighter. He danced into her mouth, and her vocabulary was reduced to two words: *Nick. More.*

Her hands explored every chiseled line of his arms and torso as he kissed her so completely. Learning him like a sculptor knew their clay. She pressed her pelvis against the hardness that poked into her stomach. Wetness and heat formed between her legs. How had she gone so long without having him, the only man she'd ever considered being intimate with?

She moaned into his mouth and stepped back.

Nick. Naked. Now.

She tugged at the loose hem of his shirt, lifting it over his abs. He followed her lead and whipped it off, dropping it on the floor. No compulsive cleaning urges—she had his total attention. She smiled and drifted her fingertips over every contour and scar. "You're beautiful."

He chuckled, but it was filled with disbelief. "You're the beauty."

She raised her arms and waited. Would he take the invitation to strip her?

His large hands were on her thighs, just below the shirt she'd worn to sleep in. His shirt. Slowly, he drew his hands up to her hips, lifting the fabric, exposing her damp panties. Higher. Under her ribs. She shivered, and he froze. She pressed her hands on top of his. "Don't stop."

If he did, she'd probably cry.

A moment passed as his eyes searched hers. She mouthed, *Please.* He pressed his forehead to hers. She held her breath. Finally, his hands moved up her body, along the outside of her breasts. He raised his head and pulled the shirt off her, dropping it on top of his. She took a shuddering inhale as the cool air hit her hard nipples.

Her bare breasts drew his gaze and then his hands. He cupped and raised them. Ran his thumbs over the tips in circles. Noelle stayed still, unwilling to do anything that might stop him, but a demanding ache rose from her core up to her heart. She arched into his grip. "Please, Nick."

He lowered his mouth to her nipple, pressing it between his lips. Then he added his tongue. Lightning shot straight into her pussy. She gripped his head, holding him there. He nipped her, and she squeaked as another flood released inside her. Her body ached in a way she'd never experienced before.

Nick moved to her other breast, teasing and loving it as he had the first. She wiggled her hips, ready to demand he enter her.

Noelle reached between them, needing to see his beautiful cock again. She pulled the string that tied his sleep pants. The knot released, and she carefully eased the fabric over his erection.

Nick lifted his gaze, his hands still wrapped around her rib cage. "Wait."

"No." She stretched the sides of the pajamas and they dropped to his ankles in one slick move.

Damn. Naked Nick was no-fooling, fucking gorgeous. She reached for him, and he tilted his hips back.

"Angel. If you touch me, I'm going to come." Nick dropped to his knees in front of her and pressed his face to her cotton-covered mound. He moaned and lapped at the fabric.

His hot breath heated her outsides like she burned from the inside. She squirmed, but his tight grip on her hips held her in place. She ran her fingers through his short hair. "Nick, I need—"

"I know what you need. Let me." He grabbed the edges of her panties but didn't move.

She wrapped her hands around his and guided them down. Once she'd started, he took over. He slid them all the way down her legs, and she stepped out, holding onto his shoulder for balance.

"Copper." Nick grazed his fingers over her soft curls. His touch ricocheted through her, and her stomach fluttered with need. He stood and lifted her. She instinctively wrapped her legs around him. Her wet core glided over his hard length.

Oh fuck, that's amazing. She couldn't wait for him to be inside her.

"Yes." It was what she'd waited for. Nick carried her to the bed and dropped her. "Wha—"

Before she could complete a word, his face was buried between her legs. He licked her with that incredible tongue of his. Repeating the dance he'd initiated in her mouth. It was even better lower. Noelle tilted her hips and spread her legs. He could have as much of her as he wanted. Her flesh quivered, and molten passion spread outward from her middle, heating her to her fingertips. Even her scalp tingled.

Nick pressed his tongue inside, stroking in and out. He sucked her clit and entered her with his fingers. The stretch pinched her perfectly, and the tremors that had rattled around her nerves contracted into a tight ball of fire. Minutes later, it exploded outward, making every muscle shake. She screamed his name and gripped his head to anchor herself. Otherwise she was sure she would have floated away with the stars that filled her vision.

"That… That was…" Noelle struggled to express herself, not even sure what she felt.

Nick rose and stood before her like a Greek statue. Except the sculptors had never made their models erect.

Holy hardness. They were missing out on an important detail. If she ever carved alabaster, or cast a bronze man, his cock would look just like Nick's. Male perfection.

Noelle's mouth watered. She could have him again. Pressing her hands into the mattress, she forced herself to sit up despite the shaky heaviness of her limbs. "I want to do the same for you."

"No, I…we—"

"Then I want you inside me."

"I don't have condoms."

Noelle had waited for that conversation. "Why is that, Nick?"

Nick's face turned red. "I haven't wanted anyone for a very long time."

"I want *you*."

"We can't."

Noelle nudged her toes against his nightstand. "Check the top drawer."

After cleaning his house top to bottom, she'd been shocked to find not one condom, or dirty magazine, or bottle of lube. Nothing. He didn't need to know how deep her "cleaning" exploration had been. She probably shouldn't have done it. But her curiosity had won out over her respect for his privacy. A thing she would never confess willingly.

Nick opened the drawer but made no move to retrieve what they needed.

Noelle stroked her hand over his cock, down to his heavy balls. "I want you inside me. Now, Nick."

"We shouldn't."

Noelle stood up, fighting her lethargy. She angled her body around Nick's, moving him with her hips and shoulders, his warm skin heating her up again. His hard cock a promise that he wanted her as much as she wanted him. When he was in the perfect position, she pressed her hand against his chest until he fell back on the bed.

She reached in the drawer and ripped open the box, extracting a foil packet. Fisting her hands on her hips, she stared down at him. His eyes had darkened with ferocious intensity, and his swollen lips were slightly pursed. "Say you don't want me."

"I...I can't." The growl that sharpened his words grazed her skin.

"Then please." She stroked her empty hand from his muscular neck, to his pecs, and down through the shadow of hair over his abs. Following the thicker trail lower, she let her fingers graze over his shaft. She paused and locked her gaze to his. "Say yes?"

He reached down and covered her hand over his hard-on, squeezing the end harder than she would have done on her own. "Yes."

That had been more difficult than it needed to be. Noelle knelt on the bed between his knees and kissed Nick. Her taste lingered on his lips. She dipped her tongue again, loving that he was branded with her, even for a moment.

Before she allowed him too much time to reconsider, she withdrew, tore open the condom, and covered him. When she finished, she ran her hand down his length one more time to make sure she had his attention. And she did, based on the way he jerked into her grip.

She moved one leg to the outside of his hips and then the other. Up on her knees, she paused, perfectly poised over him.

"Go slow." Nick placed his hands on her hips. His strength infused her with the courage to fulfill her fantasy and take what he could give.

She lowered herself until the tip of him pressed at her entrance. "Is this okay?"

"Yes. God, I want you, Angel."

She lowered her hips, taking him in. The width of his cock stretched her. She rocked her pelvis, moving him forward and back, making room for his thickness. Slowly, she sank down, pressing his flesh deep inside her until she rested on his thighs.

Holy crap, he's huge. The achy stretch blocked any other sensation. With her hands on his chest, she steadied herself.

"Are you okay?" Nick's voice sounded like he was being strangled.

She started to rise up, to release him.

"No." He held her in place.

"I don't want to hurt you." She had to be squeezing him to death.

He shook his head. "It's never been like this. Are *you* okay?"

"I'm good." She stroked her hands down his chest, petting him to sooth his worry. "But I have to move—"

Before she finished explaining what her body demanded, Nick lifted her up and then thrust up into her. He took over completely and, damn, he knew exactly what she needed. But even as he hammered into her, she screamed, "More."

The stretch, the fullness, she'd anticipated. The colors running through her bloodstream, reds and purples and pops of gold, *that* she hadn't understood. Hadn't had any idea how much she would experience each move of his body in hers. How the feel of his fingers pressing into her skin would be the best thing that had ever happened in her entire life. How her soul would crack open with a space made just for him.

No one could have ever explained what it would be in words and made her comprehend. Only the living of it made it real. So real. The colors swirled with the passion and energy building in her body. And Nick sat up under her, drawing her down tight into him. His lips pressed to hers, but she had to breathe. She pulled her head away and arched her back as the entire experience poured out of her in a wail that rattled every cell in her body. Nick shook in her arms.

He clenched her to him and buried his face in the skin above her breast, panting. "My Angel."

CHAPTER 19

$\mathcal{N}$oelle pressed herself against the naked man, his skin soft against hers. *This. This is what home should feel like.* Warm and safe and solid. She trailed her fingers down Nick's arm, following the white lines of scars, skimming over the dusting of blond hair along his forearms. Each tendon and muscle defined, even in rest.

Nick woke. He took an audible deep breath and straightened on the mattress, raising his arms.

"Good morning." Noelle rolled away and stretched, savoring each twinge of her muscles, a sweet reminder of what they'd done.

Nick froze mid-yawn. He swung his legs out of the bed and bolted for his dresser without a backward glance. He pulled clothes from the drawers and was gone.

What the hell? Was he serious? Running away after what they'd shared? She should be the one who was freaked out, not him. He'd blown her fucking world apart. A stabbing pain lodged in her chest. That was not how she'd imagined the morning after would go. But Nick. Mr. Perfect. He was probably ripping into himself because he'd been real and not the saint he tried to be. Noelle rubbed her temples and sighed. *We're back to this.*

There were two options: give up and go back to hiding her

desires or go after him. She threw off the covers and tidied the bed, smoothing the soft brown coverlet until no wrinkles remained. If he returned, he'd see her naked ass putting his well-used bed to rights. When he didn't, she picked up the t-shirt she'd worn the night before and threw it on, though without panties. Still no Nick. A quick scan of the room revealed a wad of tissue, wrapped around a spent condom. She picked it up and marched into the kitchen to toss it.

Coffee. When she'd gone shopping, condoms hadn't been the only thing on the list. She reached into the back of the shallow pantry and retrieved her new machine, filters, and the can of grounds. Tidy Nick hadn't noticed she'd claimed the unused corner. *He'll damn well notice now.*

When the can opener punctured the metal, the aroma of fresh-roasted grounds filled her nose like the finest perfume. Her body sang. She started the pot brewing, and put the can and filters back in her hidey-hole. She leaned with her back against the kitchen sink and waited.

As expected, Nick came stomping down the hall. "What's that smell?"

She smiled at him like she wasn't ready to slap him for being an ass. "I'm gonna try this again. *Good morning.*"

"Why is there a coffee maker on my counter?"

"Because it makes coffee." Noelle lifted her chin. "And I put it there. Kinda like I put the condoms in your nightstand."

Nick's neck turned red, and his gaze lifted to the ceiling.

Noelle straightened. "I need things if I'm going to live here. Like *coffee.*" She waited until he looked at her. "I enjoy *coffee.* Most adults do. Some drink coffee every. Single. Day. It makes their day just a bit better. Helps their mood. Going for a long time without…makes them irritable. Maybe you should have a cup." *Or three.*

She reached into the cabinet, her shirt sliding up to expose her bare ass to him. Taking her time, she selected two mugs and filled one for herself. Lifting it to her mouth, she pursed her lips and blew on the steamy liquid to cool it off, her eyes locked on his. Then she tilted the cup, sipped, and let a moan slip out. She licked a stray drop away. "Want some?"

Nick shook. "No."

Tension that had gripped her since he'd run from the bed released. Her man had it bad, and he was going to fight her every step of the way. Good. Fighting she understood. She sauntered past him, letting her hips swing. "Fine. I'm more than capable of enjoying my *coffee* all by myself."

NICK WIPED a hand down his face. What had he done? In one single night of madness, he'd ruined everything. He'd removed the veil from what he most desired, and all he learned was that he wouldn't be able to live without that fiery redhead. The one naked in his bathroom. And yet, he couldn't. Couldn't have her. Shouldn't have taken her. And he was as far from a saint as he could get.

He ran permutations as he prepared steel-cut oats for their breakfast. In all the scenarios he generated, only one made sense. Go back to the way things were as if nothing had happened. Keep his hands to himself. Return to training. Forget the one anomaly. No repeats. At least, not until after she had her GED. Not until he was positive she was choosing him because she wanted him, not because she needed him. He'd already made that mistake with his wife, Helena. Once was enough.

Noelle emerged from the hallway about the time the oatmeal had finished, dressed in her standard uniform of jeans and the olive henley. It looked fantastic wrapped around her luscious tits. Anything would look amazing on her, skimming over the beautiful flesh he'd feasted on hours ago. His mouth reproduced the sensation, and his tongue swirled around the recollection of her nipple between his lips. *No.* He fought a losing battle.

He swallowed hard. "Breakfast is ready."

Noelle peered into the pan. "What is that?"

"Oatmeal."

She wrinkled her nose and turned to refill her coffee cup, turning off the pot. "Not like any oatmeal I've ever seen."

"Wait till I have it all fixed up for you."

She stayed in the kitchen as he added butter, blueberries, a bit of cinnamon, and a splash of milk. He liked having her there, near him. The domesticity of the scene soothed him despite its artificiality.

He put the bowls on the table. "Grab spoons."

Noelle set her coffee at her usual spot. She had a place at his table that was hers, like the place in his heart. She hadn't asked for or claimed it—it had simply become hers. And he didn't want it back. But how much could she really want an old man like him? He was a novelty, a convenience. She'd be on to newer, younger, as soon as she had her feet under her and a basis to build from. It couldn't last.

Nick watched as she ate the first bite and then sipped her coffee.

"It's not terrible, but the texture." She wrinkled her nose. "Are you sure this is oatmeal?"

"Yeah, just not overprocessed."

"Needs sugar," she said before she took another bite.

The silence weighed on Nick. He searched for a safe topic of conversation. "When did you start painting?"

Noelle paused with the spoon midway to her mouth. "I don't remember exactly." She finished the bite he'd accidentally interrupted. "I think before I was old enough to sew, Anna used to give me coloring books to play with. So maybe three or four? She said I had an eye."

"The neighbor, in the trailer park."

"Yeah. She gave me a watercolor set with paintbrushes one year for Christmas. Really for my birthday. She didn't celebrate Christmas."

"One of those with the eight little cakes of hard pigment?" Nick hadn't thought of those in years.

"Exactly. You could mix the paint on the lid to get different colors."

"Maybe *you* did." He smiled. "All I ever did was smoosh that hard brush into them until they were pasty and I could get color on the pages. I don't think my mom gave me another set."

Noelle chuckled, and the sound lightened the heavy weight of guilt.

"I started with charcoal sketches and acrylic paint in middle school. In art class. Fell in love with the acrylic. The colors I could get, the layers. We had a really talented teacher who taught me to do portraits." She shrugged. "I kept doing it since I didn't suck at it like everything else."

"You don't suck. I mean, you have to work at reading like I would have to work at painting. But I'll *never* be able to paint. Not at your caliber."

"I guess." She ended the conversation and finished her cereal.

Noelle took the bowls and went to the kitchen. He fought the urge to clean after her—a symptom of his anxiety, his shrink would say. He could trust her to put things as he liked them. So, he retrieved their training materials, textbooks, paper, and pens from his study. Getting back to normal, resuming their usual schedule, was the best response to the catastrophe of the past night. It was a blip. An aberration. A one-off.

He laid out the math book, arranged the notepad and pencil neatly beside it. "Ready?"

Noelle sashayed out of the kitchen and dropped into her chair. "Yes, teacher."

Nick's hand itched, but he had a feeling it had more to do with his hardening cock than offering any kind of discipline.

What if she failed?

The oatmeal churned in his gut.

That was not an option. He slapped open the book. "Get focused. This is serious." She couldn't pass the test soon enough. Put him out of his misery. Or at least let him wallow in it without a witness.

CHAPTER 20

Noelle yawned, pressing her body deep into Nick's couch. He'd been insane that day. His aggression was mainly self-directed. He'd run faster and farther, had her drop him to the ground over and over, defending against his attacks. The self-defense training had been too intense for her to really enjoy the closeness of his body. Even the test lessons were more focused. She didn't mind if he wanted to work himself to exhaustion, but he was dragging her along for the ride. And it wasn't the ride she wanted.

Nick dropped the book he held to his lap. "Go to bed, Noelle."

He hadn't turned a page in the last twenty minutes. Maybe he was finally ready to give in.

He returned the book to its place on his shelves. "I'm tired."

"Fine, let's go."

"I've got the couch."

"No. You don't have the couch. It's beyond stupid, Nick. We've fucked. We can share a damn bed." The words she'd planned in her head had better work. If she didn't win that argument, he'd retreat. Forever.

"Quit swearing."

"Quit being a stubborn ass." Noelle stood, arms crossed, and glared at the man who made her want to punch him and then drop to her knees and suck his cock.

"I sleep on the couch."

"No. You *slept* on the couch. Last night, *we* slept in the bed." *And I loved it.* "The couch isn't good for you, and if you keep being stubborn, I'm moving out." There. The threat. If he called her on it, she'd have to leave.

"That's not hap—"

"It is. For real. I'm going to leave if you can't share that giant bed with me. You don't want sex, fine. But quit being ridiculous."

"It's not right."

"I'll get my things." She turned and went three steps before Nick was on her. Wrapped tight around her body, his hard cock pressed against her ass. *Thank god.*

"Stop." The low word scraped along her nerves like his stubble had scraped her thighs. Her legs went weak, but he held her firm. "You can't leave."

"Then we're sharing a bed."

"I'm not a freakin' saint."

"I don't want you to be."

The world spun as he turned her and lifted her onto his shoulder in one dizzying move. He was halfway down the hall when his hand landed on her ass in a swat that vibrated through her core. "You test me, Angel."

"Seems fair." The things they'd done the night before had changed her. She'd altered her life plans to include him. And she planned to fight for that dream.

His hand hit the other cheek, lighting her up again, then he dumped her onto the bed. He held her complete attention as he ripped off his t-shirt. She needed to lick him or draw him or both. He popped the button on his jeans and slid the zipper down a couple of inches, allowing the tip of his erection to peek out. Noelle's mouth watered.

Gripping the waistband of her sweats, he pulled them and her underwear off in one swift motion. Before she could move to ditch her shirt or grab his cock, his face was buried between her legs. She opened wider, inviting him into the space he'd already claimed. She propped herself on her elbows and watched as that amazingly sexy man feasted. His tongue danced between her folds and lit up her clit. She dropped her head back and closed her eyes. A moan rose up from deep inside, and she let it out in an approving wail. Her elbows collapsed when he slid two fingers inside and teased that perfect spot. Her shaking legs wrapped around his torso of their own volition. He chuckled.

"Don't stop."

"As if I could." He dove back in, and her world erupted in colors, every cell in her body thrumming at a different frequency. He lapped and teased her until, finally, she could take a breath and beg him to stop.

He rose from between her legs. *Damn.* A god had just eaten her out. He rearranged the covers over her boneless body. She forced her eyes to remain open while he shucked his jeans. The man's ass was the thing of dreams. But he didn't take off his boxers. Instead, he flicked off the light switch and moved almost silently around the bed before climbing in beside her. She rolled toward him, but sleep took her before she twined her body around his.

The smell of coffee teased Noelle awake. Nick was already gone from the bed, his side pulled into order. And he'd made coffee? That she had to see.

He stood in the kitchen, showered and dressed. No fair. But it was true. He had a mug on the counter for her. Guess he'd accepted her need for the evil brown elixir.

"Good morning."

Nick paused in his vegetable chopping long enough to respond, "Morning."

A thread of exhaustion wormed its way through Noelle. Every day was going to be a battle with that man. But opportunities multiplied when they were taken. She had him figured out. The man who kept *The Art of War* in his nightstand. He was first and foremost a soldier, one who understood battle. She would let him think he had the strength, the advantage. She would wear him down until losing felt like winning. But first, she had to up her game on every front.

Noelle yanked the carafe from the machine. "After breakfast, let's work on civics. And then we can go for a run."

Nick snapped his head around to stare at her.

She smiled her sweetest smile and sipped the coffee. "Then I'll get dressed and we can cover all the other subjects. Should I make the toast?"

"Um. Yeah." Nick went back to whisking the eggs for their omelet.

Noelle held in her laugh, barely. *This is going to be fun.*

Fun might have been an overstatement. Hours later, Noelle's brain was mush. "Nick, enough. You win."

"We're running out of time. October is nearly over."

"If you kill my brain, it won't matter."

"Find us a movie. I'll make dinner."

"Really?" Nick was not a fan of media. She'd been surprised he even owned a television. It wasn't huge, and he kept it hidden in a cabinet. As he started rattling pans, she started surfing the rental list, finally settling on one about a famous singer and her forbidden boyfriend.

After eating the quick stir-fry Nick had made and cleaning up the kitchen so that he could relax, she started the film.

"You can't sit there," Noelle said as Nick moved toward the chair.

"Why not?"

"Because it's a bad angle and I want to snuggle."

Nick narrowed his eyes.

"Just cuddling. I promise. I want to watch this."

Nick moved onto the couch with her, and they sat side by side, watching as a young woman fell apart under her toxic mother's career-focused treatment. The man, a cop, saw how badly the artist was hurting, but he couldn't be with her because he was being groomed to become president one day.

Noelle leaned into Nick when he wrapped his arm around her. The story was completely different from her own, yet the same in all the ways that mattered. Her heart hurt for the girl, whose career was killing her artistic expression. At least Noelle had never compromised on that. Of course, she wasn't making millions either, so maybe compromise wasn't as horrible as it looked. Noelle lay down on the couch, cocooned into Nick.

The couple in the movie had escaped to an island away from everyone. But it didn't last. Noelle could have told them that. There was nowhere to run or hide from a problem. Nick's soft snores lulled her, and her eyes drifted closed. She started to fall asleep as the couple, unable to overcome the barriers in their lives, broke up. It was too sad to keep watching.

Nick mumbled, and his arms tightened their hold. One hand slid under the waistband of her sweats and into her panties.

The TV was still on, but it was scrolling through a program guide. Noelle tried to turn in Nick's arms, but he clamped her in place. He stroked his erection against her ass in the same rhythm that he teased her clit.

"Nick." His name was a breath across her lips. Waves of pleasure washed across her body. Completely at his mercy, she laid her head back on his shoulder and let the sensations consume her. There was nothing but Nick. Slowly, the tension crested and pushed her over the cliff. She came silently, her entire body shaking from the slow build and epic crash. Nick twitched his hips a few more times.

"Angel, don't go." The words were barely audible, but the snore that followed was clear. He'd made love to her in his sleep, tormented by the belief she'd leave him. And she had threatened. In her heart, she'd created their future together. In reality, she would have to go or he would push her away. That's how real life worked. Nothing was forever. But for now, she relaxed into him. Let his body shield hers for a few more hours.

And she dreamed.

A new piece took form and drove her from his embrace before the early morning alarm had even sounded.

CHAPTER 21

Nick woke alone. His back ached from another night on the couch, which was comfortable, but not a bed. The shower spray echoed in the background.

Noelle.

She was still there, despite his convincing dreams. The tension in his chest eased. At least he hadn't slept with her. That was an improvement. He dragged himself up and went to the kitchen to prepare the coffee she loved so much and the healthy breakfast they both needed.

As Nick finished cooking, Noelle emerged from the back of the house, dressed for school, hair blow-dried. She filled the mug he'd left out and slid into her chair.

"I guess we're not running this morning?" Nick placed a plate to the side of her sketchbook.

Noelle paused her flurry of charcoal lines on the page. "You have to go without me this morning. I need to get this on paper before it blows right out of my brain."

"Eat at least."

She paused long enough to scoop up a forkful of food, but it was clear her mind was elsewhere. He quietly finished, trying to interpret what she was creating, and occasionally encouraged her to take a bite. Against their agreement, he did the cleanup, then went to take his own shower. A day of rest would be fine.

When he finished getting ready for the workday, Noelle was still at the table, hunched over her paper, a half-empty cup of cold coffee at her elbow. Nick picked it up, and she didn't even acknowledge him.

"Another cup before I turn it off?"

"Huh?"

"Do you want another cup?" He waggled the mug at her now that he had her attention.

"Oh. No. I need to go. Catch the bus." She flipped her pad closed and went to tuck it into her backpack.

"Don't leave yet," he called, emptying the carafe into the sink. He could leave the machine out for one day. He unplugged it just in case and set the still-hot glass container back in its nest.

Noelle was bouncing on the balls of her feet when he met her at the door with his keys and messenger bag full of files. "Want a ride to the stop?"

"No, I'm good." She lifted up on her toes and kissed his lips. "See you in class."

Before he could recover from the unexpected but somehow perfectly domestic gesture, she was gone. Nick glanced around his house. Touches of Noelle graced the rooms. The coffee pot. A blanket on the couch. The scent of flowery bodywash. Little things that gilded the space.

An urge to clean it away so he wouldn't become used to it again teased at the edges of his mind. A vision of his sterile space stabbed through him. He shook off the ache, opened the door, and drove to catch up to her bus.

THE SKETCH WAS NEARLY DONE by the time Ms. Julie arrived. Noelle grunted her responses at the usual morning questions her teacher asked. Dropping her pad on the table where she worked, she dove into the storage room. She flipped through her stash of prepared canvases. A two-foot-by-three-foot was the largest she had ready. It would have to do.

After setting it up on her easel, she lightly laid out the scene in pencil. Within minutes she was ready to apply the first layers of color, her base, the depth of her work. She'd add her reclaimed pieces and pull the image from the canvas, giving it dimension and life. Her brain knew how the piece would come together—it was a matter of allowing her body the time to execute it. As she dashed on the reds, oranges, yellows, blacks, and browns, mixing colors on her palette with ferocity, Ms. Julie came around behind her. Noelle didn't pause. In no time she would have to clean up and get to Nick's—*no, Mr. Christoph's*—classroom. He couldn't be Nick at school.

"Wow. That's some strong imagery."

Noelle lifted her brush and stepped back. *Yes.* An angel hovered over a man standing in hellfire, reaching for him. It wasn't completely clear, but it was coming into focus. The piece resonated with the feelings that swirled inside her. Pride overlaid them all. It wasn't often she was able to get the exact emotions on the canvas. Sometimes it was damn near impossible. But she'd opened herself, and it was there. Taking form. "I might use this one for the show."

Ms. Julie stepped back. "Might be difficult to finish it. I mean, the contest is coming up fast."

Before Noelle could respond, Ms. Julie was back at her desk. Odd. Noelle mentally shrugged and went back to work. Too soon she had to put it all away and go.

"Noelle." Nick's voice cut through her daydreams about the new artwork. "Why aren't you focused?"

"New piece. I need to do some hunting later."

Nick narrowed his gaze. "Fine. But stay focused while you're here. You can worry about your materials after school." He lowered his voice to barely audible. "I'll take you."

A warm flame flickered in her chest.

Obsessively clean Nick was going to take her dumpster diving.

~

AFTER SCHOOL, Noelle lingered by the parking lot, unsure how Nick was going to take her hunting without being obvious. The TA hadn't left the way he normally did in the rush of all the other students. He'd probably wanted to talk to Nick.

"There you are."

Nick's voice startled her.

"I've been looking everywhere. Why'd you leave?"

She tugged at her backpack strap. "Mrs. Stafford asked me why I was loitering in the hallway. I didn't want to—"

"Don't worry about it. Ready?"

"You aren't worried about someone seeing us leave together?"

"It looks weirder if it seems like we're sneaking. We're going dumpster diving, not exactly a romantic interlude." He clicked a button on his keychain, and his car chirped. Noelle opened the door and tucked her pack behind the passenger seat. Nick started the car. "What's on your wish list?"

"Wish list?" Didn't he understand that you got what you got?

"Tile, metal, something else?"

"I could always use more tile. And scrap metal."

Nick pulled out on the road, headed in the opposite direction from her usual places.

"Where are you going?"

"I thought since I was driving, we could try some more distant haunts. There's a high-end tile store where I found some of the tile for my kitchen and bathroom. We can check there."

Noelle bit her tongue. She'd accepted Nick's offer. No need to explain that it was unlikely she'd have more luck in someplace new. The best stuff showed up unexpectedly and could be gone the next day. Once, she'd made the mistake of thinking she could come back instead of overloading her backpack. But one wasted day wouldn't kill her.

They drove toward fancy neighborhoods with landscaped medians filled with saguaro, low cacti, and russet rock. He continued driving ever closer to the mountain until she could see the plants that grew on the sides of the dark rock instead of slim shadows of green. The houses became larger, stuccoed walls wrapped around gated neighborhoods. Nothing like the part of town where she'd grown up.

Nick parked in a surprisingly clean alley. It didn't bode well. Sloppy stores had lots of trash, a lack of concern about what was being tossed. Those environments led to great finds. At least he'd tried.

"Coming?" he asked, his hand on the door.

She opened her door and walked over to blue metal bin. It came up to her chest, and she peered in. Full—a good sign. She started to reach in.

"Wait." Nick handed her a pair of gardening gloves, his own already covered. "Put these on."

Seriously? But she wasn't going to argue. Gloves donned, she dug in, lifting flattened cardboard boxes and pushing aside plastic wrapping. The glove caught on something. Noelle went up on tiptoe. Metal. Carefully she grabbed the edge she could see and pulled it free. Screening. She dropped it to the ground and kept digging, more excited about the location. Apparently, they'd never heard of recycling.

"What about this?" Nick held up a small plastic tub. She released the edge of a box she held and went to him.

"Nice." The tub of dyed brown grout would be perfect for adding texture to her work after the addition of a bit of white glue. And she could always use the container on another canvas. She put the tub on top of the screen.

Walking around the bin, she attacked it from a different angle. A shine in the depths of the can caught her eye. She inspected the outside of the bin and found a foothold. Pressing her toes onto the small metal lip, she pushed up and hefted her hips to the edge of the can. Prepared to jump in, Nick's hand on her thigh froze her.

"What are you doing?"

"Going in." How else was she supposed to get the stuff out?

"No."

"But there's—"

"I'll go. What did you see?"

Mr. Germaphobe is going in the dumpster? This I gotta see. "There's something shiny at the bottom."

He lifted her off the bin and then went up and in just as she'd planned to. Two seconds later, he held up several sheets of white iridescent tiles in one-inch squares on mesh backing. Only a couple of the tiles were cracked or chipped. It was an amazing find. She snatched them out of his hands, and he extracted himself from the trash container.

"Thank you for bringing me here, Nick."

"Are we done?" He slid the gloves off his hands and held them by the wrists like they were dead rats.

"Done." She didn't need to be greedy. The stuff they'd found would be perfect to complete the artwork for the senior show. That piece would be even better than her planets.

Nick dug out his keys and popped the trunk. He dropped his gloves in and pulled out his towel. Noelle placed her acquisitions in two empty plastic grocery bags and left them in the trunk on the plastic liner. She removed her gloves and dropped them on top of Nick's. He was already arranging the terrycloth over his driver's seat. She held back a budding laugh— he'd overcome his aversion to help her. She didn't have to tease him.

As soon as they were home, Nick darted into the house. "Put that stuff on the back porch. I'm taking a shower," he called over his shoulder.

Noelle placed the bags on the cement pad behind the house and dropped her backpack in its designated spot in the study. The sound of the shower called to her, an image of Nick's perfect body clear in her mind. Impulsively, she went to the bathroom and tested the door. Unlocked. She stripped her clothes off in the hallway and opened the door.

"Any hot water left for me? I'm dirty, too." Noelle tried to sound sexy. She must have failed, because Nick slammed off the water and his arm jutted out past the curtain, grabbing his towel off the hook.

Before she could recover, he swung the curtain back and stepped out of the tub, towel firmly wrapped around his hips and gripped in place for extra security.

"All yours." He didn't even look at her or her birthday suit.

She stepped back reflexively as he darted out of the room. *Well, damn.* That didn't go as expected. Unsure what else to do, she started up the shower again. Two steps forward and one step back. Pushing the worry to the back of her mind, she contemplated her next plan of attack.

Dressed in a pair of his boxers and thin white t-shirt, Noelle tried everything to get Nick's attention at dinner, but it was like she was invisible. He was beyond stubborn. But she wasn't giving up. She'd let him retreat.

Temporarily.

"I have to go out." Nick picked up his empty plate and put it in the sink.

Noelle followed him with hers. "Something wrong?"

"Nope, just have a group session to attend."

Noelle scraped her plate and started to fill one side of the sink with soapy water. Nick had gone from every other Wednesday to every Wednesday, to Wednesdays with occasional Fridays, and now he was adding Mondays? Had the dumpster dive triggered him? Was she that hard to live with? She didn't want to be the reason he lost his shit.

They cleaned up in silence, then Nick ducked back to his study to get his things. Noelle flopped on the couch in a pout. How the hell was she supposed to enjoy that sexy man if he wouldn't hang around the house long enough? Maybe she could lie in wait for him and surprise him when he got home. A digital chirp interrupted her musing on wardrobe choices that would tempt him.

Nick's phone sat on the coffee table, where he'd dropped it with his keys when they'd returned that afternoon, not able to strip his dirty clothes off fast enough. When it chirped again, Noelle glanced at the screen: *The pictures are fabulous. Call me, love.*

Love?

CHAPTER 22

*B*efore Noelle could unscramble her brain and ask who'd texted him, Nick grabbed his phone and took off. After seeing that message, she no longer had any interest in seducing him. What if he had another relationship with someone? What if he was hiding that woman from her? He'd told her several times they couldn't have a relationship. He didn't want sex. Except that he did. But maybe he shouldn't.

Sick foreboding rolled in her stomach like a pool of filth under a garbage can. She felt dirty. With no motivation to study or clean or anything, she turned out the lights and crawled into Nick's bed. His ever-present citrusy scent didn't comfort her the way it normally did. A black haze settled inside her, muting everything.

"Noelle. Wake up. I'm right here, Angel. It's just a dream." Nick had Noelle pinned to the bed with his body. His legs held hers down, and he used his forearms to press her hands to the bed. His gaze was focused on her when she opened her eyes, panic as clear as a tattoo on his face.

"Get off." She wriggled her hips, unable to get any purchase against him on the soft mattress.

"Sorry." He released her immediately but didn't move far. "You were flailing, I didn't want you to hurt yourself."

Noelle wiped her sweaty hair back from her face, trying to clear the leftover terror.

"Are you okay?" Nick asked, his tone gentle. "What happened?"

"I don't know." But she did—the dream, so vivid it still felt real. Nick had abandoned her in an empty warehouse. She had no shoes. Rats ran over her feet. She didn't know where she was, and she couldn't get out. Every door had been locked. Nick was outside, laughing with his friends about the stupid little girl who imagined she would be his. "What time is it?"

"Late. You were already asleep when I got back."

"Where were you?"

"Therapy."

"No, before you came in the room." Noelle could tell he hadn't been in the bed with her.

"On the couch."

"Of course." She swallowed her disappointment. "Who texted you?"

"Texted me?"

"Yeah. Calls you 'love.'"

"My mom. I sent her images of your work."

Noelle blinked at his response. She hadn't even considered the fact Nick had parents. "Images of my... How did you get pictures?" She glared at him, daring him to lie.

"The images you saved. In the cloud. For our phones."

Anger replaced terror. "Why would you send pictures of *my* artwork to someone without asking me?"

"My parents are art dealers. I didn't want to get your hopes up. But I mentioned my painting." He pointed at the wall where the angel hung. "It could be a great opportunity."

"Then why didn't you tell me?"

"You've had some challenges recently—"

"I'm doing fine." But that was a lie. She'd been doing just fine with

Nick's help. Before, she'd been drifting. Noelle freed her legs from the sheets, needing to stand. "I'm not just some…some…charity case."

"Of course you're not. But—"

"But nothing." How could she make him understand? She huffed out a breath. "I want to be yours. Your lover. Not your fucking project."

He came around the bed and stopped right in front of her. She didn't move an inch, just glared up at the man who'd terrorized her dreams and made her want things she shouldn't and sent her art to people without her permission. Should she kiss him or kick him?

"I don't know what to do with you," Nick said.

Well, that made two of them. She put her fists on her hips.

He rubbed a hand over his head. "I lose my mind around you. I want to give you everything. I want to take…everything."

"Nick—"

"How do I reconcile the fact that all I want to do is protect you, save you?"

"I never asked to be saved, and protecting me isn't the same as making decisions without me. I have to be in control of my life. I have to." She reached forward and ran her hand down his arm. "I'm not helpless. I'm not a child. I haven't been one of those for a long damn time."

"I'd give you anything if you asked."

"Wait for me to ask."

Nick nodded.

"Take me to bed, Nick?"

He lifted his eyes to hers. Every fucked-up emotion she held inside her swirled in his eyes. How could they be so different and so much the same? She leaned into him. Wrapped her arms around his middle and pulled him tight. Her lips met his, and it was like she'd loosened his chains.

NOELLE'S RUNNING shoes slapped at the pavement in a rhythmic beat. Nick stayed with her even though he probably could have maintained a faster pace. That time in the morning, together with no agenda or expectations, the air cool on her body, she was glad Nick had forced her to stick with it. Not forced. Strongly encouraged.

Nick made an odd grunt, drawing Noelle's attention. She'd seen that look before. He had something he wanted to talk about. She stayed silent. Either he'd get it out or he wouldn't. Getting up early to run in the open-space park had been worth it. The native plants had bloomed in yellow and light purple in response to the recent fall rain, and everything was fresh and earthy.

"What do you think about a website?"

That wasn't what she'd expected him to bring up. *No more sex* would have been her bet on topics most likely to be discussed. "A website?"

"Yeah." He continued jogging down the path. "My parents love your work. They want to get a website set up so they can do some promotions. See if there's interest for a gallery show."

"Seriously?" Maybe she'd forgive him for sending the images to his parents. "How much would it cost?"

"Nothing. And before you protest, they've done this for other artists." Nick flicked his gaze to hers. "There's no guarantee."

"What do I have to do?"

"Give permission. They have the pictures. And I'm sorry I didn't ask first. But they do have the images and a development company they use."

"I get a say in what the layout looks like. Last thing I want is some crappy site hosting my artwork." She swiped the sweat from her forehead. "I've checked out artists online. Most of them were boring. Beige backgrounds with small photos and biographies and nothing about what inspired them." *Yuck.*

"Everything will go through you. They'll do a couple of examples, you can choose or modify, or they can start over. Whatever you want."

"What's the catch?" Nobody did anything for free.

"No catch. They want to be your agent, and you'd have a contract.

If you want to look for a different agent, you can. But you should have one. Anyone you choose would get a cut. If they get you in a gallery, they'd get a percentage of your net sales after the gallery fees."

"How much of a cut?" Just like dealing. Made sense.

"It's a standard contract my parents use for debut artists. It'll be specified in the terms."

"But what do I have to do?"

"Make art." Nick glanced over at her. "Attend the openings of shows once they get them booked."

"I don't know anything about contracts. I had Ms. Julie look over the last one with the tavern."

"I know a couple of attorneys. We can send it to one of them to review it with you."

"Really?"

"Yeah, I'm using my connections. But it's business."

Noelle concentrated on running, letting Nick's words tumble in her mind. They'd come as a surprise. She wasn't sure how to react. She made art—but websites, lawyers, agents? "This is all happening so fast."

"It's the next step in your career."

"The show in the tavern was good. I sold most of what I displayed. I might get a chance to put a couple of pieces in the gallery. But attending an opening as the primary artist?" Was that who she could be? By the time they got back to the house she was a sweaty confused mess. "I'm not sure I'm ready."

"It's up to you." Nick went to the kitchen.

She left him there and took her time getting ready for school, possibilities racing through her mind. A thousand things could go wrong. Likely nothing would come of it anyway. But if something did…

Pouring the coffee Nick had made, she said, "I have to work tonight. But when I get home, I'd like to see the contract."

CHAPTER 23

$\mathcal{N}$ick bit his tongue to keep from insisting Noelle wait for him so he could give her a ride. Her professional work outfit—dressy pants, black flats, and a black-and-white print top—made her look more like a teacher than a student. She said she was fine riding the bus, but after she finished her GED, maybe he could talk her into letting him teach her to drive. Buy her a car. Stay with him always. His fantasy of forever was interrupted by his boss.

"Mr. Christoph? Was that Ms. Michaels I saw leaving your room?" The principal's voice held knowledge. Facts that were about to tank his plans.

"Yes, ma'am." Lying was pointless. No one could mistake that mane of red hair or the way Noelle darted like a gazelle through a hallway of predators.

"She's attending school again?"

"Um. She came in today." Also the truth.

"She was absent for more than ten consecutive days. A truancy officer was assigned but didn't find her at the shelter. She left some time back."

Nick nodded, and his stomach soured on the lies. He and Julie *had* marked Noelle absent, and she wasn't at the shelter.

"Noelle is no longer a student here. And based on what I saw, it looks like she's doing fine. Do you know if she has a job?"

"At a gallery downtown."

"Good. It was nice of her to visit and let you know how she's doing, but I can't have unauthorized visitors on my campus. She has to get a pass from the office like anyone else."

"I'll let her know when…I mean…if I see her again." Like tonight. When she would likely kill him for getting her disenrolled behind her back. Or maybe it could wait a couple of days. He could have her study from home. Somehow. Give her time to get the contract with his parents in place. Yeah, the lawyers would only be available during business hours. That could work, at least until he thought of something.

Principal Lopez tapped her fingers on his desk. "I've been impressed with how you were able to turn Lucas around. The others seem to be thriving as well." She eyed his classroom. Nick was proud of the tidy stations ready for independent and guided studies. Everything charted and organized. "You're an asset to this school and the students most in need. I'm glad you're here, Mr. Christoph."

As Nick acknowledged the praise, a thread of guilt slithered up his spine. Would she be so complimentary if she knew what Nick had done with Noelle?

NOELLE DRAGGED her backpack up her arm and propelled herself out the gallery door. The waning light reflected off the glass store fronts and heated her chilled skin—Greer liked to keep the gallery cold. Barely half a block from the bus stop, Noelle's mother stepped into her path.

"Look at you, all fancy."

Noelle eyed her mother. Never a good idea to respond too quickly. It was better to assess first. Same mangy hair. Same pockmarked skin. Same chemical stench. The ankle bracelet was new.

"Got a job?"

"Yeah." *Here it comes.*

"The trailer's gone." Her mother tugged at the stained fabric of her yellow t-shirt.

It wasn't a question, so Noelle took a couple of more steps toward the stop. The other shops had already closed for the night. She couldn't miss her bus.

Her mom trailed her. "You had one job, you selfish bitch."

Noelle froze. "*I* had one job?"

"Stay in the trailer. Keep it for me and your dad. You know what happens when you don't have an address?"

Adopting her blank mask, Noelle stared down at the drug-ruined woman who'd given birth to her. *I don't have an address or a dad.*

"You don't get your checks. That's what." Her mother's hate-filled eyes narrowed to slits, focused on Noelle.

Checks. Money. The only thing that mattered. *Gee, daughter, where're you staying? How's life? Nope, just give me my fucking money.*

Her mother used to terrify her. Not anymore. Noelle kept walking. A claw latched around her arm, pinching it hard. *Damn.* She'd forgotten how strong her mom was.

"You fucked up. You owe me."

"What could I owe you? You haven't done anything for me in years. *Years.*" Noelle ripped her arm out of her mother's grasp. She'd clean the wound at home. The bus was close. "I'm not your problem any more than you're mine."

"I *am* your fucking problem. Because I'm going to be at that gallery every day until you give me the cash I need."

"All that's going to do is get me fired."

"Then you'll see what it's like to have someone take away *your* income, fucking worthless bitch."

The bus stopped in front of Noelle and doors opened. "The owner will call the cops."

"I don't have to stay long enough for them to get there. I'll just show up every day you work."

"I'll call the cops every day."

Her mom pulled back her hair, scratching at her scalp. "Then I guess I'll just have to go to the school and tell them who you're living with."

The heat from the sidewalk wasn't enough to keep her blood from freezing. "How much?"

"Two Gs."

Noelle boarded the bus, and the doors closed, separating her from the toxic troll she called Mom. She flopped into a seat on the far side so she wouldn't have to look at her any longer. Bone-deep exhaustion claimed her. She'd worked hard since the night of the arrests. But what if it didn't matter? Two thousand dollars. She had the money, in the bank, but she'd have to close the account or at least empty it. If she gave it to her mom, it would only lead to more demands. The bus lurched down the street, rattling her in the seat.

No. Noelle shook her head and forced herself to sit up tall. *Hell no.* She had a contract to look at tonight. And she could talk to her boss on Thursday. And she had a new piece in progress. And the senior show. She might have to give up Nick for a while. But she could probably string her mother along until she finished getting her life together. She had a couple of days to decide what to do.

"Noelle?" Nick's voice rang out from the kitchen when she stepped inside.

She slid the backpack from her shoulder and headed down the hallway. "I'm gonna grab a shower."

"Dinner's almost ready."

"I'll be fast." She dropped her pack in the study, alongside Nick's messenger bag. Fifteen minutes and several gallons of hot water later, she was restored. Mask back in place, she'd be able to have a conversation with Nick without telling him about her mother's visit and threat. He didn't need to know, because there was no way she would let her mom ruin his life by costing him his job.

She dropped into her chair, and Nick set a plate in front of her. "What's this?"

"Steak. Figured we should celebrate you getting an agent."

Noelle flashed him a smile, unsure what to say. She'd had steak like three times in her life. The food was good, mashed potatoes with butter and fresh green beans. Each bite reinforced her resolve to protect Nick from her crazy mother.

"Is the gallery going to be open Thanksgiving weekend?"

"Haven't asked." Why did Nick care?

"I was thinking we could go to Colorado. I have a buddy with a lodge."

"I'll talk to Greer." She'd never traveled. Hadn't had anywhere to go. But what would his buddy think of her?

"The contract came in. Do you want to look at it?"

Wiping her mouth with her napkin, she nodded. "Thanks for dinner. It was the best steak I've ever had."

Nick stacked their empty plates and put them in the sink. While he went to the study, Noelle automatically started tidying the kitchen. Not that there was much to do. Nick was a clean-as-he-went cook. A moment later, he was back.

He set the papers down and helped her speed through the rest of the dishes. "Ready?"

They sat together, and Noelle slowly reviewed each word.

"I have an appointment with a lawyer for you tomorrow. Melissa Winter. She's a contract lawyer who works with a friend of my parents. But she'd be representing you."

"Where do I have to go?"

"It's going to be a phone call. She's in New Mexico. But it's during the day."

"Can I do it on my cell phone? Maybe step out of class?"

"I was thinking you could take the day off. Stay here and take the call. I found a place that has online practice tests for the GED. You could work through one of those?"

Not a bad plan. She could take her time on the contract and do the practice test. And she could sneak off to the bank to get a few hundred to hold her mother over. "All right. I'll call in sick at school."

"No need. I'll tell the school you called me."

Noelle nodded.

"I can email the PDF of the contract to Missy tonight. She said she'd review it with Ned, her partner. She hasn't passed the bar yet, but she's brilliant with legal agreements, and there's no charge. She's doing it as a friend."

A trained lawyer was loads better than her art teacher, which would have been her solution. Noelle's relief at the price and complete trust in Nick to look out for her best interests—without taking over—let her agree with confidence.

CHAPTER 24

$\mathcal{N}$oelle scarfed down scrambled eggs and a cup of coffee while Nick set up the conference call in the study. She carried her refill into the office. The wooden desk was more beat-up and scarred than Nick. The fancy silver laptop contrasted with the old clock radio that sat on the corner. He was so funny about some things. New technology, but an ancient clock that no one would keep, much less use.

"Okay, you're ready. When the call rings in, just push this button and give it a sec to connect. When you're done, you click this red icon to hang up. Got it?"

"Yeah, looks like a cell phone."

"Uh, right. And this page here." Nick clicked an icon at the bottom of the screen. "This is the practice test. Should take a couple of hours. It's shorter than the real test but should give us an idea where we need to focus."

"Okay."

"There's food in the fridge—"

"Nick. Go to work."

He stepped back from the computer and scooped up his messenger bag. "See you tonight. Call me if you need anything."

"I'll be fine." She waved him out the door. Noelle fussed with her copy of the contract and the notes she'd written. She drew a small square next to each question so she could check them off and make sure she didn't miss any. Nick had organized the call, but it was her contract, her art, her life. The laptop made a ringing sound, and Noelle placed the earbuds as she accepted.

"Hello? Noelle?" A sweet voice came through the speakers, and a beautiful blond woman's face filled the screen. Noelle nodded. "I'm Melissa Winter, but call me Missy."

Noelle introduced herself and waited for what came next.

"I've reviewed your contract. Do you want me to share my screen?"

Once the image of the contract loaded, Missy jumped right into explaining the terms of the agreement. "First thing, the agency is asking for a cut of all geographical areas as well as online sales."

"They're going to set up a website for me."

"Oh cool. I'll have to check it out once it's up. I have an entire house of blank walls."

"I can help you with that."

Missy laughed, and Noelle relaxed.

"Excellent. So, you're okay with the internet sales. What about all geographical areas? Are they only promoting your work in Florida?"

"No, Nick says they have connections to galleries all over the world and lots of them in New York, too."

"What about where you are now? In Tucson? Do you have any art for sale?"

"Not right now. But I did and I could. I work at a gallery. And I'm doing a show through school that could lead to a sale."

"All right, I'm going to put in an exception for Tucson and a fifty-mile radius." The cursor moved on the shared screen as Missy typed the note. "The eighteen-month term is standard."

"They only want me for that long?"

"It can be renewed. It's good to have an expiration in case circumstances change or the agreement isn't meeting your expectations."

"Okay."

"Now, the commissions." Missy flipped a page, and Noelle repeated the action with her copy. "They're higher than some, but they're covering all the costs of promotion, shipping, and insurance. What do you think?"

"If I don't have to pay for marketing, then I'm good with the higher rate."

"You can always renegotiate at the renewal."

They continued through the contract, and Missy answered all of Noelle's questions. Any nervousness she'd had about signing disappeared with Missy's detailed explanations and recommendations.

"One last thing. Is the mailing address they have for you correct? It's the same as Nick's?"

"Yeah." Did Nick's parents use his address because she didn't have one or because they knew she was living with him?

"That's it. We're done. I'll make the one modification and email it to you. Your signature needs to be notarized since you're completing the agreement remotely. Do you have a bank you use?"

"Yeah, no problem."

"The bank can probably even fax it for you. Mail the original afterward."

"Thank you, Missy." It seemed so inadequate for the time she'd given her.

"My pleasure. Be sure to send me the link to your website when it's up."

They hung up, and Noelle made an exception to her limit and brewed another pot of coffee. She printed the document that Missy had already sent and tucked it into her backpack that sat on the low shelf near the door. It looked lonely without Nick's messenger bag next to it. She glanced at the red numbers on the clock. She had time to take the practice test and then hightail it to the bank. It was weird not to be at school. Not to be with Julie and Nick, but it felt good, too. Like she was getting a preview of the life she'd been working for.

The practice test went better than expected. She'd completed each section in the time allotted. Just barely, but that was a huge win. And her future studies were clear. More civics and more science. And a lot more writing. She saved the results to review with Nick when he got home from school.

Despite having accomplished so much, it was still before noon. A quick check of her backpack to make sure her bus pass and ID were where she'd left them—unable to drop the old habit from living with her parents when her things seemed to disappear constantly—and she was on the way to the bus stop. It was a short walk to the bank, but the bus would be faster. And there was one more stop to make before she returned home.

The same lady that had opened her account sat at her desk alone. Perfect. "Excuse me," Noelle said. "Do you notarize things?"

The woman glanced up and then straightened. "Of course. For bank customers."

"Good." Noelle sat down and pulled out the contract.

"Do you have an account here?"

"Yeah, you opened it. A while back?" The lady didn't have much of a memory. Or maybe she only remembered Nick. Her cow eyes had been locked on him the entire time.

"Right." She pounded on her keyboard with painted nails. Not as fancy as the school counselor's, Mrs. Harwood's, but obviously done at a nail salon. "The account number?"

Noelle rattled off the sequence she'd forced herself to memorize when first opening the account, before she'd destroyed the card they'd given her.

"Do you have some ID?"

Noelle handed the woman the laminated card. "I also need some cash." Might as well get it there instead of dealing with the ATM. "Two hundred."

"Okay. Let me do the notary first." She opened a drawer and pulled out a notebook and a big stamp. "Sign the document, then you can sign my log."

Noelle did as instructed, talked the woman into sending the fax, and tucked her cash away deep in her pack. She'd get Nick to help her mail the original contract. Another quick check of the clock. *Perfect.* She'd have time to surprise Ms. Julie.

There was a class in session when Noelle opened the door of the art room. She stepped inside and waited to catch her teacher's eye. When she finally did, the smile she'd been holding back all day took over. Ms. Julie rushed over.

"Noelle? What are you doing here? Mr. Christoph said—"

"I couldn't wait to share my news."

"Let's talk back here." Ms. Julie led the way to the storage area.

Noelle bounced with energy behind her. "I got an agent," she blurted as soon as they were away from the sculpture class.

"An agent? For your art?"

"Yeah." Noelle bit back telling her it was Nick's parents. "This company in Florida heard about my art show and viewed the pictures of my work. They sent a contract, and they're going to put up a website for me."

"Wow. Do you need me to go over the contract with you?"

"Thank you. But I did it with a lawyer this morning."

"That's great, Noelle. I'm so happy for you."

"Me too. And I'm ready to enter the contest. I decided on a piece." Noelle glanced at her stash of completed canvases. "Can we register now or after your class is done?"

"Noelle. Mr. Christoph hasn't talked to you?" Ms. Julie was wringing her hands.

"About what?"

"He was supposed to talk to you. It was *his* plan. But you *can't* enter the contest. You're…not a student anymore."

All of Noelle's excitement drained away in a second. "What are you talking about?"

"It's complicated. You should really talk to Mr. Christoph. I'm so sorry." Ms. Julie's face was red, and she stared at the ground. Wouldn't even look at her.

"Ms. Julie?"

"Talk to him." Her teacher walked out, leaving her alone in the storage room.

Noelle's vision went red. *His plan.* One he'd failed to discuss with her. Snatching up the portfolio she'd taken to leaving at school, she spun around and ran from the art class. What had he done?

CHAPTER 25

The classroom door swung open, drawing Nick's attention away from word problems and Lucas. Noelle stood in the opening, a firestorm of wrath. Nick's skin went cold.

"Class, I need to step out. I expect you to stay on task."

Nick stood up from his chair and gave his TA a quick chin thrust, then rushed to his doom.

"What did you do?" Her hissed words tangled around him like razor wire.

He took her arm and backed her out of the doorway. "Not here."

She jerked her arm out of his grasp but followed him all the way to the parking lot. When they got to his car, he stopped. "What are you doing here?"

"I guess that's the question of the day, isn't it?" Her fingers dug into the strap of her backpack, knuckles white.

"Can we talk about this at home? It's complicated."

"No. We're gonna talk about it right now. I was a student. Now I'm not. What. Did. You. Do?" Her brown eyes narrowed on him, pinning him in place.

Shit, shit, shit. He should have told her. The night before. "I should have explained this—"

"Explained?" She released her pack and pointed her finger at him. "I'm pretty sure you should have asked permission."

"I did it for you."

"Really? And exactly *what* did you *do* for me?" Noelle crossed her arms.

Nick glanced around the parking lot, making sure there were no witnesses to his confession. If he could go back a few months, he'd have handled it completely differently. He should have explained the situation to her, let her make the call. But it was too late. Noelle's foot tapped on the pavement. "I marked you absent so you'd be disenrolled."

Noelle sucked in a breath, her eyes going wide. "You *what?*" Her breath came out as a whisper.

"Look, the GED requires that you not be currently enrolled when you take the test. I didn't want you to stop coming to school any sooner than you had to, but I didn't want you to have to wait until next year either. And I figured—"

"I can take the GED anytime. You could have let me have my last semester. I wanted to enter the senior show. I've been waiting years for my turn. Ms. Julie knew how important it was to me. How did—" Noelle's mouth gaped, and she stepped back. "You talked her into this."

"I did." Nick couldn't look at her. He'd treated her like a child. He'd made decisions for her, trying to control her. Even let his desire for her drive the timeline. He had to find a way to make her understand. To forgive him.

Noelle's lower lip quivered. "When were you going to tell me that I wasn't a student? That I couldn't be in school, couldn't use the studio."

"Tonight." Nick rubbed his sweaty palms on his pants.

"Why?" She shook her head. "Why bother to tell me at all? I mean, except for the contest, I would never have known. You could have had Julie lie to me about that, too. Pretended to enter my work and then, whoops, must have lost the entry, you were too late applying, or whatever bullshit excuse you'd come up with. What the fuck else did you lie to me about? The fucking contract, Nick? Hooking me up with your lawyer? Some ex-girlfriend doing you a favor?"

"No!" He reached for her, but she flung herself out of reach. "Noelle, you earned that deal. And I've never dated Missy. My parents love me, but they don't give handouts when it comes to business."

"So, that must be what *you're* in charge of? Handouts? Clothes and food and haircuts and all that shit. How much do I owe you, Nick? I guess my virginity should be worth something." She opened her backpack and dug around.

Her words stabbed him. The pain bled through his veins, combining with his shame. "Anything I did was to help you. Not as an exchange for sex. And how can you even taint what we have like that. You had to feel how much I cared about you, how much I still care about you. Damn it. I'm in *love* with you, Angel."

Noelle remained focused on her search. As if he hadn't confessed his feelings.

Nick's eyes stung, and his throat was watery. He swallowed down the emotions. Crying at work was not something he was prepared to do.

"You love me?" She finally met his gaze. "All I see is a man who yanked me around like a yo-yo, making me do whatever he wanted me to do. Who played Daddy-knows-best with my fucking future. I'm not your angel." She flung a handful of money at him. "I'm not your anything."

Before Nick could formulate a response, she turned on her heel and ran through the parking lot.

"Noelle," he yelled, unable to move. Frozen. There was no backup to call, no sniper, no air support that could solve the catastrophe. The light of his life, his future, his angel, ran from him. It was exactly what he deserved. And there was no possible way to go back and change what he'd done.

～

NOELLE POUNDED down the pavement and asphalt. Unconsciously headed home. Not home. To Nick's house. And in minutes she found herself in front of the olive stucco building that had been safe. Wonderful. A dream. Yes. It had been a fucking dream. Time to wake up.

She unlocked the door, and the living room was as foreign to her as the first time she'd seen it. Nothing had changed in the room from when she'd left a few hours ago. But everything had changed inside her. Her eyes saw it all differently.

The blanket draped on the couch—clutter.

The lingering smell of coffee—stench.

The printout on the dining table—trash.

Like misplaced pencil lines in a sketch, she was going to erase all traces she'd been there.

Dropping her bag and portfolio at the door, she went to the back of the house. She gathered all of her clothes. Rolling them tightly, she fit what she could use in her backpack. A brown paper bag held her extra pair of shoes and her toiletries. The rest of the clothes she hid. She wiped down the bathroom, taking her toothbrush and her hair products. She folded the blanket and tucked it back in the linen cupboard where it'd come from. She folded her extra copy of the contract and slipped it between the pages of her sketchpad. The textbooks were Nick's.

No. *Mr. Christoph's.*

The only thing that remained was the coffee maker and grounds. She couldn't bring herself to throw out a perfectly good appliance and a mostly full can. She tucked it away in the pantry. Mr. Christoph could decide what he wanted to do with the last intruder in his perfect world. Maybe she'd pushed too hard, inserted herself too much into his sterile life. He could throw the machine away, but she'd see herself out.

Leaving her key and the phone he'd bought her on the counter, she picked up her things. A backpack, a brown paper sack, and a fancy new portfolio. She left almost no mark on his home. He'd added extra baggage—clothes, contractual obligations, emotions—to her already complicated life. She twisted the lock on the front door handle and pulled it tight behind her.

Blinking in the afternoon sun, she was directionless. She stood at the bottom of the short staircase to the front porch that no longer welcomed her home. There were any number of options, but she needed to go to the gallery the next day. If she could convince her boss to hang her work, that would be a start. A beginning to rebuilding the life she'd imagined with Mr. Christoph. The only solution was a hotel. But not a crappy one. He'd already proved he could find her. She'd go to a decent one, near her job. For one night. Unless she could get a second job working for the hotel in exchange for rent.

Laden with bags, she plodded to the bus stop. That line would take her only so far. Her first stop: the library. She could use their computers to research where to stay.

It took a couple of hours struggling to stay focused enough to read before she'd found a decent hotel for fifty bucks a short ride from work. If she ended up staying a few days, she might even buy a bathing suit since they had a pool. She'd also found out, after checking her email, her art agents—Nick's parents—had received her contract and would send links to sample websites soon. Just because their son was an asshole didn't mean she wasn't going to keep moving forward. She'd need to find a place to store her portfolio, and a studio space. But that was a future problem. At least she had a website going up and someone else trying to sell her art. And she was free to market her pieces in Tucson, thanks to Missy.

The hotel check-in was a total pain in the ass. She didn't have a credit card. But she finally talked the guy into taking her cash since they had hardly anyone staying at the place on a Wednesday night. Noelle wouldn't be surprised if the cops paid her a visit later, but she had nothing to hide. She'd broken up with her boyfriend and needed a place to stay for the night. It beat the I'm-homeless-again story that was closer to the truth.

After grabbing a sandwich and milk from a nearby mini-mart, Noelle sat in silence. No kitchen to clean. No books to study. No couch to snuggle on. Nick was gone. The life he'd made her want was gone. But none of it had ever really been hers. They were images he'd painted on the canvas of her mind. Pretty pictures, but not reality. Reality was finding shelter. Working a job. Feeding herself and trying to rebuild her shattered life. Picking up the remains felt too heavy. Turning it into treasure, impossible. She flipped off the lights and curled up on top of the covers, fully dressed, and cried herself to sleep.

CHAPTER 26

$\mathcal{N}$ick flopped onto the couch. The empty, cold furniture. The blanket, like all other traces of Noelle, was gone. He'd searched the city for hours. Retraced every step from the first time he'd found her. Tried hotel after hotel until he'd finally accepted she could be anywhere, and she didn't want him to find her. He glanced at her phone. It should have been the insurance policy. The tracking software on it would have told him where she was. But no. She'd outsmarted him and left it behind. Possibilities ran through his mind, each more horrific than the last. When cold sweat trickled down his shaking muscles, he recognized what was happening. Full-blown panic attack.

He dialed the one person who might be able to talk him down.

"Saint, brother. How you been?"

"Not good, man. Having a thing."

"Shit." Gabe sucked a hard breath that echoed into Nick's ear. "What triggered you, Nick? Talk to me."

"She's gone."

"We talking your student, or are we going further back?"

"Noelle. My...my—" What should he call her? His student? His lover? His woman? His life?

"Your girl pulled a runner?"

"Yeah." The word choked out of Nick's dry throat.

"Nick. Slow. Deep. Breaths. Breathe with me."

Nick focused on the sounds of the breaths through the phone. In. Out. Again and again, until he no longer sounded like he was going to die.

"One more."

Nick took a slow breath in and let it out. "Thanks."

"I'm here for you, brother. Can you tell me what's happening?"

"Maybe? I messed up. I did something. Something I should have talked to Noelle about before I did it. And she left. But she's got nowhere to go."

"You search her places?"

Had he? "Mostly. I hit the cheap hotels. That's where I found her the first time."

"She's run on you before."

"Before we were together."

Gabe flinched audibly. "Aw shit. You hooked up with her? I thought she was your student."

"She technically wasn't when it finally happened, but she didn't know that." Nick ran his hand over his head.

"You and your fucked-up plans. Always one step beyond simple."

Nick closed his eyes. Gabe was right.

"Can she take care of herself?"

Could she? Of course she could. She was the most fearless warrior he knew. "Yeah. Mostly. But she's still a small female in a big city."

"And she's yours."

Nick nodded. Even though Gabe couldn't see him, he'd know. Tears ran down his face. He didn't try to stop them. "She's mine, and she can live without me. But I'm not sure I can live without her. Not anymore. Not now that I know what it can be like."

"You want me to come out? I can be on a plane in the a.m."

"Not yet." Nick swiped at his leaking eyes. "I have some ideas where I can search tomorrow after work. If I don't find her, I'll take Friday off. That gives me three days."

"Check in with me. Latest by Sunday night."

Nick agreed. He gave up fighting the sobs after he hung up with Gabe. He howled his pain to the skies. How could he have been such an idiot. Underestimating. He'd assumed she needed him to manage her.

Not even close.

He fell asleep in the fetal position. A short while later, he woke with a start. A bad dream had left him more exhausted. Instead of eating like he should, he dragged himself into the shower. Even her shampoo was gone.

At least her scent lingered on the pillow that he held to his face when he finally crashed, sleeping in ragged spurts until the morning alarm sounded.

NOELLE WENT INTO WORK EARLY. She tucked her portfolio to the side of her reception desk at the gallery. The paper bag went underneath with her backpack. Luckily, Greer was holed up in her office. The hotel hadn't been bad. Even had a breakfast. But spending that kind of cash every night? No way would her funds last. She had to start making money off her art. The hourly wage for less than part-time covered about two nights at a hotel. No food, no transportation, and nothing for the other five nights of the week.

She smoothed the skirt she'd even ironed that morning, pulled her shoulders back, and knocked on the private office door.

"Come." Greer's sandpaper voice was clear despite the thick panel.

Noelle drew in a breath and opened the door.

"Everything okay, Noelle?" Greer looked up from her slick black laptop.

"Yes. I had a question. I noticed the new show is hung."

"The opening is Saturday. Is there a problem?"

"Not at all. But there're a couple of spaces on the back wall."

"One of the artists was short a large work. It sold to his benefactor."

Noelle swallowed. No one was going to ask for her. "May I hang two pieces? Your choice of work?"

Greer sighed and slid her black glasses off her face. "I considered that. But no."

"I don't understand."

"I create a certain environment when I do combined shows. Each artist must elevate the aesthetic of the other. Contrast in a positive way. Highlighting their unique vision and skill. These are professional artists. Not high school students gluing trash onto a canvas."

Noelle blinked back the burning in her eyes. If she couldn't hang her work, maybe she could get something else she needed. "Would it be possible for me to use a portion of the receiving area, in the back, as a studio? Temporarily? I've lost access to mine."

"That space needs to remain pristine for the arriving works. There can't be any risk of damage." Greer picked up her glasses and resettled them on her nose. She placed her hands on the keyboard. "Was there something else?"

"No. There's nothing else. Nothing for me here. I think it would be better if this was my last day."

"Really? You're going to throw a tantrum? I gave you this job as a favor." Greer spun in her chair and opened a drawer in a small black cabinet. She took out a leather notebook.

"A favor to who?"

"Your art teacher. I expected a special needs student to be more appreciative of the gift. Less demanding."

"I'm a professional artist. With a fine-art agent. My work has sold. You weren't doing me any *favors*." Noelle had worked hard for the woman. Anything she asked.

Greer laughed and tore out a check from the book. "Take your things. Don't come back."

Noelle took the check. One night. It would buy her one night of shelter. The urge to rip it in half and fling it back at the old hag crossed her mind. But that would only hurt her bank balance. It would do nothing to Greer. Noelle did as instructed.

On the sidewalk, her mother waited for her. Noelle closed her eyes briefly. Of course she'd be lying in wait to feast on the bones of her only daughter. Goddamned vulture. Choosing to ignore the addict as if she weren't related, Noelle moved toward the bus stop.

"You got my money?" The dirty woman nipped at her heels, trailing every step. She looked worse than before, same clothes, same ankle bracelet, but she must have scored at some point. There were new sores on her face and arms.

"Nope."

"What do you mean *nope*? I told you what I'd do."

"Go ahead."

"You think I'm bluffing. I'll go right into that fancy-pants shop and throw a fit about seeing my daughter. I'll do it every damn day."

Noelle laughed wryly. If only she could get that on recording.

"And I'm going to the school. Gonna let them know you're living with that Captain America teacher of yours."

"I'm not living there. I moved out."

"Where're you staying?"

"None of your business." Noelle had no clue where she was staying. But she was getting the hell away from there. She stepped onto the bus and flashed her pass.

"I'll find you, you little fucking liar. You can't hide from your mother."

Noelle rode the bus back to her neighborhood, the one she liked to scrounge for materials. She stepped into a discount department store. They gave her a hard time about her bags, so she let them hold them after pulling out a rolled-up pair of jeans. She found the item she needed and ducked into a dressing room—the dirty, cramped laminate box with its half door was nothing like the fancy place in the mall. But it didn't matter. It worked. She'd had an epiphany on the bus, letting her creativity take over during the aimless ride. A solution to one problem of living on the streets. All of that crap had been delaying the inevitable. Once she'd accepted that her life didn't belong in a beautiful house with a landscaped yard and a sexy man, her next actions became clear. She pulled on her old jeans, swapped her heels for socks and tennis shoes, and went to check out.

After leaving the store, she dropped the dressy shoes and her rolled-up skirt in the trash along with the brown paper sack. The swimsuit she'd purchased fit into the front zip pocket of her pack, the one she never used because it wasn't secure. One final thing. She rummaged to the bottom of her bag. Finally, her fingers touched the familiar fabric. Wrenching a knit cap out, she scooped her hair into a ball and tucked it in tight. Hiding every last strand. Having wiped away all the false crap she'd been fed about a new life, a better life, she wandered down the nearest alley in search of nothing and no one.

CHAPTER 27

$\mathcal{N}$ick ran to his car as soon as the final school bell rang. No checking files or making sure the kids got to the bus—he left that for the TA. There was only one person whose safety concerned him. He couldn't get to her soon enough, apologize, make amends, and bring her home.

He yanked open the glass door to the downtown gallery. "Noelle." His voice echoed in the cavernous space. He rushed in, searching behind the barriers, pieces of wall, that blocked his view. She had to be there. "Noelle."

"Can I help you, sir?" A chic, dark-haired woman dressed in black blinked up at him through black-rimmed glasses.

"I need to see Noelle."

"She's gone." The woman sniffed and crossed her arms.

"When will she be back?"

"She won't. She quit."

"No." Nick scanned the room desperate for a glimpse of Noelle. A sign it might be a lie. Nothing. "When?"

"Today. Is there a problem?"

His vision went hazy. He'd missed her. The one place he'd counted on finding her and she'd left.

Never.

Coming.

Back.

Gray ash from the emotional bomb settled over him, muting everything. He staggered outside. The heat of the afternoon hit him but did nothing to break his stupor. "She's gone," the woman had said. And she had no idea how much those words killed him—because, like every other time he'd heard them, they were true.

NOELLE DRAGGED her feet down the hard-packed dirt alley. She'd roamed for hours with no direction, not even scanning for materials. Even if she lucked out and found something amazing, she lacked a studio where she could store her finds and make her art.

"No-No." A dusty voice interrupted her pity party for one. "Noelle, *mija.*"

She halted her directionless march. "Joe?"

"What are you doing out here so late?"

"Got no place to go." The words, jagged and raw, hurt her throat.

"What do you mean 'no place'? Your parents' trailer?" Joe pushed his shopping cart toward her, the setting sun against his back.

Damn. It had been weeks since she'd seen him. He still believed she was living with her parents. "The trailer was condemned. I stayed at a shelter for a few days."

"Worst place ever." His dark eyes sparked with anger. "At least on the streets I can keep some things."

Noelle nodded. Maybe she should find a cart to hold *her* stuff, expand out from her backpack and portfolio.

"Need a place to sleep?"

"You got one?"

"Heading there now. Come on. Got an extra tent you can use."

A tent on the street was the best offer she'd get. "Thanks, Joe."

He pushed the cart forward, and she followed him like a puppy, like she'd done all those years ago when they'd been neighbors in the trailer park.

A couple of blocks later, Joe stopped behind the green dumpster she'd named Hulk. The sun was so low in the sky that only a sliver of pale yellow light cut the growing darkness.

"Here?" she asked, but the answer came in the form of a small tent being dropped in front of her.

"Gotta get some more cardboard." Joe slid a large piece from under the giant metal container. Then he climbed up the side like a spider monkey, still spry as ever despite his age. Within moments, a flat box flew out of the top, followed by Joe.

"Put that on the ground, set the tent up over it."

Noelle finished setting up her shelter. Then they shared a sparse meal of two apples and a can of cold pinto beans. Inky blackness, broken by the distant ghostly glow of street lamps, enveloped them.

"Time for bed, No-No."

Another person who still saw her as a child. And maybe he had a point since he was providing her food and shelter. She pursed her lips. She'd let people treat her like a kid—an inferior kid—because of her reading issues. She wouldn't allow that anymore. But she'd have to start owning her adult responsibilities before she could argue. So, instead of attacking from a point of weakness, she crawled into the tiny tent, her backpack a pillow and her bowed portfolio a blanket.

Noelle woke with a start. Rain dropped on her skin, interrupting her dream of Nick. She inhaled, immediately disappointed—his lemon-and leather-scent had been almost real. The touch of his hands imprinted on her skin. Her mind had created the illusion of comfort and safety.

She blinked her eyes open and turned under her vinyl art sleeve. Her neck and back barked at her. Still inside the tent, water dripped into Noelle's hair and down her neck. Not rain—condensation. When she'd run from Nick, she'd had no idea of what the cost would be to her pride.

She wrested herself and her belongings from the cheap shelter, soaking most of her shirt in the process. People used those things? For fun? There had to be ways to make it better than what she'd lived through the previous night. Since she'd eliminated all other options, she would learn about outdoor living.

Joe popped out of his tent, his body snapping like firecrackers as he straightened. "Sleep okay?"

"Mostly." He didn't need to hear about her dreams of Nick or the way her body hurt.

"Good, let's get packed. We got to move."

"Where?"

"Soup kitchen. They line up early."

Noelle slid her cardboard on top of Joe's and tucked her tent in its assigned location within his stash. Joe moved with practiced efficiency, and soon they had a foil-wrapped breakfast burrito each. Eggs and a tortilla had never tasted so good.

"Had an idea," Joe said when they finished eating.

Noelle turned her head to face him.

"Place you can maybe do your art. Store your folder."

"Really?"

"Long walk, but they'll be open when we get there, and I got some stuff to sell."

Noelle glanced down at her rumpled clothes and sniffed at her shirt. "Can we make a stop first?"

Joe agreed, and she led him to the city swimming pool. She left her portfolio with him and paid her two dollars while she held her swimsuit in her hand so they wouldn't question her. There wasn't enough time to swim that day, but she'd get some laps in on her next visit. It wouldn't be the same as her almost daily runs, but it would scratch the itch she had to exercise. Another need Nick had imprinted on her.

She shoved her pack in a locker along with her jeans and most of her clothes. Her panties and shirt she washed in the shower while she cleaned herself. Afterward, she shoved the freshly washed clothes in the automated swimsuit dryer and let the machine whir. In her backpack, she extracted a clean t-shirt, socks, and underwear, then tucked the newly washed, damp items in. As long as she stopped by every couple of days, her small stash of clothes would be enough. But she had to buy a towel soon. The paper towels in the dispenser were rough.

"Ready," she said when she got to where Joe waited on the sidewalk.

"Let's go."

NICK TOOK A PERSONAL DAY. His class would have to deal with a substitute teacher. There was no way he'd be able to focus on anything other than finding Noelle. It'd been two nights since he'd seen her. Touched her. Cared for her. His heart ached. His brain created increasingly disturbing scenarios of things that could have happened to her. Sleep evaded him. He should call his therapist or Gabe. But he had to look for her.

Since he couldn't find out where she was staying at night, he'd scour the places where she spent her days. The alleys contained the same cast of characters they had when he'd searched for Noelle the first time all those weeks ago. Drug dealers and dogs. Addicts and the abandoned. She didn't belong there. She never had. Nick turned down another packed-dirt, trash-filled road. Only, it looked familiar. He'd seen Noelle leave the bus there, before school, and search *that* dumpster behind the home-improvement store.

After a couple of quick stops, Nick returned to the familiar green bin. He parked the car and walked completely around it. Despite his irrational hope, Noelle wasn't hiding behind it. No one lingered in the alley. His plan would likely fail, but it was all he had. Dropping to his knees, he carefully placed a five-dollar coffee card on top of some flattened cardboard and then propped the coiled length of bare copper wire on top of it. Even if Noelle didn't find it, it would help someone.

He returned to his car and moved it across the road, waiting like a hunter. Except he was the prey in their struggle, trapped by her absence. She held his heart, and he was dying without her.

Hours passed. A few people roamed down the passageway, uninterested in the trash bin or the treasure lying beneath it.

His phone rang, breaking the vigil. Principal Lopez. He pressed the green icon on the screen. "Nick here."

"Hi, Nick. Just checking in to see how you're feeling. I need to arrange for another substitute if you aren't going to be in Monday. Today's will not be returning."

Guilt roiled into his desperation, making his stomach seize. "What happened?"

"Lucas had a major issue. I'll see who we have on our list that might be able work with him. But I'm not sure he'll be able to adapt."

The pieces suddenly clicked—Lucas had lost it, and the substitute had refused to return. Once again, Nick was failing everyone. "I probably need to take a leave of absence. I've been approved for a veterans' program. It's six-weeks. I'll come in Monday to complete the request. Can I talk to Lucas then?"

"Of course. If anyone can reach him, it's you."

Nick brushed his hand though his hair in an ineffectual effort to push away the pain. He'd been undecided on the program, until that call. In the state he was in, he couldn't help anyone. But he wasn't going to stop trying.

CHAPTER 28

"Where exactly are we going?" Noelle asked Joe as they walked away from the city pool. The sun baked down on her head, drying her hair through her cap in what would be an impossible mess.

"Up-Cycle. It's a used-art-supply store."

"*Used* art supplies?"

"More like surplus. Recycled. They pay for good stuff."

"Why haven't I heard about it?"

"It's new."

A couple of hours later, feet killing her, Noelle walked into the gallery-like store in a dated brown-brick strip mall that held insurance offices and payday loans. A Help Wanted sign was taped low in the large window, and an older woman with spiky silver hair sat behind the counter in the back corner of the lobby. There were at least two more rooms visible through the open, staggered doorways.

"Joe." The woman slid off her stool. "Whatcha got for me today?"

"Noelle, this is Tish. She owns the place."

Tish moved around the counter. "Nice to meet you. Do you have supplies for me, too?"

Noelle looked to Joe, uncertain how to respond to the perky woman.

"Nah, she's an artist." Joe looked back at his cart, visible through the large window. "Needs a studio or at least a place to store her work."

"Or a job," Noelle offered.

The woman ran her eyes over Noelle, then smiled. "Let me give you the nickel tour." She turned toward the first door. "Be right back, Joe."

Noelle followed Tish into the second room. *Holy cow.* Art hung on every wall. Pastels, watercolors, mosaics, small sculpture. The room was alive. Each piece had a tag with a price. "A gallery?"

"Yeah. We have an open house once a month. Get the locals in. Most of our artists live on the margins. Disabilities, physical and mental, or homeless."

Noelle swallowed hard. She was homeless and had a disability. But that didn't define her. She was an artist. First. Last. Always.

"We get the buyers in, let them mingle, realize our people are talented artists. And that all the other labels are just excuses to keep excluding them. So far, it's working."

A wave of relief washed through Noelle. There was no need to defend herself to Tish.

Noelle followed the owner through the next door into a treasure trove, a dragon's horde of every conceivable art supply, and gasped.

"I know, right?" Tish beamed. "Look it over. Dig in."

After scanning several bins, opening drawers of all different heights, and peering into glass cabinets, Noelle returned to the owner of the ultimate artist's stash. "This is so cool."

"I have one more room to show you." Tish led her through a side door into another retail space. The entrance at the front was screened off, and the windows were covered in a colorful film. Tape divided the open floor plan into squares. Most of them contained easels or desks or other art setups. Light flooded in from several large skylights. Noelle slowly walked up a side aisle between the creativity boxes. One spot at the front, near a thinly covered window, stood empty. She stepped into the virtual studio.

"That one just opened up."

"How much?" *Please let me be able to afford it.*

Tish named a figure. Lower than Noelle had expected, but it wasn't sustainable without a job. "Can I work for you in trade?"

"Do you have any experience?"

Noelle told Tish about her time at the gallery. Explained that she'd need a space if her agent started selling her work. Noelle even told her about hunting for supplies in the commercial waste bins with Joe.

Tish's eyes narrowed. Several moments passed. "Let's try it for ninety days." She laid out the pay, the same as Noelle had gotten at the gallery, but she'd have a place to store her stuff. And she'd get a discount on the studio rent and supplies.

Unable to hold back, Noelle released the smile that had built with every word. "Thank you. I won't let you down."

"I'll try not to let you down either. The ninety days is for both of us. Make sure we like how it feels."

Noelle shared her news with Joe on the walk back to their side of the city.

"Better than I hoped," Joe said when she'd run out of words. "But how're you going to get there for work? I only go when I got something good."

"I have a bus pass. Unlimited rides for a year." Nick had been generous when he'd given her the prepaid card. Even though she'd left him, he was still helping her. An ache twinged her heart. She missed him, not because he was generous, but because he was Nick. Maybe she'd overreacted when she'd left, but there was no going back. It was past time to make it on her own.

"Hey, Joe?" Noelle halted in front of a food truck after they'd walked what felt like miles. "Can I buy you lunch? To thank you?"

"You don't have to do that, No-No."

"I'm hungry. And you got me a job and a studio."

The smell of frying corn tortillas made her beg. Joe walked around the truck, then inspected the menu before he agreed. They gathered their order of tacos after a few minutes' wait. Noelle's feet and stomach thanked her when she sat at the umbrella-shaded folding table and dug into the hot food. They took their time but cleared out as soon as they'd finished, continuing the long walk back to their part of town.

The silence between them was comfortable and gave Noelle time to think. First, about how to get her art from the school to the gallery. She could hang one and store the rest in her rented space. One at a time on the bus was all she could come up with. And if Nick's parents —her agents—found a gallery... She needed to check her email. "You mind stopping by the library?"

Joe checked his wristwatch. "We got a little time."

"We have to be somewhere?"

"Soup kitchen. Dinner."

Right. Free food came on someone else's schedule. "I'll be quick."

THE SOUND of a cell phone roused Nick from the sleep he'd struggled to find. Scrambling through the fog, he snatched up the phone Noelle had left behind. *Please let it be her.* "Hello?" Desperation flooded each syllable.

"Nick? I was expecting Noelle."

His mother's voice slashed hope from his chest. "Me too."

"What? Can I speak to her?"

"She's gone." No matter how many times he heard the words, or said them, the same searing pain wrenched through him.

"Nick, honey, you're not making any sense. I just read an email from her."

Noelle was replying to his mother's emails, just not his. Weight settled in his limbs.

"We got her a show."

"Already?"

His mother's champagne laugh bubbled through the phone. "I was supposed to wait?"

"No. It's fast, though."

"She's unique and talented. The work sells itself."

His mother was right. Noelle's work was gold but unusual. He hadn't expected anyone to see it so clearly and so quickly. She wouldn't need him at all soon, but he desperately needed her. Maybe if he could get some details, he could figure out where she was using a computer. "What did she say? In the email? When did you get it?"

"It came through late yesterday. I waited to call because of the time difference. But I need to talk to her."

"I don't know where she is, Mom. She left."

"Why?"

"I did something I shouldn't have."

"You?" His mom would never see him as other than perfect.

"Yeah." Admitting that to his mother made his gut sour. He wouldn't try to explain how things had gone sideways. There was still a chance he could fix them if he could find Noelle. At least she was responding to email. Maybe he should send her another one.

His mother sighed.

"What did you want to talk to her about?"

"Logistics. Getting her artwork shipped. I've already been in contact with Bailey's."

"I can help. I'm going into the school on Monday. I'll talk to her art teacher while I'm there. I think all her pieces are still in the classroom storage." Nick had experience with what it took to ship artwork since he'd worked for his mother's favorite fine-art freight vendor in high school. It was only a matter of time before Julie would need the space anyway.

"What do you mean 'going into school'?" His mom didn't miss a detail.

"I need to take some time off."

"The nightmares?"

"Yeah." And to find Noelle. And to put his life back together. Deal with his ongoing issues. But he didn't want her to worry. "I got into a program for vets with PTSD. Gonna require some training. I was going to say no, but I think maybe it would be best if…"

"Is there anything your dad and I can do?"

"Take care of Noelle?"

"Of course. If you think of anything else—"

"I'll call you." Nick hit end on the phone. Noelle was surviving. Emailing his parents meant she was alive somewhere. And functioning. Probably better than him.

Before cleaning up to continue his search, he logged into his email and sent two messages. One begging her to respond. The other—another gift—was for her future. With or without him.

$\mathcal{M}$onday morning, Nick waited in the office for Lucas. He wasn't sure what he should tell the young man, but Nick hoped honesty would be enough to keep Lucas on track.

"What are *you* doing here?" the kid snarled from the doorway that he gripped with one hand. His other was balled into a fist—a poster child for fight-or-flight.

Nick stopped pacing. "Lucas. Will you take a walk with me? I got some stuff I need to tell you. Man to man."

Lucas's eyes closed to a squint, like a panther focusing on its prey. Nick slowed his breathing and waited. One quick nod was all he got before his student turned and moved down the hall. Nick followed until they got outside. A couple of quick steps and he was side by side with the short young man.

"I owe you an apology." Nick figured he owed a lot of people one, but it was a start. "I let my personal life get in the way of being a teacher—your teacher—after we had an agreement. And now, I need to take some time to fix my head. I should have talked to you and the others—"

"This got something to do with that Noelle chick?" Lucas jutted his chin. "You ran after her like a dog. Now you got *personal* problems? Right."

Nick clenched his jaw. One person seeing his fight with Noelle was too many. "Noelle's not a student anymore. And she's not the reason I'm going to be on leave." Not the main reason and not a topic of conversation with a teenage boy. "I'm dealing with some things left over from being a soldier."

Lucas didn't say anything. His ice-cold stare said it all. He'd heard every excuse there was.

"I'm not trying to let you down, and I will be back. But I'm doing a program, and I gotta take some time for it. A few weeks."

"Yeah?"

Nick ran his hand over his head. "I get nightmares, and it makes it difficult to work. And sometimes I let fear drive my decisions."

"You're supposed to be *the man*."

"And that means apologizing when you're wrong and admitting when you need help."

"My cousin's got the same thing. Tried to kill his woman. He's in jail now."

Nick nodded.

"Counseling and all that shit. Hector wouldn't go. Said real men don't go cry about the shit they seen."

"It's hard to talk about. But it has nothing to do with being a man."

Lucas started walking again, and Nick kept pace. "I have to ask you a favor, Lucas."

"What's that?"

"I need someone I can trust so I can focus and come back as soon as possible. Can you…help the substitute? The other guys look up to you. They're gonna follow your lead."

For several long minutes they continued to walk around the cluster of buildings that made up the school. When they'd circled back to where they'd started, Lucas paused. "Yeah."

"Thank you." Nick held out his hand. Lucas took it. "You're a good man."

~

AFTER WORKING at Up-Cycle all day Monday, Noelle returned to her old campus on Tuesday. The school had been her safe place and still held the things most important to her. Her artwork and Nick. She wavered between dying to see him and taking every precaution to avoid him. Rather than decide, she made her way directly to Ms. Julie's classroom.

Noelle had gone early, like she always had when she'd still been a student, but the classroom was locked. Good thing she'd stopped for coffee before boarding the bus. Joe had discovered a gift card and spool of wire when he'd pulled out their cardboard. Noelle suspected Nick had left them for her. But why? And if he knew where she was sleeping, it was only a matter of time before he'd confront her and try to drag her home. Back to *his* home. But gift cards and copper wire did not appear under trash bins, *ever*.

Maybe she'd stop by and thank him before she left campus. No big deal, just poke her head in and say thanks, then leave. Her stomach fluttered at the thought of seeing him. It was difficult to remain mad when she missed him. And even though she should stay away, her silly heart whined for one more glimpse.

"Hey, Noelle. I didn't expect to see you here." Julie's arrival shut down Noelle's conflicted musings.

Noelle rose from where she'd been sitting on the floor and swiped a hand across her ass to knock off the dirt. "I came to deal with my art. I know it can't stay here."

Julie opened the door and let Noelle enter first. "I'm supposed to send visitors for a pass, but I don't think the office is open yet. Did you talk to Mr. Christoph?"

Even the sound of his name made her heart pump faster.

"He said your agent got you a show."

"They did. I do. In Florida. That's why I'm here. I need to figure out how to get my artwork to this company that's going to ship it. I figured I could take them one at a time on the bus, maybe?"

"But Mr. Christoph met the shipper here yesterday. They crated everything that was complete. I still have your work in progress. The one with the man reaching up?"

Nick had taken over the shipping. Relief and a bit of guilt hit her. She'd been dreading the logistics of getting her paintings to the shipper. She couldn't even fault him for not asking since she'd been ignoring his attempts to communicate. She owed Julie an explanation.

"I've been—staying at a shelter. Haven't had a chance to check my mail since Saturday." She'd tried to go on Sunday, but the computer area had been packed with people, and more had been waiting. Then the day before, they'd been closed by the time she'd got off work. No matter what, she'd get on a computer and read her email before she slept that night.

"I hope it was okay. I guess I should have checked with you first, but I didn't have a way to contact you and—"

"It's fine. This makes everything easier. I can just take the last one to finish at my new studio."

"You have a studio?"

"Yeah. I got a job with Up-Cycle, and they have studio spaces."

Julie tilted her head. "You're not working for Greer?"

"It didn't work out." There were so many things Noelle could say about that situation, but it would only upset her former art teacher. If Julie needed the story, she could get it from her friend.

"I'm sorry about the gallery job, but it sounds like things are really going well. I'm so happy for you." Julie's smile was genuine. Noelle could hang on to her anger about the lies and being kicked out of school, but why? It would have all ended soon enough. It wasn't Julie's fault Noelle was homeless, and she'd tried to help by getting her the job.

Noelle grabbed her unfinished work. "I better go."

"Get me on your agent's mailing list for the gallery opening. I want an invite even if I can't go."

"Okay. I'll get you on the Up-Cycle list, too. They do a monthly show." She finished her goodbyes with Julie and left with her unfinished piece.

The visit left her unsettled. They were no longer connected by necessity, only by choice in the most casual of connections. An invite to some future show. Occasional updates. Julie was a person who'd been in Noelle's life for years, and it was basically over. By leaving with her painting, she'd severed the last strand of their bond. Her teacher hadn't changed.

Noelle had.

Would it be the same with Nick? Would he be some distant connection in her history that no longer mattered? Noelle raced to his classroom. The bell would ring soon. But he would be there, preparing for the day. She flung open the door. A trim woman with short brown hair looked up from the planner on the desk.

"Mr. Christoph?"

"He's out. I'm the sub. Is there something I can help you with?"

"No." Noelle shut the door and left campus in a daze.

NICK PARKED at the end of Noelle's alley. The last gift card had been used for a large, plain coffee. He'd loaded more money on it and come back next with a gift card to a sandwich shop that provided lots of fresh vegetables, and some kind of expanding strainer he'd found in the cooking section of a local store. It was so difficult to know what she might want, but she'd told him about searching behind restaurants. Maybe the petaled colander would be valuable in her eyes.

As he slipped the items onto the flattened cardboard, he heard a rustling behind him. It was an old man with a shopping cart packed to the gills.

"Whatcha doin', *hombre?*" The man's stare was filled with suspicion.

"Looking for a friend. Well, leaving some stuff for her. Maybe you know her? Red hair. Wears a knit cap?"

The gnarled man jerked his head up. "Who's asking?"

"Nick Christoph." Nick thrust out his hand. "I lost my friend Noelle."

A rough chuckle like a car backfire burst from the guy. "Nobody loses No-No. If she wants to be around you, she's like a tick. Sounds to me like she don't want to be around *you*."

"You know her? Is she okay? Does she need anything?" Electric spikes of urgency raked Nick's nerves.

The man's eyes narrowed. "She's fine. Known her most of her life. Don't know you."

"I'm her…I'm…" How was Nick supposed to explain who he was, who he should've been, who he wanted to be, for Noelle? He wasn't sure. "It's complicated."

"It usually is." Another chuckle rumbled out. "You got it bad."

"I do." The admission pinged through his empty chest, rattling in the space where his heart had been.

"I'm Joe." The name triggered Nick's memories. Noelle had mentioned a neighbor who'd taught her about salvage.

"Nick."

The man finally shook his hand. "Buy me lunch and tell me about it."

They walked to the front side of the home-improvement store, where a hotdog vendor was making his living. Nick ordered dogs and chips and drinks and sat with Joe on a bench outside the entrance, his overstuffed cart parked next to him. As they ate, Nick explained how Noelle had been his student and what had happened with her parents.

Joe shook his head. "Never did trust her mom. She was mean *before* she hooked up with that *pinche pendejo*. After that, they didn't pay any attention to the girl. Just drugs. Day and night."

Nick's chest tightened at the reminder. "I took care of her the night of her parents' arrest, but I couldn't—I mean—she went to a shelter."

"Shit."

"She didn't stay long."

"Good."

"I kept her at my place after that. Fell in love with her. But I messed that up, too." It was getting easier for Nick to admit, but words didn't change the situation.

"What'd you do?" Joe's eyes narrowed.

Nick described his grand plan to keep Noelle in school without being enrolled so she could take the test.

As Nick talked, Joe's expression softened until he laughed. "That plan was never gonna be right. With that kind of logic, I'm amazed you ain't working for the VA."

"You served?"

"Twenty years. Left after the first Gulf War." Joe looked away, unfocused, like he was back in a different desert.

"Why are you on the streets?"

"Had a trailer. Lost it after I got buried in some medical bills. Couldn't focus on the paperwork. Tried the shelters." Joe shrugged. "They work for some people, I guess."

But not Joe. And not Noelle. "Would you let me help you? Get a place. Where you and Noelle could stay—you're like family. And I could do some legwork on your benefits."

Joe waved it off. "We're doing fine. And teachers ain't got no time and even less money."

Nick laughed. The time thing was right, except he had all the time in the world since he wasn't working. "I've taken a break. Gonna start a new therapy program soon."

"Got some battle fatigue, son?" Joe's warm brown eyes focused on him, and Nick understood why Noelle loved the man.

"A bit."

"Ain't no shame. Some saw more than others. Some felt more. Some carry it longer." Joe nodded sagely. "Ain't no shame."

"Thanks." Nick meant it. Understanding without questions. It was truly powerful. He cleared his unexpectedly tight throat. "Will you let me help you?"

Joe nodded once. "For Noelle. For now."

Nick gave Joe the sandwich card and the strainer. They made arrangements to meet again. In the meantime, Nick knew where Noelle was. And he hated it. But he could watch over her and her friend Joe. Make sure they came to no harm until he could get them to a safe place.

CHAPTER 30

$\mathcal{N}$oelle stood back from her canvas and chomped down on the other half of the turkey sandwich she'd saved from her lunch. The sandwich card, like the coffee card, continued to be refilled. Joe had refused to answer when she'd asked where he'd gotten it. As if it were a mystery. The only real question was if Joe had spoken to Nick. Her friend refused to provide answers not matter how she phrased the queries. He was a vault when he wanted to be. She could see them together, two former soldiers grunting back and forth in a language no one else would comprehend. The image made her long to be near Nick again. Noelle forced him from her mind and focused on her artwork.

Working in a real studio, with other artists, was amazing, but having the place to herself that afternoon was better. She'd broken up the strainer, trimming the pieces and painting them to suit her purpose. It was another mysterious gift from Joe, only because it was so obviously new. With the addition of the metal "feathers", her angel transformed into a warrior. The shadowy figure, a man by his physique, was clenched in the grasp of the fierce savior. The man's arms were strong and straight, saving as well as being saved. Fire consumed the lower part of the canvas, licking at his legs. Forgetting her sandwich on her stool, Noelle picked up a wet brush and added fine white accents to some of the thick flames.

"Hey, Noelle." A voice dragged her away from her painting. Tish. Her boss stepped closer to the tape that defined Noelle's workspace. "Wow, that's really coming along."

"Should be ready for the show," Noelle responded. The monthly gallery event was too soon. But a deadline prevented her from tweaking the image until another one inspired her to start a new canvas. She'd muddled more than one painting by overworking it when she'd first started working with acrylics. No way was she going to ruin that one. In fact, she'd be a little sad if it sold, but not as sad as if it didn't.

"We haven't had a debut artist in a while. Everyone will want to meet you."

Noelle swallowed down the sandwich that rose in her throat. *People*. At least Julie would be there—she'd called the store that morning to put her name on the list. If only Nick... She shook her head. "That's great. But I won't be able to stay the whole time. I—"

"No problem. Leave when you need to. There's no rules."

Noelle relaxed. She wasn't forced to explain that she had to stick to the bus schedule.

"Everything good up front today?" Tish asked as she moved back down the aisle.

"Yeah. A couple of sales. I left the register totals in the top drawer."

"Cool. You gonna be here awhile?"

Noelle glanced up at the wall clock. "Not much longer."

"All right. Let me know if you need anything. I'll be poking around in the supplies. Gotta make room for some new stuff. I'll lock up tonight."

When Noelle left a little while later, it was already dark. After two transfers and a short walk, she was at the alley. Joe didn't have his tent set up like usual. "What's up?"

"Got a place. I can move in anytime."

"Really? I didn't even know you were looking."

"Wasn't, really." Joe's eyes left hers. "A friend helped me out. Found a program. Pueblos or something."

"Is it a group-home shelter thing?" Noelle dreaded the idea of losing her companion, but Joe shouldn't be living on the streets, no matter how effortless he made it seem. She knew first-hand what work it took work to maintain hygiene, a decent diet, and to stay safe.

"Apartment. Not far. Would you go with me?"

Joe got an apartment without looking? If someone had squirted lemon and leather up her nose, it couldn't have smelled more like Nick. He was rescuing her friend. Tears pricked her eyes. "Of course I'll go with you."

Pale white streetlights lit their way. Joe pushed his cart. Noelle followed, not really seeing anything. Hero Nick was saving someone. Always. And she'd been mad for the way he'd tried to save her. Yes, he should have talked to her, but maybe she should have talked to him, too, instead of throwing a fit and running away. Her behavior had been immature. Someday she'd have a chance to apologize.

The apartment was on the ground floor of a two-story, boxy building. There were four apartments on the bottom. Joe's was a corner unit. He fished in his pocket and pulled out a key. Instead of putting it in the lock, Joe stared at it.

"Been a long time since I had one of these."

The key she'd left on Nick's counter had been her first. Hopefully, not her last.

Joe finally opened the door. He reached around the entrance and must have found the lights, because one came on over the door and one lit the interior. The furnished interior. Joe popped his cart over the threshold and moved inside. Noelle followed him and shut the door, locking it with a twist of the knob.

She turned and took in the tiny but homey space. The floor was smooth vinyl that looked like wood. There was a kitchen in an alcove with a full-sized stove and refrigerator and brown-painted cabinets. The long, narrow room where they stood had a futon couch flanked by little square storage blocks, a chair that looked comfy, and a small

TV mounted to the wall between the kitchen and a door. Under the far window was a slim desk and chair. With a laptop.

Noelle stepped around Joe's cart and opened the first door, closest to the kitchen. A bathroom. It was narrow but had a tub with a shower. Nice. There was even a new roll of toilet paper. Lastly, she peeked into the second door. A full-sized bed with a blue plaid comforter, one storage cube, and a lamp. The simple bed had four pillows with an extra blanket folded along the bottom. Did Nick think he was fooling anyone? The extra bedding and the futon might as well have been a poster with exclamation points.

Joe shouldered his way into his new bedroom, having finished banging around in the kitchen. "It's got everything, No-No. Even food in the fridge."

"Your friend is a planner."

"You should stay."

Noelle sighed. She should be finding her own place to live, not relying on Nick through an intermediary.

"I need help figuring out where I am," Joe said. "You gotta teach me the bus. I got appointments I have to go to."

"The bus? Appointments?" Her Joe? He never left his cart behind.

"Yeah, new VA doc. And the housing people."

Noelle suspected he had a shiny new bus pass, too. Nick always thought about the details.

"And I need help unpacking. Can't keep that cart in here."

"You're giving up your cart?"

"Gettin' too old for the streets, *mija.*"

He was right, but the words stung. Joe was getting older. And too soon, he'd be taken from her. "Of course I'll stay. Until you're settled."

They ate a simple meal of ham-and-cheese sandwiches with grapes. And glasses of milk. Noelle noted there was even a coffee maker with ground coffee. Joe excused himself to the shower after retrieving a brand-new pair of pajamas from a drawer and tossing Noelle a long navy t-shirt from the same source. She couldn't help but smile. While she waited her turn for the bathroom, she checked out the laptop. There was no password, and it was connected to a community Wi-Fi with the same name as the apartment complex.

Noelle logged into her email and paused, cursor hovering over the confirmation about the GED test. The one she'd received almost two weeks ago. She opened it. *Holy crap.* Nick had paid for the tests, all of them. The only thing she had to do was set the date. With a little more studying, she'd be ready to take the exam. Tish wouldn't care if she studied at work. If she didn't at least try, she'd be no better than that Huck Finn character. Blowing out a huge breath, she clicked the "Schedule Your Exam" link and completed the registration before returning to her inbox.

There was a new message from Patricia. Noelle read the information about the opening and looked at the website from the link she'd included. The gallery was beautiful. A dream space for her art, light and spacious, perfect. But there was one problem. Patricia wanted to send her a plane ticket to Florida for the show. She'd never flown. Never been to the airport. Seen it in TV shows, all the searching and restrictions on the bag and what you could bring. And she'd thrown away her nice outfit. The rest of her clothes were hidden at Nick's. She hadn't been able to take everything, yet she couldn't bring herself to give them up. Not the things he'd bought her. But she didn't even have a suitcase.

The shower water stopped. Noelle closed the email. She'd deal with it later.

Tonight, she was sleeping in a bed. She'd better enjoy it while it lasted, because once again, it wasn't her bed. And it wasn't her home. It was temporary, and she would still be sleeping alone.

CHAPTER 31

$\mathcal{N}$ick pulled out of the apartment parking lot once all the windows were dark. They were safe. At least, safer. And she'd stayed. A long day in his PTSD program, followed by watching the alley while Joe waited for Noelle, then making sure they got into the apartment okay, and Nick was ready to sleep. A true, deep sleep, not one riddled by nightmares of something terrible happening to the woman he loved.

His phone rang as he pulled into his driveway. Gabe. He took the call, making his way into his too-empty house.

"Checking in. How's things?" Gabe asked.

"Better. Started my training. Got a vet, Joe, into some community housing. He was on the streets." Nick dropped his keys on the counter and peered into the fridge.

"Really? How'd you hook up with him?"

"Friend of Noelle's. He's been helping her out. Known her since she was a kid." Nick pulled out the makings for a sandwich. Cooking for one had lost its appeal.

"You found her? Is she home?"

"She doesn't know I know where she is. She's staying with Joe. For now."

Gabe took a loud, disappointed-sounding breath. "That might wreck the dude's housing situation. Better check the terms of the lease."

"He can have short-term guests. I've got a couple of weeks." Nick tucked the phone into his cheek with his shoulder and cut his sandwich. He hoped he'd have her back long before that much time passed. He had to—the gallery opening was coming up fast. "How's the lodge?"

"Moving along. The outside is better. Can actually park a car out front."

Nick laughed. "That's good. Guests like parking."

"No kidding. I've about got all the windows and everything caulked, so it's not leaking like a sieve."

"Get any snow yet?"

"Hell yeah. Wish I had rooms ready. Looks like I'm gonna miss most of ski season this year."

"Sorry about that."

"No worries. Come up when you're ready."

The men finished chatting while Nick ate his sandwich, too starved to wait. When he hung up, he could only manage a quick cleanup of the kitchen and himself before he crashed hard, finally able to relax.

A few days later, during the mid-morning break at the VA, Nick found a text on his phone from Julie Balinchek: *Are you going to the Up-Cycle show?*

Nick: *What's that?*

Julie responded right away: *Noelle's new gallery. On the west side of town.*

Nick: *When?*

Julie: *Tomorrow. 6-9.*

Nick: *I'll be there.*

Julie: *Can I get a ride? My car is acting up.*

Nick: *Sure. Give me your address.*

Noelle was having a show and she hadn't let him know? Fuck waiting. As soon as he was done that day, he was going to the apartment. The time for being patient was over. But before he could be upset at Noelle for not contacting him, another text came through.

Mom: *Nick, have you heard from Noelle? I know you're in your thing, but I'm getting nervous. The show's in 10 days. She HAS to get on that plane.*

Nick: *I haven't, but I'm handling it tonight. I'll call you afterward.*

His mom sent a thumbs up and a smiley face.

Once he was released for the evening, he drove to Joe's. He rapped sharply on the door, ready to do battle with a sexy, feisty redhead. Joe answered the door after a short wait. His eyes met Nick's.

"She's not here." Joe stepped back into the apartment and swung the door open wide.

Nick took the implied invitation. The place was too small for her to hide, and she wasn't the hiding type, at least not in close quarters. "Where is she?"

Joe shut the door. "Either at Up-Cycle or on her way here."

"I'll wait."

"Her show's tomorrow. And it's her job. Don't cause her stress."

"She's got a huge gallery opening in Florida, and she has to get on a plane. She's not answering her agent's emails. This is her big chance. She can't break her contract."

"Go to the show tomorrow. Or…she's taking her tests in a week. Been studying. Got it marked on the calendar." Joe pointed at a picture of puppies on the kitchen wall.

Nick beelined to the marked-up page. "She's taking the GED?"

"She said you paid for it."

"I wasn't sure she'd schedule it." From the moment he'd seen her in the hallway of a bar all those months ago, she'd surprised him at every turn. And he loved her for it. Nick memorized the information on the date, time, and place. That gave him two more chances to convince her to get on the plane even if she didn't want him back. He'd be low-key at the show, but they were running out of time.

"You gotta go." Joe held the door open.

"What?"

"Don't upset her tonight. Let her get some sleep."

Nick let Joe kick him out. He would see her in one more day.

Except he didn't. Noelle wasn't at the show when he'd finally arrived. His program had run late. He'd gone home to shower, then driven to Julie's, but there'd been a problem with her mother-in-law. By the time they made it to the show, Noelle and Joe were already gone.

Nick shuffled through the crowd. The din of happy conversation might as well have been in a foreign language. He scanned the wall. *There.* Noelle's painting. Another angel, but nothing like the one in his bedroom. Her art had gone to the next level. And he was relieved to see the price better reflected her skill, even if it was still too low.

"You didn't find the artist, but I see you found her art." The woman who'd told him he'd missed Noelle stood at his elbow. "There's been a ton of interest. Two serious buyers who I expect will battle over it."

Nick named a figure, several multiples of the asking price.

"Sold." The woman chuckled. "Noelle will be thrilled."

"Don't tell her who bought it."

So, instead of taking Noelle home, he took home her painted angel. Warrior. Savior. Paint on canvas instead of flesh and bone.

The week of waiting tortured Nick. He'd been distracted and nearly lost his place in the PTSD support program after failing one of the certifications the first time. He forced himself to focus, saving all his worrying, planning, and wishing for the evening hours that crawled by. At last, it was time.

He arrived at the testing center shortly after the test had begun. There was no way of verifying Noelle was in there, but after so many hours together, studying her, learning how she tackled challenges, there was no possibility she'd hesitated to face the battle. She'd been committed when she'd used a black marker to ink in the time and place for her test. In his gut, he knew she was inside. So he waited. Listened to the radio. Texted his anxious mother an update. Every hour that passed without her coming out of the building was a good sign. Noelle still fought.

The closer it got to the end of the time window, the more people started trickling out. Nick left his car and leaned on the front of it. Arms crossed. Waiting.

A pimply young man in a mechanic jumpsuit stomped out. An older man came out a few minutes later, spine straight and a smile teasing his lips. Two girls holding hands squealed into the open space, "We did it!"

Nick's attention was drawn from the celebration back to the doors. Noelle. She was close enough to see clearly, not a shadowy shape in the distance. His heart lunged in her direction, ripping at his chest. She was familiar and different. The same knit hat covered her flaming locks. The same paint splotched her jeans and hands. But she glowed, her celebration even louder than the bubbly duo, but all internal. It sparked from the cells of her skin. She'd done it. She'd finished the tests. Tears pricked his eyes. So damn proud of her. Nothing held her back. She was even more fierce than he'd ever given her credit for. God, he loved her.

She turned. Her gaze pinned him in place.

A tear ran down his cheek, and he couldn't swipe it.

She froze, poised at the top of the stairs. "Nick."

CHAPTER 32

He's here.

Noelle couldn't move. She'd planned to go by his house, later that day or the next, to thank him. But he was there.

Nick straightened from where he leaned against the car. His intense gaze locked on her. He wore a dark, long-sleeved knit shirt that clung to him exactly like she dreamed of doing. Her fingers itched to undo his jeans, free him, and suck him until he screamed with pleasure. She'd been the one to run, but he'd been hiding from her. Lurking in the shadows. It was like seeing him for the first time. Only there was no mystery—just burning, agonizing desire.

She took a step, her legs so stiff from sitting in the test for so long that she tipped forward. Before she crashed into the concrete, his arms wrapped around her and lifted her to safety. Their lips met. Salty tears seasoned their kisses. Hers or his, she wasn't sure. The kiss went on forever but was over far too soon when she leaned back. "You're here."

"You took the test," Nick said at the same time.

She laughed. "Yeah. This bossy man made me study for it and paid the fee."

"I'm sorry. I shouldn't have…" His voice faded to nothing.

"Well, I'm not. I'm pretty sure I passed. I wouldn't have done it without him. He's kind of amazing, even if he is a terrible communicator."

The twinkle was back in Nick's eyes. "If *you* say I'm terrible, I must be."

"Who's this?" Noelle pointed at the medium-sized, golden-haired dog wearing a vest and trailing at Nick's heels.

"This is Mackie. Say hello, Mackie."

"Hello, Mackie."

Nick chuckled. "I meant the dog should say hello to you."

Sweet brown puppy eyes pleaded up at her as if he was campaigning for her forgiveness, too. "Can I pet him?"

"He'd like that. You can pet me, too. If you want."

Noelle leaned down and stroked the soft fur between the dog's floppy ears. His vest was embroidered with the words *service dog* in bright blue. She turned her attention to Nick, letting the question fill her gaze.

"I'll explain everything." He scooped her up into his arms.

He was carrying her to the car. "Nick, stop. We should talk."

"Does it have to be here? Can't we go home?" There were dark shadows under his eyes.

Guilt reared its head. Nick hadn't been sleeping. Because of her? But if she let him take her home, they would fall into bed. Noelle bit her lip, unsure what to say.

"Let me at least buy you lunch." He set her down.

Nick's pleading tone shocked her. She said the first place that popped into her mind. "Mario's?"

He agreed, and they rode silently to the restaurant where he'd taken her before she'd kissed him the first time. Mackie curled up under the table at his feet. After they ordered a pizza to share, the space filled up between them.

"Thank you—"

"I'm sorry—" Their words tumbled over each other.

Noelle closed her eyes. Nick sighed.

"You first," he said.

"I owe you an apology." Noelle couldn't lecture Nick about communication without addressing her fit. "I shouldn't have run away when I found out about not being a student anymore."

"I should have discussed it with you first."

"True." Noelle hesitated. "Why'd you do it?"

Nick glanced at the ceiling before meeting her eyes. "I was afraid."

Afraid? "Of what?"

"That you'd give up. I know better now. But when I set the wheels in motion, I didn't know just how strong or…how stubborn you are." He rubbed a hand over his head. Mackie rose and moved to his side.

"Stubborn? Seriously?"

Nick raised his eyebrows.

"I'm determined. Not stubborn. But you could have explained it at any time."

"I was planning to, that night."

Noelle found the words he'd used to describe Lucas. "You acted from fear instead of love. You didn't trust me to make the right decision."

Nick nodded. "I tried to control you."

"Don't do that again."

His head jerked up. "Never."

She considered him. His hair was longer and his face thinner. Their separation had been hard on him, too. "You helped Joe, didn't you?"

"I asked him before I did anything." His words came out in a rush.

"Thank you. He's my family."

"Our family."

Tears stung Noelle's eyes. She swallowed back the emotions and nodded. The waitress appeared with the pizza, a small, but it was still huge. The hot, gooey cheese and crispy crust was the perfect post-test, emotional-boyfriend-discussion food. *Boyfriend?* The word felt right even though they'd been apart. She still loved him. Every generous, messed up, overbearing cell in his gorgeous body. *Stop.* Loving him didn't mean they didn't have things to discuss before she jumped back in his bed. *If* she returned. She took a sip of water to clear her throat. "Tell me about Mackie."

"While you were…away, I completed a VA program—training and testing—so I could…" Nick rubbed his head. Mackie nudged Nick's leg. "I know, buddy. I'm okay."

Noelle's heart clenched.

"He recognizes when I'm stressed. Interrupts my nightmares before they take hold. We completed the certification two days ago, and he's helping already. It'll make it safer for you to live with me."

"I was never unsafe. You made sure of that." Noelle bit into her pizza to avoid the living-arrangements discussion. Should she move back in with him? She didn't want to rely on him for everything the way she had before she'd left. But she missed him to the point of pain. Not everyone had to be good at everything or strong all the time. And Joe always said, when you love someone, you support them. Noelle had done that for Nick, hadn't she?

"Did you get a plane ticket?"

"What?" She'd been reviewing all the moments they'd shared. His words made no sense.

"Your show. It opens in two days. My mom, Patti, said she's been emailing you."

Right, the show. Her stomach knotted, and she set her slice on the plate, then wiped her hands on the paper napkin. "I wasn't sure. She said she'd buy the ticket, but I don't even have a suitcase or clothes."

"I found the bag of clothes you left. Washed everything and put them back where they belong."

"If I go, will you come with me?" Noelle couldn't look at him. What if he said no? He probably had to work.

"Do you want me to?" His voice was rough.

"Of course I do." She reached out and wrapped her hand around his. "I wouldn't have this show without you."

Nick gave her hand a light squeeze and shook his head. "It may have taken a bit longer, but I've given you *nothing* you wouldn't have been able to get on your own."

"What did I give you, Nick?"

"Everything. A reason to feel again. A reason to heal. To live."

Noelle wasn't sure if she believed that. She released his hand, attempting to return to practical matters that had concrete answers. "How do we get tickets? Can Mackie fly? We need to go tomorrow, I guess."

Nick blew out a breath. "Mackie's cleared for travel. Can I take care of the arrangements?"

Noelle smiled and nodded, pleased that he'd asked.

They finished their slices and had the leftovers boxed. Nick paid the check. The silence became heavy once more. He cleared his throat. "Will you come home?"

Home. She'd never really had one. Then she had and she'd given it up over pride and anger. He was offering it to her again. Asking. The tears she'd been holding in slid down her face as she choked out one word: "Yes."

The car ride took forever. When Nick pulled up in the drive, a sense of peace rolled through Noelle. The stress from the test floated away as she left the car. Each step to the front porch eased the uncertainty of the last few weeks. Nick opened the door for her, letting her lead the way. He removed Mackie's vest and told him he was off duty. Everything was tidy, exactly how Nick always kept the place, except at the end of the couch where Nick's pillow rested on a folded blanket.

Overwhelmed by a flood of emotions, Noelle spun around to Nick. As she wrapped herself around him, she whispered, "I'm so sorry."

The words hadn't completely left her mouth before Nick's lips were on hers, repossessing her with kisses. He turned and pressed her against the door. His fingers dug into her flesh where her thighs met her ass, and he moved between her legs. Hard heat ratcheted through her core. She broke their connection. "Bed."

Nick didn't argue. Kissing her the entire way, he carried her back to his bedroom. Their bedroom. He dropped her on the soft mattress, but before she could miss his touch, he began stripping the clothes from her body, starting with her shoes. Noelle whipped off her shirt and tossed it, followed by her bra. She was naked and staring up at her beautiful, sensitive, broken man, who was wearing entirely too many clothes. "Hurry."

His t-shirt followed hers. Noelle sat up to touch his lean, scarred torso. She held her hand steady, letting his body move under her fingertips as he toed off his shoes and dragged his jeans and boxers off in one motion. She giggled and pointed at his feet.

He raised an eyebrow and sat on the edge of the bed, addressing the last item of clothing.

Socks were the most difficult thing to remove during seduction, especially working around a hard-on like he was. But even naked with socks, he was still damn sexy.

"There." He flung them onto the pile of clothes. Leaning forward, he opened the nightstand and grabbed a condom, dropping it on the bed. Then he pounced on her.

"Wait." She flipped him over easily because he let her. Her pussy settled on his hard cock, and she placed her hands on his chest. "I missed you. The feel of you. The sight of you."

Nick rested his hands on her thighs. Slowly, he slid them up to her hips, over her belly, along her ribs. "Me too."

His husky, needy voice and his strong caress shot fire through every nerve. She ripped the foil packet open and slid the latex down the length of his hard shaft. Lifting her hips, she guided him inside, her wet heat easing his way. And fuck, wasn't that more like coming home than walking through the front door? Molten pleasure slid across her skin, making her limbs heavy. She pressed her hips into him, pulling his cock deeper. A moan of satisfaction and desperation escaped from her lips.

Nick rolled them, taking control with slow, even thrusts in a measured rhythm. His lips kissed every bit of skin he could reach. His hands held her in place, no retreat from the pleasure he was painting her with. She glided her hands over his cheeks, down his neck, and across his chest—everywhere. Reconnecting to each line and plane of his gorgeous body. Reclaiming what she'd thrown away. Reminding him how important he was to her.

She came in soft, slow waves over and over again. And when the shades of Nick's pleasure washed over her like a beautiful watercolor, she let oblivion take her.

CHAPTER 33

ick dropped his lips to his sleeping angel. Her hair spread across the white pillow like gorgeous flames. "Noelle, wake up. We have to get ready."

She moaned and stretched and blinked up at him. Her gaze moved past him, over his shoulder. "Is that my—"

"No. It's *my* new painting. I bought it." He rolled back on the bed next to her and stared at the striking image. Hard to believe that she worked with just five colors—red, yellow, blue, white, and black—to produce such a stunning work.

"You can't keep buying my paintings."

"Who says?" He dragged her into his arms and held her close.

"But you already had an angel. And where is it?"

"I had it shipped to my parents as a gift. I loved the image, but it was time to let go. I'm done living in the past."

"Nick," she breathed out before kissing him deeply. His body responded, and he would've liked nothing more than to stay in bed, but they had a plane to catch.

He broke their connection and smacked her sweet ass. "Let's go. We still have to pack. There's a suitcase waiting for you in the closet."

Noelle nipped his lip and then bolted out of the bed.

After a flurry of packing and an easy drive to the airport, Nick bypassed all the usual departure lanes and drove to the private hangar. As he parked the car, two men in coveralls rushed over and lifted the bags from the trunk and carried them toward the belly of a small jet parked a short distance away. Noelle remained in the passenger seat. He led Mackie from the back seat around the front and opened Noelle's door.

Her eyes were wide and locked on the plane. He held out his hand to help her from the car.

"What is this?" she asked.

"Our ride." Slowly she took his hand in hers and pulled her backpack out with the other.

"Is this a private plane?"

"Technically, yes. But it's not ours. It's chartered." Everyone assumed he was a broke teacher. And he would be if his family money, inheritances, and insurance settlements were ignored. He lived easily on his military benefits and paychecks, even though they'd shrunk after he'd quit doing the private security. Since he hadn't *earned* the other sources, he didn't spend it. Usually.

"What?"

"There wasn't enough time to get my parents'…" Nick swallowed down the confession. Noelle was back to gaping at him.

"You rented a *plane*?"

"Yes. And we should get on it. It's a long flight." He took her elbow and guided her to where the pilot was waiting. They showed the woman their identification and climbed the short flight of stairs behind Mackie. An attendant greeted them and offered them drinks. Then the uniformed man stowed Noelle's backpack into a storage compartment. Nick was surprised she let him take it.

Nick settled Mackie at his feet and buckled up for the ride. Noelle spent several minutes inspecting the interior with probably as much attention to detail as the pilot was spending on her preflight checks. After covering the entire space, Noelle dropped into the seat next to him and sipped her ginger ale. "I feel like an even bigger idiot for throwing twenty-dollar bills at you."

"I deposited that back into your account."

Noelle nodded, but her forehead was furrowed. "How did I not know you were rich? You were out of my league before. Now…"

And that was why he never shared the fact that he was wealthy. "It's just money. Yes, you have to have it. I try to put it to good use. But it doesn't make me better than anyone else, just makes things easier. I don't let it define the way I live."

"I can't imagine. It's weird. My first plane ride is on a private jet with my super-rich boyfriend, who I didn't know was rich, going to my first real show."

"Third. Your show at the Fried Egg was a real show. And so was the one at Up-Cycle. And you sold at both of them. You're a successful artist. That's at least as rare as a super-wealthy boyfriend, if not more so." God, he loved that word, *boyfriend*. But it was just a start. "I'm the one in awe. And your opening is going to be amazing."

Patricia and his dad met them at the plane. They were casual and tanned as if they were on a beach vacation. His mother's smile warmed Nick to his bones. "Noelle, this is my dad, Bill, and my mother, Patti."

"It's so nice to meet you in person after all the emails." His mother, dressed in white shorts and a flowy top, held out her arms.

When she embraced Noelle and whispered something in her ear, Noelle's happy glow told him what he'd already known. She was the one for him. But it was not the time for grand announcements. After sharing hugs all around and introducing Mackie, they loaded into his parents' huge dark SUV, and his dad took the wheel. Noelle relaxed into Nick, her fingers stroking the soft leather of the seat, her backpack at her feet, Mackie at his.

"Nick, honey." His mom turned in the passenger seat, holding the seatbelt away from her body. "You're staying with us. The rooms are ready."

"That's fine. But we're sharing a room. Right?" Nick turned his attention to Noelle, who'd squeezed his hand hard. Pink crept up her cheeks and he held back a chuckle. "Is that okay with you?"

She nodded as her skin continued to darken. He couldn't wait to get her alone and confirm that it covered her entire body. The image of her pink tits slipped under his defenses, and his dick hardened. He redirected his thoughts to prevent *his* embarrassment. "What time is the opening tomorrow?"

"The Diamond VIP pre-event starts at four-thirty. Then at six, the private show opens to the rest of the VIP ticket holders. It's completely sold out. I was over today checking on the setup. It's perfect. Worth Street has a ton of galleries, but there's nothing like what you do, Noelle. They blacked out the windows so no one can get a sneak peek. It's all anyone is talking about at the clubs and on the courses. Your father's been hounded to play more rounds than there are hours in the day. People are hoping he'll let something slip."

"I never thought I'd be sick of playing golf," Bill added as he navigated the exit off the freeway.

"So, I have hair and makeup scheduled for after lunch like we discussed in the email. I'm having my usual people come in. Is that all right?"

Noelle nodded slowly. Nick tightened his arm around her. He whispered in her ear. "Don't worry. It'll be fun."

"We'll need to be on the way by three-thirty. Black tie, boys. Nick, I had yours aired and pressed already."

Noelle started to shake. He gripped her tighter.

"Oh, and I have my stylist coming over in the morning with some dresses and things for you to try. Even a satin tux if that's your style. If you hate everything, she can get more. But I gave her your coloring and the sizes you sent. There should be something you'll feel comfortable in. With the tight timeline, we just don't have time to shop."

"That's great, Mom. But it's been a long day. I think for tonight, if it's not too much of an inconvenience, we'll do dinner in our room and crash early." Nick could tell Noelle was getting overwhelmed. The plane, his parents, black-tie events, and all that after they'd just reconciled. If he didn't get her to a quiet space, alone, there xmas a good chance she'd panic.

"Of course. We need our artist well-rested." They pulled past a large gate and up a wide paved drive. The house was a pale stucco and red tile monstrosity. He'd only been there a few times since his parents had moved to Florida while he was in the service. He probably should have warned Noelle, whose eyes were like saucers when they parked under the portico in front of the six-bedroom, two-story, on-the-lake-and-golf-course mansion.

When they walked through the massive entry, the first thing Nick saw was the painting he'd sent to his parents. "You got my gift."

"We love it," Patti said. "I had to hang it so it's the first thing guests see when they come in."

Noelle's voice was low. "You didn't have to do that."

His mom patted Noelle's shoulder. "I'm an art dealer. People expect me to have the best. And thanks to my son, I do."

As soon as they were alone, in the room farthest from the master, Noelle spun on him. "I can't do this, Nick. I'm a homeless trash-artist from a trailer park. What have you gotten me into?"

"You belong here. As an artist. As my lover." He held out his arms to her.

"This is a mansion."

Nick dropped his arms when she didn't move into them. "I didn't grow up here. My parents bought the place because they had to reinvest the money they got when they sold our home in New York. There were tax reasons. I get that it's over the top, but we're visiting. And my parents don't care where you came from. They like you. You heard what Mom said about your art. And what did she say when you got off the plane?"

Noelle poked her navy canvas shoe into the thick pile of the carpet. "That she was glad I was here, and she thanked me for forgiving you, because she'd never seen you look happier."

"See? Normal, nice people. This"—Nick swung his arm to gesture at the room—"is just stuff. A bed to sleep in, windows to let in the light, and a shower for washing."

"It's a little fancier than the shelter or even Joe's apartment."

"Or even *my* house. Which I love." He held out his arms again, and that time she fell into them, warming the chill that had begun to take hold. "But let's just pretend we're on a super nice vacation and this is a luxury hotel. And we have to have hotel sex, because I hear it's the best."

"Hotel sex?" She peeped up at him with half-lowered lids. Naturally sexy.

"New place. New bed. We don't have to clean up. We can be as loud as we want, no neighbors."

"We're always loud."

"Is that a yes?"

Noelle pushed out of his arms, shucked off her t-shirt, and kicked off her shoes. She raced toward the bathroom with a squeal. "Last one naked has to be the oral slave."

Nick picked up her shirt, tucked her shoes into the closet, and slowly removed every article of his clothing, folding or hanging each piece. Then he strolled into the spacious tiled room. Steam poured out of the glass enclosure. He opened the door. "How can your slave serve you, mistress?"

Noelle laughed and yanked him under the hot water.

HANDS CLENCHED TOGETHER and a smile plastered on her face, Noelle focused on breathing during the ride to the gallery. The temptation to pick at the gorgeous dress nearly overwhelmed her. The stylist had left her hair loose in shiny waves of flame that grazed the rose gold and merlot halter of her long dress. The delicate, flowing skirt cascaded to toes that had been painted in the same metallic color as the top. A subtle slit went up to her thigh, but the dress stayed closed, mostly. Her low-heeled sandals matched the soft wine-colored fabric. She'd felt like a princess, and then the makeup artist had applied colors with the lightest touch, making her brown eyes huge and her lips pink and slightly glossy. Patricia had finished her look with a sparkly rose gold collar necklace. Noelle had been sure she'd been overdressed for the evening until she'd seen Nick waiting at the bottom of the staircase.

It should be against the law for a man to look that good. The tailored black suit wrapped itself around the length of his muscular body the way she had the previous night. His silvery-blond brush cut and sparkling blue eyes were the only accessory he required. If she'd seen him like that, model-gorgeous, before meeting him as a teacher, she'd never have been able to take his hand the day she'd been run over by the jocks. But in that moment, he'd held out the same hand to her, and she'd floated down the stairs with no hesitation. That gorgeous, solid, loyal man was hers.

They were seated facing his parents in a limousine. First the private plane, then a limo. The extravagance was uncomfortable, more like a nightmare than a dream. The car pulled to the curb on a busy street lined with expensive shops and competing galleries.

"Let's go meet the owner," Patti said before taking her husband's hand and sliding out of the car.

Nick went next with Mackie, who was sporting a black bow tie on his collar for the event. When Noelle failed to follow, Nick stuck his head back in. "I'll be right by your side the entire time."

Noelle took a deep breath and let him guide her between the palm trees and into the building's canopy-covered entrance. Light wood floors and crisp white walls made her artwork the focus. The canvases filled the modern space, perfectly lit, professionally framed, and discretely priced. A space she'd dreamed of, and so much better in person than the pictures on their website. Floating on a cloud around the room, she glanced at the tag under her orbiting planets and bit back a gasp. She quickly calculated her cut after the gallery and agent fees. There had to be an extra zero.

"I know they're a bit underpriced." Patti moved in close, her light floral scent and gentle voice enveloping Noelle like a hug. "But, technically, this is your debut. The next show will be more in line with your worth."

Before Noelle could respond, a trim man in a dark suit with a red flower in the lapel appeared. "Is this our *artiste*?"

"Noelle, allow me to introduce Lawrence Robertson." Patti put her hand on the man's shoulder. "He's a visionary when it comes to art and owns the gallery."

He held out his hand, and Noelle shook it. "Thank you for hosting my show."

Lawrence beamed. He chatted with Patti about the evening, everything from the food the caterers were serving, to when Noelle would be introduced and how long her speech would be.

Fuck. The speech. It was on the list in the email. How did I forget? Now what? Noelle turned to Nick, every instinct screaming for her to run.

Nick gave her hand a gentle squeeze. "Don't worry. You just say a few words. Thank the gallery and Lawrence. Thank Patricia and Bill for representing you. Leave it at that."

The first patrons arrived, a small gathering, and Noelle was introduced to each person. Nick stayed by her side and only wrapped an arm around her if a man lingered too long or leaned in too close. But then the doors opened again, and the gallery filled with even more people in sparkly dresses and large jewels, dark suits and polished shoes. Noelle pressed herself against Nick. His hand rested on the small of her back, and he leaned in to whisper in her ear. "You're doing amazing."

"Ladies and gentlemen." Lawrence's voice rang out over the crowd. He welcomed and thanked them, and then he said, "I'd like to introduce the incredibly talented artist. We are so privileged to be the first to feature her work on the East Coast. A rising star. Come up here, Angel."

He called her by the name she'd used to sign all her paintings, reminding her with a word who she was, who she was destined to be. Her heart thundered in her chest. With a deep breath, she slowly strode to the front. The only thing on her mind for the last half hour had been that speech. And she had something she wanted to say.

"Thank you, Lawrence. You have a beautiful gallery and have showcased my work exquisitely. I'd also like to thank Patricia and Bill Christoph, my agents. Without them, this show would not have happened." Noelle took a deep breath, fighting the Jurassic-sized butterflies that batted around in her stomach. She lifted her gaze to focus on the one person in the crowd who mattered. "And lastly, I'd like to thank Nick Christoph."

She swallowed and raised her voice so he wouldn't miss a word. "I'm a reclaimed artist. I transform what some might call trash into the treasure it is. Nick did that with me. He saw beyond what I showed the world. He helped me to shine. He believed in me and gave me everything." She paused to swallow down the tears that were building. "And I gave him the only thing I owned, my heart. Nick was —" Before she could continue, he was there, his lips on hers. She barely heard the clapping that filled the room.

The rest of the evening was a blur. Lawrence waved them away while he was still completing some last-minute sales. Patti chattered in the car about how great the event went and how she would be looking for a gallery in New York next.

Noelle half listened while she watched Nick fidget and stare out the window. He'd cut off her speech. Granted, with kisses, but had she embarrassed him? She spent the rest of the ride second-guessing her spur-of-the moment confession.

CHAPTER 34

As soon as Noelle crossed into the marble-clad entry way of the Christophs' too-big home, Nick spun her into his arms and pressed his lips to hers. She wrapped her arms around his neck and let her body relax against his, all the tension from the car ride gone in a moment. His parents were probably watching, and she didn't care. But he stopped kissing her way too soon. The apology for the speech that formed on her lips was interrupted as Mackie bumped into Nick and nosed his hand.

"I'm okay, Mackie. Just nervous. Remember we talked about this, boy." Then Nick reached in his pocket and then dropped to one knee.

No way. Wishes never come true.

He opened a ring box and held it out. "Marry me, Noelle?"

Mackie barked.

His mother squealed.

"Give her a chance to answer, darling," Bill said.

"Really?" The word escaped when Noelle had meant to say yes.

Nick took the ring from the box and held it up to her. "I'm completely serious. We're completely serious." He glanced at Mackie, who sat by his side and stared up at her with soft puppy-dog eyes. "Bill and I went shopping this morning. I wanted to ask you at the gallery, but that was your moment. I can't wait another minute. Please say yes."

Noelle held out her hand and nodded. Nick slid the single diamond on a silver-colored band over her knuckle as she found her voice again. "Yes."

Nick's lips found hers, kissing her passionately until she lost all sense of time and place. Mackie brushed up against them, and Noelle reached for him, receiving a doggie kiss on the hand. Nick released her mouth, but his gorgeous blue eyes were locked on hers, filled with love and promises.

"Oh my goodness," his mother said. "You have to get married here. There's plenty of time. You can get the license on Monday. We have the weekend to put it together. Bill can call Judge Franklin. I'm sure she'd be willing. We could do it Friday, after Thanksgiving. It's perfect."

"They just got engaged, Patti."

"But she said *yes*."

Nick's focus never left Noelle as his parents bantered. "It's your decision, Noelle. Any kind of wedding you dreamed of. No rush. As long as I can be yours."

Warmth flowed through every cell of her body. Hers. He wanted to be hers, like she was his. "Let's do it. I don't want to be apart from you ever again."

Nick rose and wrapped her in a tight embrace, twirling her around. "Go for it, Mom. Plan it all."

"Can we get married in this?" Noelle pointed at her gorgeous dress and Nick's tux.

"An evening wedding. Perfect." Patti clapped her hands. "I'll start making calls in the morning."

Eight days that passed like eight minutes later, and they were husband and wife.

Noelle clutched the still-fresh bouquet of lavender Ocean Song roses in her hands as the plane took off to return her and her new husband to Tucson. The wedding arrangements had come together so quickly with Patti's connections and organizational skills. They'd shared a quiet Thanksgiving dinner, just the four of them, their last meal as an unmarried couple. Patti had insisted they not see each other at all on their wedding day, making them sleep in separate bedrooms. But the ceremony that Friday night had been perfect.

Candlelight had flickered over the living room walls while Noelle and Nick spoke their personal vows. The judge had smiled at their sweet promises and love-filled commitments. Mackie had acted as the ring bearer, and Nick's parents had signed the paperwork as witnesses. They'd even recorded it so Noelle could show Joe. She'd watch it with him. Nerves had prevented her from remembering all the details.

She yawned. Nick had been intent on blessing his wife on her wedding night with way too many orgasms. Something about starting as you meant to go on. She rested her head on his shoulder, the humming of the plane's engines quickly lulling her to sleep.

"Noelle, we're here." Nick stroked his hand down her arm. Her bouquet lay on a seat opposite them.

She grabbed the flowers and lifted her backpack over one shoulder as the attendant opened the door. The pilot stepped out of the cockpit.

"Thanks, Captain." Nick shook the man's hand.

The wail of sirens interrupted anything else he might have said. Police cars pulled up to the plane, lights and sirens blazing.

"What's going on? Nick?"

"Stay in the plane."

"No. I'm going with you."

Nick went down the stairs first, gripping Mackie's lead. Noelle followed him, still holding her flowers. As soon as he was on the concrete, three officers rushed him. One took Mackie's leash, and the other two put Nick in handcuffs.

"Nickolas Christoph, you're under arrest for kidnapping and..."

Noelle didn't hear the rest of the charges. A female police officer held her by the bicep and guided her to the back of another squad car. "Nick. Wait. Stop." Noelle tried to wrest her arm out of the woman's grip unsuccessfully. "He's my husband."

"Noelle, don't fight them," he said. "I love you."

Before she could answer, the officer firmly put her in the back seat and shut the door. The woman sat behind the steering wheel. "We'll sort out everything at the station. I'm sure you think you're married, but there're laws against what he's done."

Nick hadn't done *anything* against the law. "But what about Mackie? Where are you taking him?"

"Animal control will take him to the shelter until the training organization can retrieve him. Or some judge releases that monster on bail."

"You can't take them from me." Noelle rode silently, too shocked to cry. They'd arrested her husband and his dog. What did they think Nick had done? Kidnapping? Who? When?

When they entered the building, she searched for any sign of Nick. A blur of uniforms faded to the background as Noelle focused on the hell-bitch who'd given birth to her almost twenty-one years ago. It all made sense. Dressed in clean black slacks and a long-sleeved, printed top, her mother appeared deceptively normal.

"Baby girl! You're safe. I was so worried." Her mother ran to her and grabbed her in a bone-crushing hold, ripping her backpack off her body. Her bouquet fell to the floor, the dusky lavender petals scattering. Lips to her ear, her mother hissed, "Not a word or I call reporters and see what the public thinks of a teacher fucking his student." Standing back, her mom continued her performance. "We'll get you checked by a doctor, therapy. Anything you need, sweetheart."

Noelle slipped her ring off and tucked it into her pocket before her mother saw it. If she could linger long enough, she might find Nick. She craned her neck to see beyond an overweight officer coming toward them, but snapped back to his face. It wasn't the first time she'd seen the man—he'd been at the trailer, but never in uniform.

"Your daughter's back. Safe and sound." The guy laughed, and it sounded completely faked. But there was nothing funny about what her mom was doing with that seedy bastard's aid. If she had cops on her side, how would Noelle ever get Nick freed?

"Thank you so much for your help, Officer Stebbins." Her mother blinked up at the man, putting on a show. Bile rose in Noelle's throat, and she swallowed hard.

"Here's your baby's birth certificate. Only *fifteen* years old, and that guy conned her into marriage. Scum, huh?" The uniformed man handed her mother a paper that couldn't be real. "Doesn't matter how old they get or what they do, we still love them. Right?"

Oh fuck. Her mother had set it up. *But seriously?* "Fifteen? I don't even look fifteen. I'm twenty fucking years old. This—"

"Noelle, you have *got* to stop lying. If you keep acting out, they're going to send you to juvenile detention."

Officer Stebbins stepped too close to Noelle, fingering the hand-cuffs on his belt. "Ms. Michaels, are you sure you can handle her?"

"Oh, absolutely. I'm going to take her home. She needs to recover from her ordeal."

"That's fine. But you let me know if you need help with this one." The man ran his hand down her mom's back, all the way to her ass. His body blocked the action from his co-workers. "We have all your contact info. We'll be in *touch*."

The scripted conversation had been observed, and judgmental eyes focused on Noelle from every direction. No one was going to believe a word she said about Nick. Not until she got away from that crazy woman and could prove it was all lies.

Her mom grabbed her elbow, digging her nails in, and dragged her outside. "Keep your mouth shut."

Noelle searched the area for Nick. Nothing. Biding her time until the opportunity was right, she followed her mom onto a bus, letting the woman pay her fare. Her bus card remained hidden in her pack along with her ID and bank card. Whatever plan Noelle came up with, it had to include getting the wallet out of that pack. "Why are you doing this?"

"Payback's a bitch." Her mother's answer confused her more. Payback for what? For not giving her two thousand dollars? Not saving the trailer destroyed with chemicals and neglect? Not turning into a drug-dealing addict like they'd tried to train her to be?

After a long ride, her mom stood up from the seat. "Let's go."

Noelle peered out the window into the deepening gloom. There were a few scattered businesses and an apartment house, but nothing she recognized. She followed her mother off the bus.

Her mom tugged on her sleeve with one hand and scratched herself with the other. "I gotta make a stop."

Translation: she needed to score more drugs. "Do you need some money?"

Her mother froze. "You got some?"

"No. But I can get some. I bet that gas station has an ATM."

Her mother half ran as she beelined for the lit-up sidewalk. Noelle followed, gauging the environment and watching for the perfect moment. She stood behind her mom, who was panting in front of the unbranded machine.

"I need my wallet."

Instead of handing it over, her mom unzipped the pack and reached in. Several minutes passed. "Where is it?"

"Let me." Noelle hovered one hand over the bag. Her mom held it open and out to her, not releasing it. Noelle dug beneath the fake bottom and slid the slim wallet from its hiding place. Before pulling it from the bag, she opened it and palmed her ID.

"Got it." She held the wallet up, letting her identification slide into her loose shirt sleeve.

Her mom snatched the wallet and yanked out the bank card, then dumped the rest back in the pack. She pushed Noelle by the shoulder toward the machine and shoved the card into the slot. "Get as much as you can."

Noelle tucked her hand in her pocket, letting the ID slide back down her sleeve. "I can only get two hundred at a time."

"Do it."

Noelle entered her PIN and completed the selections. Ten twenty-dollar bills emerged from the machine.

Her mom snatched the cash and nudged her arm. "Again."

Noelle went through the motions of entering her PIN again but keyed it incorrectly. "I messed it up."

"Dumb bitch. Do it again." The smack to her shoulder was expected.

Noelle did, twice more. The machine sucked her card in. A message flashed up about calling her bank. "I'm sor—"

Her mother's forearm rammed into her face so hard that her head hit the ATM. The store clerk rattled the locked front door and screamed out that he was going to call the cops. Noelle took the moment of her mother's inattention to bolt.

NICK RAN his free hand through his hair. Nothing made any sense. He'd been sitting in the interrogation room of the station for hours. Where was Noelle? He'd violated no laws. Noelle was an adult. She was legally married to him. But there he sat, handcuffed to a table. A panic attack built, his panting breath getting tighter, and they'd taken his dog. Supposedly, Mackie'd be held at the shelter. If anything happened to either his wife or his dog—

An officer walked in. The same one who'd booked him. Stebbins. "So you like little girls, you sick fuck."

Little girls? No. What's he talking about? Nick opened his mouth to argue, but in a moment of clarity, he recognized the bait. If he said anything, it would be used against him. He clenched his jaw. Took a slow deep breath. "I want to call my lawyer. And I need to use the facilities."

"You stole a little girl from her family. Took her across state lines."

Family? Her mother. But how would Noelle's mom have convinced them she was a minor? "I want to call my lawyer."

"There ain't no lawyer who's gonna be able to get you off these charges."

Nick continued his slow breathing and as calmly as possible repeated, "I want to call my lawyer."

The door opened again. "Stebbins. What are you doing in here? There's no one answering the phones at the front desk."

The trim middle-aged officer held open the door until the portly bully sauntered out. Then he undid the cuff on the table. "Your lawyer's here."

Lawyer? I haven't called anyone.

The officer opened the door again and Ned walked in. Edward Strauss. The man who'd hired Nick that summer for his last security gig and had taken care of all his parents' legal issues for years. His calm, commanding presence filled the room. Relief washed through Nick. "How did you—"

Ned held up his hand and looked pointedly at the officer who ducked out of the room. "Nick, are you all right?"

"Where's Noelle? They took my service dog. I don't know where either of them are."

"They have you on some serious charges." Ned folded his tall frame into the chair on the opposite side of the table, adjusting the lines of his gray slacks. "Did they read you your rights?"

Nick shook his head. "How are you here?"

"The pilot called your mother as soon as he saw you being cuffed. She called me, and I got on the next flight here. I happened to be in Albuquerque, having dinner with my family."

"How are Jack and Missy?" Nick felt guilty dragging Ned away from his partners.

"They're fine. *They* haven't been arrested for kidnapping."

"The cops keep saying that, but I don't understand."

"From what I have ascertained between the call with your mother and the discussion with the detective, they're under the mistaken impression Noelle is underage." Ned's calm explanation only made the last part more shocking.

"She's *not*. She'll be twenty-one in a matter of weeks. On Christmas."

"Do you have any proof?"

"She has identification, and her birth certificate is in my safe at my house." Nick rattled off the combo and his address. Ned would have to get his keys from the cops. "Where's Noelle?"

"They released her to her mother."

Acid shot through Nick's gut. "That's not good. Her mother's a meth-head. Can you find her?"

"One thing at a time."

"And they have my service dog. Said he was being taken to the pound."

"Standard procedure. Let's take care of you first."

"I can't believe this is happening."

"I'm going to get you out of here as fast as possible. Then we'll get your dog, find Noelle, and deal with the botched false arrest. Someone knew you were coming in on a private charter. With Noelle. Something about this stinks."

NOELLE RECOVERED from her long-distance run on the front stoop of Nick's house. Her home. The home she couldn't enter because her set of keys was in her backpack, currently in the possession of a deranged junkie. As she'd escaped, the only thing she could think was to go home. Having gotten there, she didn't know what to do.

Headlights filled the driveway as an unfamiliar car pulled into Nick's space. Noelle forced herself to stand, backing into the shadows of the porch. Her feet screamed, but she'd run again if she had to. A tall man got out from the driver's side. "Noelle?"

At the sound of her name, she paused. "How do you know me?"

"You're Nick's bride." His deep voice held the trace of an accent and the promise of assistance.

"You know Nick?" Tears welled in her eyes.

"I'm his lawyer, Edward Strauss. Ned. Melissa Winter's partner?"

"Oh thank god. You have to help him."

"I've already seen him. I'm here to get your birth certificate." He held up a keyring.

She helped Ned retrieve the document. On the way back to the station, she told him everything that'd happened since the day her mother had been arrested. The threats for money at the gallery, even her suspicion about the officer. When she got to the part where her mom had bounced her head off the ATM and stole her backpack, a low growl erupted from the man. Noelle peered at him through the darkness. Ned's jaw was set, and his spine was rigid. Moments later, they parked in the police station lot. He flipped on the overhead light and inspected her face.

"Your *mother* did this to you?" Disgust dripped from his words.

Noelle nodded.

"She's going to be arrested. Any problem with that?"

"No." She'd seen it before.

"We're going to go in there to have your injury documented and your husband released." He grabbed his cell phone. "First, I need to make some calls. We need to alert people outside this 'police' station."

CHAPTER 35

*N*ed escorted Noelle into the police station. He opened the doors and stayed right at her side until he approached the desk and then stepped directly in front of her, blocking her from view. "Officer Stebbins. I'm Edward Strauss, attorney for Mr. and Mrs. Christoph. Detective Anderson is expecting me."

The bully picked up the phone without a word. A few moments later, a man in a light blue button-down shirt and dark slacks opened a door. Ned turned to allow Noelle to go ahead and made a horrified sound when his gaze hit her face. "Your mother did this?"

Noelle reached up to her cheek. "Is it bad?"

Ned turned to the detective. "I want pictures of this injury for the report."

Anderson's expression gave away nothing as he nodded. "Come on back. I've already started a file."

Ned gave Noelle a sly wink.

The man led them to a conference room. Another detective was pouring coffee into a mug, but the action barely held Noelle's notice. Nick slumped in a chair on the far side.

"Nick." Noelle darted around the table. Her husband stood and embraced her, his face buried in her hair, like they'd been apart for days instead of hours. She ran her hands along his shoulders and down his back, reassuring herself he was okay. His pulse raced. She held him until his breathing slowed.

"Your face." He grazed his fingertips over the bruise she'd yet to see.

"My mom." It throbbed more intensely since Nick noticed it.

Nick glared at the others in the room.

Ned spoke first. "We're filing a police report for the assault so they can pick her up. As well as the robbery and any other charges related to filing a false report and…" He dropped Noelle's birth certificate on the table. "Providing false documents."

Noelle placed her official Arizona ID next to it and slid her wedding ring back on her finger.

"Care to explain why my client's wife wasn't asked to provide identification when she disputed the claims of a woman with a felony arrest who's on a court-ordered monitor?" Ned crossed his arms, his face a stony mask.

The detectives glanced at each other, then back at the paperwork. Anderson loosened his tie and sighed.

Hours passed as the details of the night and previous encounters were documented. They took pictures of Noelle's face and her statement. They recorded notes on the possible involvement of Officer Stebbins. Sometime in the early morning hours, a uniformed officer came in and whispered in Anderson's ear at the door. The detective closed the door and returned to the table. He addressed Noelle. "Your mother was arrested a short time ago. She won't be getting pre-prosecution probation this time."

Noelle tried to question him, but he "wasn't at liberty" to discuss the details. All the charges against Nick were dropped, and he was released.

"Is your car still at the airport?" Ned asked as they walked toward the front exit of the station.

"I guess so," Nick replied. "We need to get Mackie."

"It's past midnight. The shelter isn't open until noon. Let me take you to your car. I need—"

Ned's voice was cut off by the screams of a banshee from the back of the building. Noelle sighed. Her mother had arrived.

"*You fuckers*! You don't know who you're dealing with. I fucking *own* you. Stebbins. Get these goddamned cuffs off me now."

Noelle hesitated. Nick grabbed her hand and guided her outside. "That's not your problem. Not anymore. Not ever again."

No, that woman wasn't anything to her. Nick was her family. And Joe and Mackie. And Patricia and Bill. And she had friends, too. Like Ned and Missy and Tish. That fucked-up, drug-addled, crazy person no longer mattered, was owed nothing. Noelle squeezed Nick's hand and then got into Ned's car, so ready to put that part of her life behind her.

Once they got home, Nick led her to the bathroom. He stripped off his clothes, and she started to remove hers. Brushing her hands aside, he said, "Let me. I've been your husband for less than two days and I haven't taken care of you."

"We get to take care of each other. It's not all on you." She ran her hands down his back.

Naked, under the water, they washed each other. Noelle paid close attention to every inch of Nick's skin, as careful as he was with her. He lathered her hair, pressed so tightly to her that the water didn't come between them. The tension leaked away. They returned to being newlyweds, kisses and caresses more important than arrests and assaults. Nick dried them and applied some kind of cream to her face that would help heal the bruise.

"Will you let me make love to you? I need to be inside you." His husky voice shot straight to her core.

She took his hand and led him to their bed. After rolling on a condom, he moved her on top of him, the tip of his cock parting her folds, nestling, not pressing in. Her gaze locked to his beautiful blue eyes, and love poured out, blanketing her. He pulled her hips down and thrust up, filling her in one stroke, stealing her breath. Perfection. Every damn time. That man, that beautiful, understanding man was hers. For always. She rose up on her knees and rode him, taking ownership, marking him as hers with small nips on his chest. Then he rolled them and took control. She parted her thighs, encouraging him to go deeper. His fingertips dug into her skin perfectly. His hips pounded her, making her his. She reached up and grabbed him behind his shoulders, holding on as she flew, her soul soaring from the bed and taking him with her. She'd never let him go.

NOELLE WOKE to Nick thrashing in his sleep, making pained sounds that wounded her heart. A night terror. No surprise after the stress they'd been subjected to. There were still a few hours before they could retrieve Mackie, who might have been able to prevent the episode. But once Nick was fully in the nightmare, there was nothing she could do but let him ride it out. She slid from the bed so that he didn't hit her by accident. Leaving him was awful, but he would hate himself if he hurt her. With her pillow under her arm, she padded out to the couch. The blanket she liked to use was draped artfully over one end. Rolling into the soft fleece, she found sleep instantly.

"What are you doing out here?" Nick's voice cut through the fog of Noelle's morning snooze.

She blinked up at him. He was still shirtless but wearing sweats. "You were having a nightmare." She got up and kissed him. "How about some breakfast? The shelter should be open by the time we eat and drive over."

The kennel staff brought Mackie out on his lead, his vest askew but in place. As soon as the dog laid his sweet brown eyes on Nick, his thick golden tail wagged so fast that it blurred. Nick ran his hands over his protector, checked each paw and inspected his ears, petting him and talking to him in a low voice the entire time. He thanked the woman for taking good care of Mackie, and they left.

After they settled into Nick's car, still filled with the scent of lemon and leather, Noelle turned to him. "We should give Mackie a bath and a good walk, then we can go shopping."

"Shopping? *You* want to go shopping?" Nick shook his head lightly.

"We need dog treats and a Christmas tree."

"A Christmas tree?"

"Yeah, I've never had one. It's time to start new traditions for our family."

Nick smiled. "Okay, but we're celebrating on Christmas Eve. Because the twenty-fifth will always be dedicated to celebrating the love of my life's birthday."

Noelle leaned across the seat and wrapped her arms around him before giving him a slow, deep kiss.

EPILOGUE

 ick rushed into the house, ready to celebrate Christmas Eve with his wife. Mackie trotted at his side, his golden fur flowing around the service vest. Nick flicked through the mail. One envelope caught his eye. *This is it.*

Noelle wasn't curled up on the couch as he'd expected. The tree lights reflected against the back window, but he saw her through the sparkling reflections. Earbuds in her ears, paintbrush in her hand, she wiggled her yoga-pant-covered ass to sounds only she could hear.

Drawn to her, he opened the back door. His dog started to follow. "Hold up, Mackie. How about you take a break?" He relieved his loyal assistant of his uniform. Mackie retreated to his fake fur bed and curled up for a snooze.

Nick crossed the backyard to Noelle's painting shed. Not really a shed, more of a mini-house that acted as her personal studio, supplementing the one at Up-Cycle, where she still worked three days a week. As he moved inside her space, she turned to him and smiled. The brush was abandoned in a tin of dirty water, and the buds ripped from her ears. "You're home," she said. "You were gone forever."

"Took longer than I expected."

"What did?" She pressed herself against him.

"Uh-uh. You have to wait until tomorrow."

She morphed her face into a barely believable pout. Nick dropped his lips to hers as he freed the flames of her hair that she'd captured in a loose ponytail. He moved his hand down her side to caress her luscious body. His other hand still clutched the important letter. He let her go, wishing they'd already purchased a daybed for the space. Soon.

"You got some mail." He held up the envelope.

She reached for it but couldn't grab it. "Another check from the gallery? I thought we got them all?"

"Nope. Better." Nick hoped it was good news. Either way, he'd deal with the outcome. He let the paper fall into her grasp.

"Oh." Noelle slid her finger under the sealed flap, ripping it open. She pulled a single page out and unfolded it. Nick let her take her time to read it without pushing for the information, no matter how urgent the situation felt.

"I passed." She raised her gaze to his, eyes sparkling like the lights on the tree. "I got my GED. We did it."

Nick whooped and spun Noelle in a circle. "You did it."

"We did. Together. We can do anything."

"Absolutely, my love." He kissed her again and again. She might think she needed him, but she could do anything. Thank god what she wanted to do was be with him.

Nick let her catch her breath. "Is Joe coming over for dinner?"

"No. We had a good visit. He loved the video of our wedding. Said I should have had a white dress." She kissed him again, as she always did when they talked about their wedding. "He's coming for lunch tomorrow to celebrate my birthday. But he wants to let us spend our first Christmas together."

"As long as we get to see him before we leave." Working on Gabe's B and B wasn't the best honeymoon, but he'd sneak in a ski lesson or two while they were there. And probably make Gabe's ears ring with hotel sex. "Come on, let's eat. Then presents."

Noelle put away her paints and finished rinsing her brushes.

After they ate the extravagant holiday meal, Nick tidied up the kitchen. Noelle lounged on the couch, staring at the tree, while Mackie curled up on his doggy bed by the back door. Christmas carols played in the background. Everything exactly as it should be. Nick joined Noelle in the living room. "Ready?"

Noelle sat up, hands clasped in her lap. Nick plucked the red hat from the side table and fit it on his head. "You've been a very good girl."

Noelle giggled. "Have I, Santa? I thought I was pretty naughty this morning."

"Ho ho ho. No, that was *very* good. Deserving of a present." He handed her a wrapped box.

Noelle tore off the paper with childlike enthusiasm. "A backpack?" She looked from the flattened turquoise bag to Nick. "You got me a backpack."

The heartfelt tone and the quick kiss she gave him reassured him that it'd been a good selection. The one her mother had stolen had been lost in the chaos of her arrest. An arrest that had led the FBI to bust three dirty cops, including that loser, Stebbins, and an airport baggage handler so far. The best part was Noelle wouldn't be needed to testify since her mother had pled guilty to lesser charges and turned on her collaborators.

"My turn." On her knees, Noelle bent over in front of the tree and pulled out a familiar-sized box. Familiar for anyone who'd celebrated Christmas. On top was an envelope. "Open the box first."

Inside, Nick found a navy-blue henley in the perfect size. He held it up to his chest. "Love it."

"I sort of owed you one." Noelle pointed. "Open the other one."

Nick pulled back the loose flap and slid out two tickets. He turned them over and peered at the words printed on them. "A concert? In Vegas?"

"Yes." Noelle bounced up and down. "During spring break. And I'm covering the entire trip with my earnings from the show."

"You don't have to—"

"I want to. It'll be like a real honeymoon. Since you're making me work at Gabe's." She stuck out her tongue teasingly.

"Thank you. A completely perfect and awesome gift."

"And I'll buy you a t-shirt at the concert."

It would be his new favorite. Although he still enjoyed it when she wore his old ones.

"Are we done?"

"One more for you." He reached behind the tree and retrieved a bulky box wrapped in white paper with a silver bow. Thank goodness stores had wrapping service.

Noelle opened it and pulled out a teal-blue suit. "What is it?

"Ski pants and jacket. We have lessons scheduled in Aspen."

"Skiing?"

"You'll love it."

Noelle set them in the box and moved it to the side. "I love you."

She met him halfway, equally eager in her efforts to find his skin. He reached for the Santa hat.

"Leave it on," she said.

Nick finished unwrapping his wife, the best gift of his life. He sat back on his heels. The lights danced off Noelle's creamy skin, her red hair splayed out across the rug. If he were at all talented, that would be the image he would paint. Fire and ice.

Noelle slid her hand down her belly and teased two fingers inside. "Nick, I want you."

He didn't move a muscle, let her take her pleasure, her performance riding his cock, as hot as if he were inside. She glazed her pink lips with her shiny wetness. Nick wrapped his hand around her wrist and brought her fingers to his lips, sucking them clean. Craving more, he knelt between her parted thighs, spreading them wider, and then buried himself in the source. His tongue savored every sweet drop and searched for more. He sucked her clit between his lips and teased it.

Noelle arched off the floor, her voice drowning out the sexy song that currently played. Nick slid his own fingers inside her hot sheath. It might be cold outside, but Noelle was on fire. Her flesh rippled, gripping him.

Nick replaced his fingers with his swollen cock.

"Fuck, Nick. Yes." Noelle screamed her need and dug her fingers into his ass, pulling him even deeper.

Being inside her bare was the best present ever. With almost no chance of pregnancy since she'd insisted on getting birth control, he could love her, give her all of him and not miss the slightest twitch, the intense heat, the sweet wetness. Nothing muted and all for him. He tried to last, to drive her through another orgasm, but she felt too good. His hips moved faster without his conscious effort. He pulled her up from the rug and held her naked chest to his. She moved with him. Dancing together perfectly. He exploded, and Noelle carried him through it, her own body reacting to his, softening, giving, everything.

Hours later, they went to the bedroom. Mackie was on duty to make sure Nick could sleep. Their routine was comfortable after just a few weeks. The next day was Noelle's birthday, and it would be as perfect as their first Christmas.

Nick woke early and slipped silently from the bed. He provided for Mackie and then let him off duty. With candles on the cake and a covered cup of coffee for Noelle, he returned to her side. He kissed her awake. "Happy birthday, my love."

"Mmm. Thank you."

Nick lit the candles and attempted a sexy rendition of the traditional song. Noelle laughed and clapped her hands.

"Make a wish." Nick held the cake out to her.

"What could I possibly want that I don't have?"

"Not sure. Trip to Paris? Art school? More yoga pants?"

"That last one would be for you." She closed her eyes, then she blew, extinguishing the four flames on their tiny breakfast cake. Nick had a bigger one for later when Joe came over. He handed Noelle her coffee, pulled out the waxy candle leftovers, and picked up the single fork. They took turns eating the white cake covered with whipped cream frosting and filled with fruit.

"This might have to become a tradition." Nick hadn't imagined he'd like having cake for breakfast, but it was really good.

"Okay." Noelle held her mouth open, waiting for him to feed her another bite.

Not even halfway through the cake, they both gave up trying to finish it. Nick set it on the nightstand and took the empty cup from Noelle. "I have a present for you."

"A *birthday* present?" Her voice was whisper soft.

"Yep. Meet me in the kitchen." He took the remnants of their feast, allowing Noelle to get dressed because if he saw her naked, she wouldn't get her gift for hours.

"I'm ready." Noelle had clearly thrown on her clothes from the previous night, eager for her present.

Nick took her hand and led her to the rarely used garage door.

"My present's in here?"

Nick opened the door and turned on the light. Noelle gasped. She faced him, mouth still agape.

"Do you like it?" She had to like it. He'd spent hours negotiating and then the transport nearly hadn't arrived in time for her surprise.

"What do you mean? It's a *car*."

"A red-hot metallic sports car that's perfect for my wife." Fiery, powerful, and sexy as hell, exactly like her.

"But I don't drive."

"I'll teach you." Nick braced himself as she leapt into his arms and kissed him senseless.

~

ACKNOWLEDGMENTS

First, I have to thank my husband who gives me all the time and space to write and never gets upset when I use him for research. I love you!

Thank you to the Land of Enchantment Romance Authors (LERA) who provided a place of support and education, especially Robin P. whose advice on the opening was inspiring.

To my Reines, without whom, this book would not be what it is. Thank you for everything.

And a special thank you to all those who have served in the U.S. military, who continue to serve, and their families. Your service is recognized, remembered, and treasured.

ABOUT THE AUTHOR

Award-winning, best-selling author, Jordyn Kross, is an unapologetically naughty novelist who spent years honing her writing skills with tech manuals and marginal poetry before finding her passion for writing sexy, boundary-stretching happily-ever-afters.

When she's not writing, she's attempting to garden in the desert Southwest, hiking with her insane pound hound, and admiring that handsome man wandering around her house who continues to stay.

Jordyn enjoys saucy double entendres, pretending to be an extrovert, and is well-known for having no filter. And when she's not in social media jail, she can be found on Facebook, Instagram, and Book-Bub. Unless she's feeling particularly bold on TikTok.